GREY GHYLL

When Kit Talbot's mother leaves him the money she has earned by running a high-class brothel in London, Kit buys a farm in the Lake District. At first, Judith his wife, loves the place and does all she can to transform it into a home, but aware of Kit's penchant for women, she becomes unsure of his love and blames him when the attractive dairymaid becomes pregnant.

Gipsies camp on Kit's land and he resents their refusal to leave until they are ready. He makes a condition that Ben Boswell provides two of his grandsons to help on the farm, and a girl to work in the dairy, who brings in more than her fair share of trouble.

GREY GHYLL

Grey Ghyll

by
Anne Rundle

MAGNA PRINT BOOKS
Long Preston, North Yorkshire,
England.

British Library Cataloguing in Publication Data.

Rundle, Anne.
  Grey Ghyll.
  I. Title
  823'.914(F)   PR6068.U7

  ISBN 0-86009-730-7

First Published in Great Britain by Robert Hale Ltd, 1978

Published in Large Print 1985 by arrangement with Campbell,
Thomson & McLaughlin Ltd, London and St. Martins' Press Inc.,
New York.

Photoset in Great Britain by
Dermar Phototypesetting Co, Long Preston, North Yorkshire.

Printed and bound in Great Britain by
Redwood Burn Limited, Trowbridge, Wiltshire.

For Ruth
with Love

PART ONE

THE GIPSIES

1

Judith yawned and stretched. It was dark and the place beside her was empty. Sitting up, sleepiness vanished, she lighted the lamp that stood on the bedside table. The warm glow through the pink glass of the shade revealed rumpled bedclothes, Kit's dented pillow, the white ghost of his nightshirt on the floor. The smell of lavender crept out of the linen.

She grasped one of the oak bedpoles and slid to the floor. The bed was high and she always had to stand on the chair to get into it unless Kit were there to pick her up and deposit her on the patch-work spread. Lifting her houserobe, she shrugged herself into the garment and pushed her feet into slippers. The moon was full so there was no need of a candle to find her way to the kitchen. The big brown jars stood around like funerary urns. Moonbeams left murky gleams in the scoured pans. Kit was not there and she was touched with unease. She'd imagined him hungry or thirsty—Kit was a man of large appetites—but there was no sign of crocks or crumbs. The room was just as she'd seen it after supper when she'd come to speak to Madge.

Judith shivered. The nights were cool in late September and she regretted the necessity of leaving the haven of bed to search for her husband. She deplored, too, the fact that she found it essential to know where he was. Certain of her own love for him, she could never quite believe that it was similarly reciprocated. Kit had had relations with many women before he married her. He was good-looking, lusty, bedworthy, and Judith was horridly aware that she sought for constant reassurance that he remained faithful. Not that there were too many temptations at Grey Ghyll, but Deborah Broome always stared at him when she fancied herself not watched. Only this morning she had craned her pretty, little neck at the dairy window to see Kit ride by towards the pasture and her shapely body was not uncomely. Plumper than it had been, but still bonny.

Hating herself for her suspicions, Judith went to the farm door. It was not bolted. Opening it, she looked down the slope towards the Broomes' cottage. There was no light in any window but a lamp was not needed for what Kit or Deborah might have in mind. Between Grey Ghyll and the cottage stood the cow-byres and Judith saw, just before she heard the low, agonised bellow, a tiny crack of yellow between the lime-washed stone.

Flinging on the cloak that hung on the hook, she began to run across the grey carpet of grass. Judith had never seen a cow calve before so was unprepared for the sight of Kit, sweating, his forearms a mass of blood and dung, straining at the small roped legs that were all that could be discerned of the coming animal by the light of the storm lantern.

'What are you doing here?' Kit asked more sharply than he'd ever spoken to her.

'I woke and could not find you.'

'Then you should have had the sense to go back to bed.' Kit pulled again while the cow gave vent to another grumble of distress. There was still no more to be seen of the obstinate calf.

'Should it be so difficult?' Judith en-

11

quired, revolted, yet fascinated. She'd not imagined one would be faced by the sight of the calves legs protruding almost obscenely from the cow's backside.

'It's a tight fit,' Kit admitted, 'and likely I've been too clever imagining I could manage it alone. I fear I'll have to call on Jim Broome after all. Could you go and rouse him? They must sleep like the dead. I'd rather not leave the poor beast at this stage.'

'Yes. I'll fetch him. Can't I help?'

'No.' Kit was definite. Already he had withdrawn from her as though she no longer existed. But the sufferings of an animal in labour were of more immediate import than the reassurance of a wife whose doubts, on this occasion at least, were unfounded.

But, as she panted on towards the darkened cottage, the face of Deborah Broome returned to haunt her with its youthful vivacity. She was an attractive girl, not pretty, but striking with those black eyes and mop of raven hair, though she'd have to be careful not to run to fat like her mother.

A light came on in the Broomes' kitchen just as Judith drew level with the window.

Through it, she could see Deborah hanging over a chipped bowl, retching. The black hair tumbled down a back that still contrived to look well-proportioned through the enveloping folds of a calico nightgown, then the back disappeared behind a man's nightshirted body. Rough, toil-worn hands seized the now unseen shoulders and shook until the curly head nodded frantically. 'You're a bitch, our Deb. 'Ad my suspicions I 'ave, this time past though your mam wouldn't 'ave it. Warned you agen making eyes at married men, I did. A dirty little bitch, that's what you are, and us left to clean up the muck. Couldn't rest content wi' a man as'ld marry you, though you'd still 'a been a slut. No, get yoursel' wi' bairn wi' someone already wed.'

The man's arm came up and dealt a smashing blow to the side of the girl's head. She shot across the room and fell, sprawled against the white-washed wall in a shower of pots and pans, mouth open on a shocked scream.

Judith felt sick, stomach muscles compressing themselves into a painful knot. It was obvious Jim Broome knew who had impregnated his daughter. A married

13

man who wouldn't be too far from this cottage. The Broomes had not the money to go travelling any distance. A weekly trip to market was the limit and Mrs Broome usually there as chaperon.

The scene she had just witnessed, Judith thought, would be very similar to the one in Chrissie Ashton's home when her fisherman father discovered she was with child by Blain Heron from the big house on the hill. That child had been Kit, brought up by Blain's childless sister Jo who'd married Gil Talbot, the local doctor. Kit had a bad reputation in Cramble though he swore he'd always been honest in his relationships and taken no girl who wanted or expected marriage. Judith, he maintained, was the only one he had loved, but words were easy and leopards did not change their spots.

Jim Broome made a move in the direction of the weeping Deborah, and Judith, unable to bear a repetition of what she had seen, moved to the door and knocked loudly. A pan rattled as Deborah squirmed against the wall away from her father's threatening shadow. There was a silence, the sound of bolts being drawn, the damp, protesting creak of the warped door. Jim stood against the gap, his face suffused with angry colour. His expression changed. 'What's wrong, Mrs Talbot?'

'A calf arriving. The cow's in trouble and my husband needs your help.'

'O' course, Mrs Talbot. Just gi' me five minutes to dress.'

'I'll tell Kit. Thank you, Jim.'

She moved away as the door closed, averting her eyes from the uncurtained window. A weight lay on her spirits. Deborah had shown unmistakable interest in Kit, who liked women. There were nights when Judith had not been able to have relations with him. It all added up to a picture she could not bear to contemplate. 'Oh, Kit,' she whispered. 'Kit—'

He was still struggling with the recalcitrant calf when she poked her head round the byre door. 'He's coming in five minutes,' she said, surveying the weary cow, its eyes dulled with pain it probably could not remotely understand.

'Good girl,' Kit told Judith, his hands still steady on the reddened rope. 'Now go back to the house. It won't do you any good to stay. Surely you know why I don't want you here? I don't want you hating the thought of motherhood. Off you go and heat some milk. I'll manage with Jim. Forget you came and saw what you did. It's a messy business, childbirth. Oh, and make sure you don't lie in in winter or I may have to deliver you myself. I'd prefer to confine my activities to cows. Judith? Is anything wrong?' His voice had changed.

'No. It's cold, that's all.' She would have to become used to reproduction. That was what farming was all about. Procreation, copulation—

'Some warm milk will send you back to sleep. I have no idea when I'll be back.'

'Would you like anything?' she asked. 'Food? Drink?'

'Not really. Jim and I will share a bottle. We'll keep warm enough.'

She turned away. He had most likely forgotten her already. There would be no time to think of anything beyond the struggle that could go on for hours.

Madge was up when she returned to Grey Ghyll, fussing and exclaiming, making her change her wet slippers for dry ones. Her kind rosy face and grey hair were comforting. 'I heard you go out and then I heard that dratted cow so I knew Mr Talbot would be in the byre. I'll see he gets his breakfast.'

16

'Jim Broome's with him.'

'Then they'll both get breakfast, never you fear. Now bed, Mrs Talbot, you look tired. I'll fetch you the milk.'

'Have some yourself. Oh, Madge, is Deborah really useful about the place?'

'Useful as any other dairymaid.'

'I wondered, has she any young man?'

'Not that her mam's mentioned. They are mostly older men in the dale so she'd need to look further afield. I must ask Amy sometime—'

'Oh, please don't tell her I was asking!'

'No, ma'am.' Madge was studying her with the beginnings of curiosity.

Judith flushed. 'You must find us very different from the Brandons.'

'Old they were, and past coping long ago. Nice couple, though. Miss Lucy was a lady and Mr David a kind gentleman. But a farm's for the young and strong.'

'Neither of them married, ever?'

'Not ever. Not that Miss Lucy didn't have a beau or two as a girl but she had invalid parents and men don't like other folks' dependants that much.'

'I suppose it does call for unselfishness.'

'Never had the children she wanted, Miss Lucy. But you'll never have that trouble, Mrs Talbot. Not with a strapping young husband like your Mr Kit.'

A curious pain lacerated Judith. It was only her own jealousy that had the power to hurt, she told herself. Broome had named no one and those glances of Deborah's were perfectly understandable, a young country girl with no contact but with hired men, then Kit, six foot three and handsome into the bargain. Virile. She'd known from the start she'd have to fight to keep him.

'I won't have any trouble,' Judith said.

'There's been a difference in Grey Ghyll since you came. Lucky Mr Kit was left that money by his mother. Many a farmer works all his life and the place never his own.' Madge watched the saucepan into which she had just poured the best part of a pint of milk.

'The Broomes will never own anything, certainly,' Judith agreed. 'It's not even their cottage. I wonder if they mind?'

'It's all they've ever known, so why should they mind? They're fortunate to work on a place where a cottage goes wi' the job! But as I was saying, Mr Kit was lucky.'

Judith wondered what Madge would say if she told her how Kit's mother had

18

earned her fortune. Chrissie Ashton had become one of the most succesful whores in London, not that they called them that when the aristocracy and Members of Parliament were involved. Then they became courtesans with connotations of near respectability. Madge's grey eyes would grow round as marbles, round as her disapproving mouth. She could understand the fact of Deborah Broome's pregnancy when it became obvious but for a woman to make a business of selling her body to the highest bidder would shock her beyond measure. And the fact that Grey Ghyll had been purchased from the elderly Brandons with the accrued earnings of such a dissolute life would appal her even more. But no one would know. The disreputable secret was quite safe.

'We have been lucky, Madge. The milk's hot enough for me.'

Madge took a pewter pot from the dresser and transferred the steaming liquid over the sink to avoid drops on the table. She was a careful person, Judith reflected, and she was lucky to have her. Luck. How that word persisted in cropping up and what a mockery it seemed without peace of mind.

Taking the hot drink back to bed, she sat against the pillows, reliving the scene in the Broome's kitchen that had crystallised all her suspicions. It was not that she thought Kit had any real feelings for that girl, but she had imagined her own hold on him was greater. The knowledge that it was not filled her with a dread of the future. Deborah might go, or lose her attraction, but there would always be someone to fill her place.

* * * *

Madge was in the kitchen when Kit returned, tired and filthy, from the byre. She had hot water ready and he washed at the sink, revelling in the sensation of being clean again, wolfing down the well-cooked food.

'I left Mrs Judith abed,' she said. 'She'd difficulty getting back to sleep. Saw her light for a long time, I did. She thought Jim Broome would be back for breakfast?'

'He had some business at home.'

'Oh?'

'Didn't say what it was. Thank God there's Robbie and the others to see to things for the next hour or two. I must go to bed myself. Can you manage the hens this morning? If Judith was so wakeful I'll try not to disturb her.'

'I can manage fine. Don't need so much sleep when you get older.'

'Thank you, Madge. That was good.'

'Glad you enjoyed it.'

'Wake me in two hours or so?'

'Three would be better.'

'Can't spare too long. There's the first of daylight.' He peered through the crack in the curtain. 'It's a good feeling to stand in your own kitchen and look out on your own land, your own cowshed.'

'I was telling Mrs Judith how lucky you were. Your own property and you still in your twenties.'

Kit heaved a sigh of pure satisfaction. 'I never expected it. It's like a miracle.'

'And a bonny little wife into the bargain. Uncommon pretty she is. Couldn't really describe her, could you, and manage to do her justice. Why, there's Mrs Broome ready to go somewhere and—is it?—yes, it's Debby with her.' Madge pulled back the curtain for a better look down the slope. 'Jim said he'd something to sort out. Looks like family business.'

Kit took a look. 'He should have told me if it's to keep the girl from the dairy. A death in the family? Who can we get in her place? Funny he didn't mention it.'

21

'Robbie's niece? He'll be up here soon. I'll ask him, shall I?'

Together they watched the two cloaked figures walking towards the stile that led to the main road. Kit gave a great, self-indulgent yawn.

'You should have made Jim and Robbie stay up with the cow,' Madge told him. 'You're the master.'

'I've always preferred to do things myself. Particularly the difficult things.'

'That's probably why Grey Ghyll's going to be a much more successful farm than when the Brandons had it. But don't stand about thinking you must talk to me. You'll have to be up soon enough.'

'The best day's work we did was taking you on, Madge.'

She looked pleased, then, looking again through the gap in the curtain, said, 'now, just where is Amy taking that girl?'

'You're a nosy old woman,' Kit answered good-humouredly. 'I could think of a few in Cramble like you.'

'That was the village you came from?' Madge turned and began to clear the table.

'Aye, and glad I was to get away from it in the end. Fine country but gossips can spoil a place. This is a fresh start—the

22

problems left behind.'

'Are they ever?' Madge reflected, giving the cloth a brisk shake out of the door.

'Pessimist!' Kit laughed, stretched copiously as though he embraced not only this comfortable kitchen that was the hub of his house, but the surrounding fields and buildings that were all his. A thrill of possession ran through his weary frame. All his life he had been made to feel shame, that he was inferior, but here he was the master and his word was law. The knowledge was heady as strong drink.

He had taken off his boots and now padded, soft-footed, in the direction of his bedchamber. The door was slightly ajar as though Judith had left it so in order that he might enter quietly. It gave a slight click as he closed it and Kit froze, half-expecting his wife to move. But she did not. He took off his breeches and his warm shirt, tossed his socks into the far corner, then tried to slide unobtrusively between the sheets, only he was too large for such a manoeuvre. A bull in a china shop he'd been called before today and it was true, he reflected ruefully.

Judith still did not move and he knew with a sudden certainty that she was foxing. A vague disquiet possessed him. Ordinarily, Judith was responsive, in a marked degree, to his proximity, and, while he was too tired to avail himself of her body, he was certainly not averse to falling asleep in her arms.

'Judith?' he whispered.

She did not answer. A tentative exploration revealed a small, stiff back and tightly jammed thighs. Even the neat buttocks seemed set against him. He tried to think how he could have offended her but failed.

'I know you're awake. What's wrong with you, girl?' His fingers teased at her flesh until she became soft and compliant, turning to him with a desperation of fierce kisses and clinging embraces as though to reassure herself of the continuance of good relations between them. The insistence of her attempts almost resulted in a resolve to take her and be hanged with the necessity of facing the day without the snatched sleep he'd anticipated, but the long strain of the night had told more heavily on his strength than he realised and he knew he could not easily satisfy her obvious need.

'Steady,' he whispered, hearing Madge pass the door. 'I'd like to love you, my own girl but it will have to wait. Tonight

24

it will be different. Hold me, while I sleep?'

She grew still and quiet.

'It's not like you to resent me without cause. What have I done?'

'That's what I wonder!'

'Judith? Stop speaking in riddles.'

She flung off his arm violently.

'If you will not let me rest, I must find another bed,' Kit said, annoyed at last. 'We will be short of hands today and I cannot afford to sleep for long.'

Judith raised herself on one elbow. Her long hair touched his face. It had a scent all of its own. 'Short of hands?' she repeated, puzzled.

'Amy Broome and Deborah have gone on some journey. I saw them leave.'

'Oh.' Her breath was expelled on a little gasp of awareness.

'You sound as if you know why. You've not quarrelled with them and kept it from me?'

'I have not. I should have thought that you would know better than I, the reason for Deborah Broome's departure.'

A cold silence settled between them. First Judith, then Kit, sat up fully and stared at one another resentfully in the gloom, all thoughts of sleep or loving gone.

'Speak your mind,' Kit said softly but there was a bite at the back of the restraint.

'If she had gone of her own accord *I* would have seen to it—'

'I am master here!'

'A stud bull, you mean. Leaving Cramble has not changed you. We heard about your grandfather. He was no better. His taste seemed to run to serving wenches—'

'Why, you insufferable little upstart!'

'At least I am not loose!'

Kit got up on his knees. The mattress sagged under his weight as he seized the tress of black hair that had seduced him only minutes ago and pulled it hard. Judith gave vent to a restrained scream. She, too, had heard Madge and wished not to advertise the quarrel. 'Come to the nub of the matter, vixen,' he growled.

'Miss Broome is pregnant. To a married man, according to her father.'

'And I am the only married man in Cumberland!' Kit released the the thick tangle, drawing away from Judith as though she had some disease.

'She cannot keep her eyes off you! And it is not only since I heard her condemned by Jim Broome that I noticed that. I suspected before—'

'Thank you for your touching faith. But when did you come to know the Broome's secret? You were eager enough last night for my despised attentions.'

Judith smacked his face, then shrank from the black anger that changed his features to those of a stranger.

'I asked you a question,' he said in a hard voice. Judith, used only to his better nature, was afraid of what she had done.

'I—I saw through the kitchen window when I went for Jim. Deborah retching and her father accusing.'

'He's not the only one, is he.' Kit shivered as though he had just become aware of his near nakedness and the chill of early morning. The room had grown tangibly lighter.

'If I was wrong, I am sorry.'

'But your tone suggests the kind of stiff-necked pride that is almost worse than the insult. You are obviously unconvinced. I do not feel that I wish to continue the discussion. I'm weary and if you do not mind, I'll find another corner—'

'Do not bother to find another chamber unnecessarily. I will not be here. I've slept sufficiently and as you point out, we are short handed—'

Judith began to climb over Kit in an effort to get out of bed but he put out an arm to keep her there. 'Be careful,' he warned. 'Be very careful. There are things that can be ruined by shrewishness—'

'Let me go.'

They surveyed one another over a chasm.

Kit released her slowly. Judith was aware of the smell of drink on his breath. He had been up all night bringing a calf and now that he should have been at peace, she had spoiled everything. One part of her wanted to grovel for forgiveness but the other saw pictures of his intimacy with the girl down the hill. She hated Deborah Broome.

Taking hold of the polished bed-pole she lowered herself to the floor. Stop me, she said to herself. Please stop me. It isn't too late. But Kit did nothing.

* * * *

The gipsies came that day. They came every year around this time, so Madge said, and the Brandons, though they had tried, had never succeeded in driving them off. They camped in the copse to the far left of the big grey house and the smoke of their fires had risen in a blue pall above the changing trees. Kit was angry at the sight of the haze that blurred the autumn colours of the dell, and, still bitter about the first quarrel with Judith, and tired with lack of proper sleep, had ridden out with his fowling-piece to have it out with the Boswells.

Ben Boswell had his various sites for particular times. He was much in the Borders and the lowlands of Scotland but the Lakes always drew him at summer's end. A truce had come to exist between him and the quiet sheep-faced Brandons. So long as he kept his tribe under control and the woods were not spoiled, the Boswells were not harried. David Brandon had been essentially kind, and recognising his own inability to eject the tough young Boswells who ran to pugilistic strength and features, realising that the resulting vengeance of the tribe could be more painful and costly than the concession of a small area of land that could never be otherwise used, he had turned a convenient blind eye to the few weeks that the gipsies were encamped. True, the game vanished and sometimes the farmyard hens, but the foxes could do as much damage, and there were always newly-whittled pegs on the step when they left, or a plaited basket, even, ironically, a couple of Grey Ghyll rabbits with dull, protruding eyes, or pheasants that were not peppered with buck-shot. Once it had been a deer with furred antlers and trout from the stream that was the main attraction of the illegal site.

'God's truth!' Kit ground out, his eyes pouched with weariness, 'as though I had not enough to worry about! They'll foul the water and leave their miserable rags and refuse. I'll *not* be intimidated!'

Madge counselled caution. 'A bad old bugger, Ben, if you get on his wrong side.'

'Maybe. But that's where weakness gets you, and I paid good money for this land. I'll not be held to ransom by a pack of tinkers. Brandon may have been a gentleman, but not I. Isn't that true, Judith?'

She stared at him, miserably, knowing that yesterday she could have refuted the suggestion light-heartedly. Today, everything was different. She did not answer, conscious of Madge's surprise. During their weeks at Grey Ghyll, she and Kit had been loving and teasing. The woman must recognise their present estrangement. Unable to bear the condemnation in Kit's look, she got up and went out into the yard where the hens still pecked busily at the morning's meal. Out of the corner of her eye she glimpsed the Broome's cottage. No smoke issued from the chimney to drift over the hill-flanks. There was only Jim, his sleeves rolled up to show sinewy forearms, slashing at thistles with a scythe and an air of hating the world.

Judith went into the byre. The cow was recovering from her ordeal while the calf, a bonny brown and white creature, lay in the straw, watching her with a limpid gaze that was half-obscured by a stiff fringe of sandy eyelashes. She both hated and loved it. Loved it for its smallness and newness, detested it for having been the indirect cause of Kit's disillusionment with herself. She had not known she could be so jealous. The fact shocked her as much as it disturbed her husband. Surely she had not thrown away all that had existed between them because of a little slut like Deborah? How could he need another girl when she had tried so hard to be a proper wife?

She flung herself out of the cowshed and was arrested by the sight of Kit on his large roan, the fowling-piece held purposefully, profile frowning. Her heart thumped erratically. He was only one and the Boswell youths were many Madge said, and wild as the country that spawned them. Judith ran to the stables and saddled her mare. Kit's anger was triggered off by her behaviour and she felt responsible for the consequences of his ill-humour.

Following the distant brown of his coat, the red sheen of the stallion, she made her way through the slanting spear-shadows thrown by the trees. The sound of the water was soporific, reminding her of the broken night. Again she saw Deborah sent flying across the kitchen by her father's heavy blow to fall in a rain of pots and pan. She would never care for kitchens in the future for that picture would be superimposed over the earthen crocks and the big scrubbed table where the genteel Lucy Brandon had never sat. There had been a fussy little parlour for Lucy, with antimacassars and sprigged rosebud china. Judith had detested it on sight, replacing all the knick-knacks with

32

polished silver and stained floorboards, curtains of bright marigold. There was a goatskin rug in front of the hearth where she and Kit made love when the bedchamber seemed too far away and desire was urgent. And now she had driven him away.

The smoke was stronger now and the quiet of the wood infiltrated with a murmur of voices, the more staccato sounds of children. Kit must be furious, Judith thought alarmed that so many strangers were making free with his property. He had grown progressively more proprietorial over Grey Ghyll and his unexpected ownership.

She spurred on the mare and stopped just before the trees ended to scrutinise the encampment. There were three large waggons covered with black tarpaulin, some grazing horses, a scamper of ragged children, thin but brown and foreign-looking. She counted at least six burly young men, all with greasy black hair and neckerchiefs, moleskin trousers. One old dame with a face composed of wrinkles out of which a hawk nose protruded and more than a suggestion of a chin. Her eyes were magnificent, dark and snap-

33

ping, seeing everything. Two or three girls in kirtles and shawls were busy around the fire that burned cheerfully, casting a golden glow on dark skins and patched clothing, the worn pattens of the women, the suggestion of slim, bare ankles and supple wrists. Music too, as strange and alien as the Boswells themselves. A strong smell of stewed rabbit.

There was a sudden silence as Kit forced the roan through the water and reined in by the group nearest the fire. The swarthy faces were blank as glass but the powerful shoulders and muscular forearms looked all the more dangerous in their immobility.

Judith became aware of patches of red that were 'kerchiefs and gowns, the reflections of firelight in glittering eyes, the mouths of the younger girls. Black and red were the colours she would always associate with the Boswells, those and the sweaty brown of their skins against which their teeth showed white and vulpine. The old woman in her rusty black assumed a queer dignity as she rose, leaning on a blackthorn stick, her nose Wellingtonian, her gaze piercing. A queen—

Judith could not hear what Kit said,

nor what the woman replied, but she saw all too clearly, that three of the youths went up to stand beside the old lady, their stance threatening. Kit shouted, one of the youths seized the weapon and twisted it from his grasp. It was discharged during the struggle and an explosion of shot tore into the tree-tops dislodging frantic swarms of rooks and smaller birds. The air was rent with bird cries.

Calling out, Judith spurred the mare into the open and splashed across the stream.

'Stay away!' Kit said fiercely. 'Go and fetch Jim and Robbie. Go on, girl!'

Judith hesitated and that was her undoing. One of the Boswell men leapt onto a brazing horse and was round the encampment in a flash though the beast was unsaddled. He seemed glued to the wide, piebald back. A broad hand clamped itself round her wrist.

'Let me go!' she cried indignantly.

Plum black eyes laughed back at her anger. Through the opened shirt she saw a tangle of strong black hair matting a broad chest. The eyes that appraised her quite openly were admiring. Her hand looked small and pale in comparison with that of her captor.

Kit struggled to free himself. 'Take your hands off her!'

Judith never knew what might have happened next. The nearest wagon flap opened to reveal a broad man of about sixty who bore a strong resemblance to the old lady who still held the stage through the sheer force of her personality. Dark eyes flickered from one to the other of the young gipsies who held herself and Kit prisoner. A harsh voice barked out words she did not understand. Her arm was released so suddenly that she swayed and almost fell. Kit surprised that he was free, reacted angrily. 'Anyone would think you were master here! This is my property now. My woods. My river.'

'Mr Brandon was a good man,' Ben Boswell said without any trace of sycophancy. 'Never had any trouble with Mr Brandon, not in all the years we camped in this place. No one can say different.'

'They laid their hands on me and my wife,' Kit said hardily. 'And let off my fowling-piece into the bargain. How can you expect me to overlook that. Intimidation—'

'I think they did not realise that Mr Brandon was no longer the owner. I feel my sons saw you as but a new overseer. One who knew nothing of a bargain made years ago. A bargain I feel you would not willingly break. They are stupid, my sons.'

'I know nothing of the bargains. Brandon said nothing—'

'We do no harm,' Boswell said, his eyes gathering up darkness, his gaze hard on the youths who had manhandled both owner and wife of this so desirable camping-place. 'I will chastise them, never fear. As in a pride of lions, the younger try to oust the chief. But I am still chief, just as you are master of this land. This area grows nothing, will never be more than a watering-place. A week or two and we are gone. We are nomads, owning nothing. A persecuted race.'

'Is there no common land?'

'Little.' Boswell made a deprecating gesture. 'Everywhere beset by magistrates—'

'Let them stay,' Judith said, thinking of the children. Their beds would be hard and cold enough in another month or two. 'What harm can it do? If the

37

Brandons had found them so much of a liability, they'd have enrolled the help of the authorities long since.'

Kit ignored her. 'And what do I get out of your presence? Depleted stock. The river polluted?'

'We'd never taint the water,' Ben refuted strongly. 'Spoil what matters most? The stream's safe enough. And what's a rabbit or two? Vermin.'

'I'd want these louts horse-whipped,' Kit said curtly, eyes cold as icebergs. 'I'll not be intimidated on my land, or see my wife restrained by a showground bully.'

'They shall be whipped in front of you, if that's what you wish.' Boswell's voice crackled like the lash itself and the snaky blackness of his eye flickered over the bulging shoulders and powerful chests of his young with serpentine menace.

'No—' Judith protested and was cut short by Kit's look of contempt.

'I do not see why I should play benefactor without some recompense,' he said, his mouth hard. 'If you want to stay, without the Military being summoned from Carlisle, I'd expect some help from your young parasites. There's always work on a farm. And we've lost our dairymaid. One of your girls for the dairy. Two of your bucks and we'll say no more except that I'll countenance no river dirt, not one bush burnt and anyone I see from the windows of Grey Ghyll will find his hide full of pellets. And these mongrels—' he indicated a scatter of thin, yellow-eyed dogs, 'keep those from my sheep and cattle or you'll be in gaol quicker than you can say Talbot. And you can pass back my fowling-piece.' He glared down at the man who had disarmed him.

The dark, gipsy face flashed hatred.

'Do as he says,' Boswell ordered with dangerous quiet. 'We cannot afford to do otherwise.'

The youth bent to retrieve the discharged weapon. Kit's hand fastened round the stock and he struck the boy's knuckles as a blow that made him close his eyes with pain. There was a murmur of threatening disapproval, quelled swiftly by Ben speaking to his tribe in his own tongue. The eyes of the old woman grew strange and mesmeric. She seemed inexplicably taller.

Judith, aware of the hostility that surrounded them, said, 'let us go home.'

'Very well.' Kit did not even glance at her. 'You know my conditions, Boswell. Keep them and all may be well between us. Disregard them and you'll take the consequences. Is that understood?'

'I understand.'

Judith, her gaze ranging the gathering, felt a sensation of danger. If she and Kit turned their backs, she thought, they could be set upon, trampled underfoot in a minute, the dogs worrying at what was left. The gipsies could surge up to the farm, overwhelm Madge and the others and set fire to the buildings. Panic flickered in her like the flames she envisaged. But—and the thought was a buoy—someone would know who had done it. The Boswells would have been seen by others in the neighbourhood. They'd not want to be taken and hanged, twelve at a time on a multiple gallows like those Bread or Blood rebels of the past. Boswell might hate them but he'd be no more anxious to die than the next man. His revenge, and she was sure it already existed, would be of a more subtle nature.

Kit motioned for her to move and she did so, glad of his bulk behind her, welcoming the splash of the water against the mare's hooves, the embracing shadow of the woods. All the way back to the house they said not one word.

* * * *

Boswell was as good as his promise. He had sufficient sense not to send those sons who had any part in the rough-handling of the Talbots, not that these two appeared any more friendly. Both were tough, surly and uncommunicative, yet there was a sort of pride in them. They did not shuffle about on the step, only stood there, straight and silent, waiting for Kit's orders. Jim Broome, understandably, did not appear enamoured of their presence but set them to cleaning the byres and splitting logs in the paddock. The sound of the axe-blows contained the same menace as that of Boswell's regard of his tribe.

The girl came like a shadow. Judith saw her darkness slanted over the kitchen window as Kit rose from a late breakfast. He had been out with Broome since six-thirty, arranging the day's work. The carter had harnessed the horses, Madge was in the dairy, the shepherd had passed

41

by with his crook and the handsome black and white collie called Ruff, and Kit himself was to inspect the pregnant cows, then go on to the sheepfold. Someone must search for a missing goose—

A hesitant tap at the door brought Kit to his feet. Judith, stone-faced, for they had spent the night at opposite sides of the bed with a gap like a field down the middle, saw the door open. She was unprepared for the girl's looks. The brown skin was expected. So, too, the black tangle of hair, the jetty eyes. The nose was a trifle long but did not detract noticeably from the hollow-cheeked splendour of the composite features. A faded red gown, almost pink in the parts that covered the girl's breasts and thighs as though the sun had shone more fiercely on these protuberances, and bare, shapely feet, completed a picture both compelling and dangerous.

'Well!' Kit said. 'So Boswell has sent you. You'd best come inside until one of us can take you to the dairy.'

The girl obeyed, standing in the middle of the kitchen with no sign of gaucherie, looking at nothing in particular.

'She should wash her hands,' Judith heard herself say harshly. 'And I do not think bare feet advisable. She should have pattens.'

'Have you none to lend her?'

'Even if I had, they would not fit her. She is so much larger.'

'My dear, you make her sound like a carthorse,' Kit observed acidly.

'That was not my intention. But the dairy is a place for cleanliness—'

'Then for heaven's sake give the wench a bath and a clean gown!'

'I ain't dirty,' the girl said, her voice deeper than Judith had imagined, and there was something in the now direct gaze that could be construed as amusement of a sort. Judith could have struck her but for the fact that the action could worsen the gulf between her and Kit.

'You will find we are more scrupulous,' Judith told her unemotionally. 'I shall leave you here with soap and water, clean clothing and a cap for your head.'

'Must I wear the cap?'

'We'd soon lose a market for butter and cheese if there were hairs in our products.'

Kit still had not gone, though that had

been his intention before the arrival of the girl.

'What shall we call you?' he asked.

'Pan. Pan Boswell.'

'The old man's daughter?'

'Aye.'

'Not—wed?'

As if that mattered, Judith thought hotly, and hoped she was.

'Not wed, sir.' The deep voice contained disturbing inflections.

'I'll need the kitchen, Kit,' Judith said, biting off the words in spite of her resolve not to allow him to see her dislike. 'And tomorrow you must come earlier, Pan Boswell.'

'We've no clocks.'

'Then bang your head on the pillow six times.'

'Ain't no pillow.'

With those looks she'd not need a pillow, Judith reflected sourly. There'd be a glistening brown shoulder for her head. She'd couple like an animal— Shocked by her thoughts, she turned away, the pink of the gown still visible on the edge of sight. 'Are you going, Kit?'

'I can see where I'm not wanted.' His voice was dry.

Not wanted! She turned her head so that he could see all of her torment. His expression changed and for a moment it was as though they were alone, that they were to come together on the goatskin that was their refuge when they could not wait to go up the long stair to bed.

'Goodbye, Kit,' she said softly.

'See someone looks for the goose,' he said and smiled.

'Perhaps it's in a certain pot that I can mention. Not a hundred miles from here.'

'I told your father, no taking what's mine,' Kit told the girl more curtly.

'We don't have no goose. Rabbit, that's all. Ain't nobody owns rabbits.'

'If they're on my land, I do. It's my grass, my crops that feed the wretched things. I may have to consider the use of traps—'

'Oh, not traps!' Pan cried out. 'My brother Ben caught 'is leg in one of them things. Died o' the bleeding, he did. Cut 'is thigh nearly through—'

'Don't upset yourself, girl,' Kit growled, seeing the glitter of tears in the black eyes, and took himself out before he made matters worse.

Pan. What a stupid, barbaric name.

Judith, disturbed by the story of the lethal man-trap, but unmoved by the girl's distress, poured hot water in a large bowl and fetched a clean gown, underclothes, and the harshest towel she could find, a faded bonnet and Madge's oldest pattens, set aside for disposal but good enough for this gipsy. She felt tired and disinclined, vaguely nauseated. Judith was strong-stomached and the queaziness didn't suit her plans for the day. The best antidote to unhappiness was hard work.

'Get on!' she said sharply. 'And no going through the drawers and cupboards after I leave you.'

'Ain't no thief,' Pan objected, slipping herself out of the pink-red gown in one movement to reveal her body, splendid in its nakedness, dusky gold with crimson-rimmed nipples.

'Is—is that all you wear?' Judith resented the girl's beauty more than the hint of the pagan.

'Ain't got no money for no more. Woman give me this, Peebles way. T'other was in rags.'

'I'd prefer it if you wore those under-things while you're working here.'

'Don't care to be too much dressed.

46

T'ain't natural—what's it matter if me bum's not covered? Can't *really* spoil cheese and butter.'

Judith gritted her teeth. 'I know more about hygiene than you do. And before you ask, hygiene means being spotless. Particular. I'll be back in ten minutes and I'll know if you haven't washed from top to toe.'

'How will you?' Pan picked up the sponge unwillingly.

'I do have a nose.'

'Ain't nobody told me I smell before.' The girl wet the sponge and soaped it gingerly, then began to wash her breasts in a slow-circling motion that was curiously sensual. She made no movement that was not graceful. She'd be a lazy bitch, Judith decided resentful and angry, banging the door behind her.

She made her way to her bedchamber. Like Kit, she preferred to take part in the running of Grey Ghyll even though most women in her position would have employed a maid as well as housekeeper. But Judith had been brought up in the house of a solicitor father with pretensions, her only function to perfect her deportment, piano-playing and her handwriting. There had been more servants than family and she had been bored to distraction. When she married Kit, she had approved his methods of complete involvement. The local gentry would despise them but Kit was Radical and had no time for bootlicking. There'd be time later for frills, he told Judith. There were only the two of them, and though Grey Ghyll was large and rather grand, much of it could remain under dust sheets till they had real friends to invite. Chrissie's money would not last for ever and ownership of the farm had made a big hole in it. Chris Ashton had been inclined to extravagance, the natural result of having made a fortune after impoverished beginnings.

Pushing a stool against the front of the bed Judith began to pull up the top sheet but the smell of Kit rose from the coverings. That dent in the front pillow was put there by his head. A red hair straggled across the creased linen, evoking the image of him. Heart-sore, she leaned forward and put her face against the place where he had lain. Tears came, not softly and easily, but harsh and painful as a flagellation. True, they had made their peace in that last moment before he left,

48

but the knowledge of Deborah, pregnant with his child, remained to torment her. She wondered what Jim Broome had told Kit, remembering the vengefulness of the scythe's slashing of the thistle patch. A hired man could hardly accuse his master and remain popular, but in any case he blamed his daughter more. Who had started the affair? Not Kit! It would be that sly little cat.

Dry-eyed now, her senses smarting, Judith straightened and finished the chore. She pushed the stool away, tidily, and made herself restore personal objects to their proper places on the dressing table. She wished the unpleasant lethargy would lift, hoping it did not presage some illness. Men did not care for ailing wives who had not the energy to cope with physical demands.

Pan Boswell was fastening the bonnet clumsily when she returned to the kitchen. The washed-out gown was too short and tight but not unbecoming. The cracked pattens had the effect of beautifying the portions of feet that remained visible, the brown, smooth ankles. Even the bonnet showed off to advantage the undeniably exciting face.

'You have not thrown away the dirty water,' Judith snapped, glad of an excuse to chide the disturbing hussy.

'Ain't 'ad time, 'ave I,' Pan pointed out, finishing the lop-sided bow.

'Well, do it, then. I have not got all day.'

Pan obeyed, face impassive.

'And squeeze out the sponge.'

The kitchen having been tidied to her satisfaction, Judith picked up the old red gown gingerly and dropped it into the clothes basket.

'I ain't got no other dress!' Pan cried, alarmed.

'It will be washed before you get it back.'

'I wish my father'd sent one o' the others, 'stead of me.'

'So do I,' Judith agreed with feeling and set off dairywards. Pan at her heels, her feet flopping in and out of the pattens in an annoying fashion. No matter how Judith tried to make excuses for the girl and her not unnatural ignorance of civilised custom and behaviour, she could feel only irritation that bordered on detestation.

They crossed the cobbled square between the two wings of the house where the fountain stood, the copper green as moss. Virginia creeper swayed against the wall that was the colour of mistletoe berries and late flowers danced like butterflies. Pan's eyes were everywhere, staring into the stables as though she'd prefer to be with the horses, peering upwards at the long, shuttered windows that marked the disused rooms.

Passing the dark cave of the brewhouse where the hogsheads showed dimly, Judith went into the dairy. It was large and cool and stone-flagged, the cheese press taking up one corner. Pan touched the mesh over the small window with a careful finger.

'That's to keep out the farm cats,' Madge said from her place at the wooden milk pails. Churns and cream skimmers gleamed in the dimness, scrupulously clean. Judith saw Pan shiver, grimacing as though she were afraid of the sterile character of the place, the lack of light and freedom. She experienced an obscure pleasure that was almost a triumph.

'I've told her she must come earlier tomorrow,' she told Madge, 'and she's not to have her own gown back till it's washed within an inch of it's life. She can keep those things she's wearing. I certainly wouldn't want them back afterwards!' Then aware of Madge's suddenly knowing gaze, she flushed. 'You show her what's required, then come back to the house. A pity we'd not just settled for Robbie's niece but this was Kit's idea. His pound of flesh from Ben Boswell. I feel he'll live to regret it.' And Judith turned her back and went out into the sunshine. She certainly would.

Staring almost unseeingly into the bleak maw of the brewhouse, at the flittering butterflies, she fought against the inclination to go and lie on the sofa and close her eyes. She had never felt like this before and the realisation frightened her. She must not be ill. The sound of the axe-blows rose and fell, perfectly spaced, coldly mechanical. It was as though they struck some nerve in her head. Already the Boswells had left their indelible mark on Grey Ghyll, on herself and Kit.

Returning to the house she went to the parlour from which she had eradicated every trace of Lucy but the lingering smell of pot-pourri that hung inside the drawers. She could see the reflections of

52

the furniture in the black floorboards, the
orange glimmer of the curtains, misted by
the prick of tears so that they were only
shifting shapes. She had intended to get
out the polish and cloths from the oak
press, to clean the silver that was her
pride, but the sound of a footstep outside
made her turn towards the door, brushing
the wetness from her eyes.

'Kit.' Surprise and contrition filled her
voice.

'Have you got rid of the Boswell
wench?'

'She's with Madge. I daresay it'll be
hours before she knocks any sense into
her.'

'Just as well.' Kit kicked the door shut
and locked it behind him as she ran across
the room.

'Shouldn't you be looking for the
goose?' she said, weariness forgotten.

He lifted her up against him. 'I've
found it, wouldn't you say?'

'I'm sorry.' The feel of his body
reminded her of her stupidity, of those
acres of empty bed. Every time she showed
her jealousy it would be a nail in the
coffin of their relationship. She should
turn a blind eye. Take what was left—'I

didn't mean it,' she whispered.

'What was it you called me?' he went on.

'I don't remember.' She stroked his back, her nails grooving the stuff of his shirt.

'A stud bull. That's what I recall, and somehow, the expression reminded me of nights that were preferable to the one just ended.'

'I'm sorry.'

'Don't be.' He let her slide onto the goatskin rug. 'I'm just about to prove the truth of what you said. Do you mind?'

She did not answer but there was no need.

* * * *

The Boswells were still camped by the stream. The leaves had changed colour and were flying off with every twist of the wind. Fences were all mended and the winter wood-pile ready for the first snows. Pan Boswell had mastered the intricacies of the dairy though her hours were erratic. Some mornings she would be there when Judith came down to breakfast, others, she would arrive later and with no proper explanation. But whatever time she came, she was made to wash thoroughly before her day's work.

'*Every* day, Mrs Talbot?' she asked in disgust.

'Every day. Would you care to drink milk or touch butter and cheese prepared by dirty hands?'

'But I ain't dirty! Washed yesterday and the day before—'

'So long as you are here you'll do as I say. I did not want you and your tribe. You're none of our responsibility, but, like my husband, I do not see why you should occupy any part of Grey Ghyll without some kind of recompense. You and your brothers are paying your father's dues.'

'Mr Brandon didn't—'

'Mr Brandon was soft,' Judith said crisply. 'Now get those things off. You'd best wear your own gown today and the other can go into the laundry basket. And there is fresh underwear—'

'Underwear!' Pan muttered under her breath. She hated the silly constricting things as much as she detested Judith and the regimented hours in this place. Before she was out of sight of the house at the end of the day's work she divested herself of the long white drawers and pushed them inside the hollow tree at the entrance to the wood. They irritated her crotch since her legs were longer than the person's for whom they were originally intended.

'What did you say?' Judith asked sharply.

'Thinking of my gran,' Pan replied untruthfully. 'Got a fever, she 'as. Shilale.'

'Shilale?'

'Aye. Fever from marshes and the like. It's a gipsy word.'

'And how will she cure that down in the damp of the woods and water?' Judith asked sarcastically.

'With the lungs and livers of three frogs—'

'Don't be stupid!' Judith laughed unkindly.

'T'ain't stupid, ma'am. Dried and powdered mixed in a cup and drunk. And then Gran says "Frogs in my belly, devour what is bad. Show the evil the way out." And it goes. Usually—'

'Superstitious twaddle.'

'You can believe what you like, ma'am—'

56

'Oh, I shall! Never you fear. Now get on. I shall want the kitchen soon.'

Pan, deflated now that her enemy had gone, took off her clothes and put them in the wicker basket. She recognised it as one that her sister Peg had woven for young Mrs Lucy two years back. They'd leave nothing for young Mrs Talbot. Didn't deserve anything with her carping ways. She picked up the sponge and wet it, rubbed it on the cake of carbolic soap. Judith had an eye like an eagle. She'd know immediately if the soap had not been used. All these pernickety restrictions were gall after a life bounded by tinkering, peg-making, telling a farmer's wife her fortune by the Tarot cards. Running wild with the dogs, the stars through night branches. The smell and feel of the wind and camp-fire.

The outside door opened suddenly in the middle of her ruminations and Mr Talbot stood there, staring, while the leaves pattered in to rustle against the kitchen floor.

'I'm sorry,' Pan muttered, the sponge held against her magnificent breasts but covering nothing. 'Your missus did say I must always bolt the door. But I forgot—'

Kit said nothing. How green his eyes were. Pan shuddered as the chill wind licked around her bare body and he closed the door against the weather as if he had only just come to life.

'Your mistress,' he said at last. 'Where is she?'

'Gone upstairs. Be back in a few minutes. Been slow I have—' Her voice died away under the intentness of his stare. It was as though he had, for the first time, become aware of her. She seized the towel, afraid that Judith would surprise them, and wrapped it around her. 'I'd best hurry. Don't like me to dawdle, she don't.'

'No,' he said after a minute. He'd never taken his eyes off her. Not that many men would do any different, confronted by a naked woman at this time of the morning, or at any time she amended, half wanting him to go, the other half conscious of the fact that, given half a chance he'd be at her like a ram at a ewe. But she couldn't, of course. Old Ben would kill her for going with a gorgio. It would be bad enough taking a Lovell. Only a friendly tribe, like the

58

Faas, would meet with Boswell's approval.

But it would serve Mrs Judith right if she let Mr Kit do as he so obviously wanted. Pan Boswell smiled. 'Don't want to get me in no trouble, do you, sir?'

'Better hurry up then, hadn't you,' Kit told her. 'That's not the way to keep out of mischief but I suspect you know that already.' His half-smile told her he was not in the least angry and that he had no intention of mentioning this unexpected episode to that termagant wife of his. Only five minutes ago she had wanted more than anything to be gone from Grey Ghyll but now Pan was content to stay. Even in that tight, old charity gown Kit Talbot was going to see her as she was at this moment. She'd prick at his memory like a thorn against the flesh.

'Don't know what you mean,' she said softly, willing him to touch her.

He slapped her rump in passing. 'I'll see my wife doesn't come down too soon. But get moving, girl, before you really make her angry.'

' 'Ave already, I'm afraid.' She laid aside the inadequate towel and picked up the cotton drawers to cover up the dark triangle of hair he had already seen.

'You must not think we both disapprove,' he said carefully.

'Oh, I don't think that, sir.'

He looked back just before he left the room. He didn't want to go, Pan thought exultantly. It was just that he had to. Damn Mrs Judith Talbot for a lucky bitch. She threw down the drawers in a gesture of defiance, then bent to retrieve them. It could be exciting to have someone else take them off. Someone not a hundred miles from here. Someone with green eyes—

2

'Jo and Gil are coming,' Kit told Judith, laying aside the letter from Cramble. Quite clearly he saw the wide, pale beach, the slate roof of Heronbrook, the pantiles of the village below. The smell of kippers seemed to invade the room. Life was all a matter of the senses and what one experienced in boyhood was what lasted though one never realised it at the time.

'That will be pleasant. I'll get Robbie's niece in while they're here. She was disappointed over the dairy, but once those shiftless Boswells have gone, she'll take over. When are they going?'

'Oh, any time, I expect.' Kit's tone was evasive. He did not meet her eyes.

Judith sat up very straight. 'You don't want them to go, do you. Not that girl, at least.'

'You are not, by any chance, going to show the kind of obsessive jealousy you did over Deborah Broome, are you?' How cold his voice had become.

'I'm not blind.' And how she persisted!

'Can I not admire anything, or anyone, without incurring your displeasure?'

'Admiration is one thing. Impregnating skivvies is another!'

'My dear, you sometimes manage to sound exactly like your pompous father. You have not the slightest proof that I was responsible. And the girl has gone now and her secret with her.'

'And her father, which seems very odd. For a man to leave his work and a cottage—'

'He obtained employment elsewhere.'

'In order, I suppose, to remove his

61

daughter so that she'd not be brought to bed yearly of your bastards?'

There, it was said, and Judith knew with a terrible inevitability, that she had gone too far. She had sworn not to interfere with his doings so long as he still wanted her but it had proved too difficult. And whenever her jealousy overcame her, there would be a reconciliation of sorts, but every time the spell of estrangement would last longer, the tenuous peace be more uncertain, until, eventually, there would be nothing left. She had known it on the first day she came here. Why could she not behave as other women did, be wife when it suited one's husband and pretend ignorance when he took a mistress? But not all husbands had a hold over their wives. Many women were frigid, experiencing nothing but boredom and a longing to have the whole sordid business over so that they might sleep. She wanted Kit so badly that she often wakened him during the night so that he'd take her again, or sometimes he would do the wakening and that was when she received the greatest pleasure. The gradual growth of consciousness, the delicious awareness of what he was doing. He could never find anyone who needed him more. She'd die if she'd driven him away for good.

Kit pushed back the chair, thrust aside his unfinished food and went from the room. Judith tried to justify herself. He would come back in a minute and all would be well. But he did not return and the world was a desert.

She picked up Jo's letter and looked at it almost unseeingly. Tenderness for Kit exuded from the closely written sentences. Here was a woman who had brought up someone else's child and had revelled in the exercise. Her brother's bastard. That was the real motivation. There was a strong tie of blood and Jo had been childless. She'd thought of Kit as her own.

That was the real reason for Judith's present desperation. Deborah Broome could conceive and she herself may never do so. There was always difficulty with her periods. They were sparse and infrequent, not conducive to procreation. She had known this since she had visited Dr Bassett in Keswick and had been unable to communicate the worry to Kit for fear of disappointing him. He would want a son, especially now that he had come

63

into property.

Blinking away two blistering tears, she continued with the news of Cramble. Her father had not changed. Still, he ignored any members of the Heron or Talbot household; growing meaner and sourer with the passing months. He never mentioned his daughter Judith since she ran off to marry her disreputable lover. How he must have deplored the spoilation of his plans to marry her off to Sir Carne Amberwood. She might have been mistress of that cold, golden house, married to a man as obsessed by her as she was with Kit, but that was all gone like a dream or a nightmare. Even then she had been jealous of Kit—

She threw down the letter and went in search of Madge. Preparing Grey Ghyll to welcome the Talbots would fill her time for long enough to win Kit back again. Jo might be able to advise her and Gil might suggest some remedy for barrenness. He was a doctor, after all, not that he'd managed to do anything for his own wife.

* * * *

64

Judith and Kit had achieved a cautious truce by the time the Cramble visitors arrived. Robbie's niece, Betty, had been very useful, a clean, rosy, willing child, and Judith, still lethargic and suspended uneasily between listlessness and bouts of energy, had decided to keep her as a general help. Her sister Joannie could go to the dairy. She was taller and stronger than Betty for all that she was eleven months younger. Between them, they'd lift some of the load from her and from Madge who had been over-worked since Amy and Deb Broome had gone. The thought of Deborah brought back bitterness that was undiminished.

Once Jo and Gil were at Grey Ghyll, there was little time to brood on past wrongs. There was always something to do and Judith was worn out at bedtime, past caring even that Kit might be looking for more than the sight of her back in the big, shadowy bed.

'We must ride,' Kit told Gil at breakfast on the third day.

'Oh? Are we not included?' Jo teased. She seemed, Judith thought, to become more beautiful as she grew older. Her likeness to Kit was extraordinary until one remembered that Blain Heron, Kit's father, and Jo had been twins. 'It would do Judith no harm to be released from the necessity of chores. She's looking pale.'

'Judith is always pale.'

'Paler than usual,' Gil put in. 'And I prescribe fresh air.'

'Very well,' Kit said equably. 'Come and choose a mount.'

'What about neighbours?' Jo asked. 'I thought we might have seen some by now.'

'We have the Boswells,' Judith said rapidly and clearly. 'They camp on our land.'

'My land,' Kit pronounced as quickly. 'And I see that they pay their dues.'

'Indeed you do,' Judith agreed, thinking of Pan Boswell and her plentitude of charms, her sly eyes watching Kit's progress as Deb Broome's had done. 'I'm sure they give excellent value though the merchandise may be somewhat soiled.'

Jo frowned, all too aware of undercurrents. 'I thought we might see some of the less civilised country before we left. There was a wild valley Brandon Amberwood used to love. At the end of

66

nowhere, my mother said, and a huge purple rock like organ pipes—'

'That's Pillar,' Kit said, his anger held in check, 'but to go there calls for feats of mountaineering I think beyond you, Jo.'

'Well, that's plain-speaking enough,' she answered with mock indignation. 'To throw my age in my face so churlishly. But if it's so difficult then it's as well Judith will not be called on to make such an effort. You should give your wife a holiday, Kit. From everything.'

'She may take one with pleasure,' Kit said impersonally.

'Come back with us,' Jo suggested. 'The sea air would be beneficial. No worries—'

'You sound just like a doctor's wife,' Kit told her, only half amused.

'I *am* a doctor's wife.'

'Do you wish to go back to Cramble?' Kit asked.

'Another time, perhaps,' Judith answered. Not now. Not with the Boswells still here. 'I think I could not face meeting Father and Mother. It would be dreadful. He must have been so enraged over the business of running away from

67

Amberwood where he had such hopes of me becoming Sir Carne's lady. Then marrying you over the blacksmith's anvil at Gretna Green, knowing how he'd disapprove.'

'I know how you must feel. But if you'd stayed you'd have contracted the typhoid as Carne did. They'd have lost their only child,' Jo said.

'They'll never see it as you do. Father will have made up his mind, that, had I agreed to marry Carne earlier, Carne would not have contracted the disease and I should now be mistress of a great house in Hampstead. A house that would have been a prison as my own home used to be.'

'You had not the happiest of childhoods, I agree.'

'The only thing that made it bearable was being able to look out of my window and seeing Kit riding around Heronbrook. Do you remember that spinney, Kit, where we planned to meet one night after the household was asleep, only Father saw me with my cloak on, at the back door, and whipped me within an inch of my life?'

'I—remember.' Kit's face had whitened.

'He was really set against me.'

'And then, Carne, who was visiting his mother at Heronbrook, asked Father to send me to Hampstead to be a companion to his daughter, Faro. You remember Faro?'

Judith was looking at her husband with an expression that disturbed Jo. She'd expected to find them in the still ecstatic state of young married bliss but neither Kit nor his wife appeared in the least happy. Judith was hag-ridden and Kit short of temper, and both were quite obviously at loggerheads. One would have thought they'd have tried harder to conceal the fact. It could not be a small disagreement or it would have been easier to dissemble.

'I remember Faro particularly well,' Kit agreed loudly.

'I thought you might.'

Silence descended, thick and hostile. Gil threw down his table napkin. 'About that ride? Should we not go?'

'Yes,' Jo said quickly. 'Your Madge will manage perfectly well without you, Judith, now you've got—what's her name?'

'Betty.'

'They'd get on much faster if we were not here.'

They were all rising and the chairs were scraping against the shiny floorboards, then they were dispersing to put on their outdoor things for the outing that held out no promise of pleasure.

'My God,' Gil said to Jo, in the privacy of their room. 'You cou⸬ l cut the atmosphere with a knife. What do you suppose is wrong?'

'That girl is desperately unhappy. You only need to look at her. But she'll drive him away and I love Kit. I couldn't bear to see his life spoiled—'

'It might be his fault. I recognise the signs. She's jealous, and remembering Kit as he used to be, one hasn't far to look for the possible cause. Cherchez la femme, my dearest Jo.'

'I hate to admit to Kit's clay feet, but you could be right. A pity she wasn't happily pregnant and oblivious to anything else.'

'How do you know she isn't?' Gil said unexpectedly. 'The early stages can make women hard to live with.'

'But if it was that, Kit would be overjoyed. He'd fuss over her, bad humour or no. Now that he's a landowner, children will have assumed their own importance in his mind.'

'I still thinks she looks like a girl who could be enceinte without knowing it—'

'What? Married to a lusty young buck like our Kit and still not knowing the whys and wherefores of the business! And you'd think that living on a farm would teach her the mechanics of the entire process. She can't be that green after all these months. How many is it? Five? Six?'

'Something like that.'

'Oh Gil, we must do something! Thank God we don't have such problems.'

'I seem to remember rather precarious beginnings.'

'Well—perhaps. But that was different.' Jo reached out and took his hand.

'It's always different when it's ourselves, a useful thing to remember. Our early marriage was no bed of roses, my sweet, however well it turned out afterwards—'

'It proved to be—a miracle. Once I came to my senses.'

'Perhaps it can for them. I'll talk to Kit—discreetly. And you must do the same with Judith. We do know some of the pitfalls, after all. And in spite of what I said, I'd not exchange one day we've spent together. I love you, Jo, always have, always will.'

'And I you.' Jo took his thin, dark face between her palms and pulled him towards her. Their kiss was not gentle.

'I don't know that I want to go, after all,' Gil murmured.

'We must. It's hardly decent to drag me back to bed after breakfast and our hosts kicking their heels at the stables—'

'I find the notion titillating. But I suppose you are right. Perhaps we should put *them* to bed and let them sort out their differences there.'

'I suspect they've tried that. Let's face it. Kit being Kit, that would be his idea of a reconciliation. He's a Heron, after all, and we are notoriously over-sexed. It's no secret.'

'Not from me!' Gil slapped his wife's rump and pushed her towards the door. 'But I have no complaints. I can see,' he continued, with a look out of the window as they hurried downstairs, 'why Kit wanted this place. It's quite beautiful.'

Crisp air met them as they crossed the yard to the stables. There was a slight film of frost over the cobblestones and the fountain turned to a milky green.

'Look! Hogsheads. That must be the brewhouse,' Jo said, lifting her green skirts from the damp. 'I wonder if they make their own ale? And I suppose that's the dairy. Yes, I see churns and a corner of the press. Oh, and a girl.'

'As you say,' Gil agreed thoughtfully, 'and *what* a girl.'

'I suppose she's that gipsy creature.'

'It's not like you to show your claws, Jo.'

'We must all sometimes. I think I begin to understand.'

'But she's just a bird of passage. Gipsies never stay anywhere for long.' Gil took long strides in the direction of the stables. 'It's against their nature.'

'She's already been here long enough to do damage. I wonder if that old man—Boswell—sent her as a sort of revenge? Because Kit insisted on a return for his hospitality.'

'Hospitality! But you're an astute lady. That young Diana sent to sow seeds of discord, eh? She appears to have succeeded and I can't say I altogether blame Kit, either.'

73

'Gil Talbot!' She slapped his hand.

'Now, now,' Kit said more easily, emerging from the stable, a grey on a leading rein. 'Having a tiff?'

'You have not the prerogative,' Jo replied, stroking the grey's nose.

Kit stared at her unsmiling. 'I might have known you'd ferret something out.'

'Plain as the nose on your face, my boy,' Gil supplemented. 'Shall we go ahead and leave Jo to follow with Judith?'

'If you like.'

'Am I to have this lovely mare?'

'Yes, Jo. I thought this one for you, Gil.'

'Anything with four legs.'

Judith emerged, white and subdued, dark rings of weariness round her eyes. Jo studying her narrowly, wondered if Gil might not be right. She had looked much the same when she first realised she was with child. A child that was lost and gone this twenty-five years and more. The pain was still there, perhaps a little blunted but sharp enough.

Judith had her own troubles, that was evident, and suddenly, Jo was, for the first time, angry with Kit. This girl had

74

suffered for him, given up position and riches to be his wife, estranged herself from her parents—not that that was much loss—the Lammeters were an unprepossessing pair. Jo put her arm round Judith's shoulders and felt the slim, young body lie for a moment against her own. She'd get the girl's secrets out of her easily enough, just as Gil would disinter Kit's.

Pan Boswell, her face pushed up against the mesh of the dairy window, watched the small party mount and clatter away over the cobbles. There was something about the red-haired lady that put her on her guard. A different kettle of fish she was from young Mrs Talbot.

Something fluttered in the lower branches of the hedge beyond the courtyard. A wren. The witch-bird, Pan thought, alarmed. As though one of them had left behind some part of themselves to watch her. The tiny bird moved so fast and daintily, never leaving the spikes of hawthorn, its eyes catching sparks from the sun so that they were red sequins. Red, like the strange woman who had come from Northumberland.

Pan became aware of her chilled hands

and heels, the discomfort of the detested drawers. She kicked out at one of the wooden buckets and gained a warped satisfaction as the milk slopped out over the flagstones. But the witch-bird remained and she could not concentrate for thinking of it.

* * * *

They had skirted the gipsy encampment, everyone busy, the fire leaping as usual, the savoury odour of rabbit and fowl mingling with the smoke. The children hung from the branches of trees, showing their genitals under the skimpy clothings. Dogs bared their fangs and ran, snapping at the horses' legs until they were called away, still snarling as they slunk back to the waggons after Kit's fierce shout of protest.

The trees dwindled to leave a graveyard of huge white stones, brown hills patched with cloud shadow. A tarn grew out of distance, black in the shadow of the fells, then was left behind. There was nothing in the wilderness beyond but a lace of dark branches and a mass of stained rubble that had once been a house.

Jo stared at the ruin. Behind her, Kit was saying, 'I wish I'd met Cobbett. To think that a man who was once a ragged boy scaring the rooks from the fields should accomplish all that he did. He became a clerk in a lawyer's office—'

'Must have taught himself more than just to read, then,' Gil commented. 'You'd need to have a special head on your shoulders to cope with law. Never understand official papers myself.'

'He was in the army for a spell—'

'And didn't he teach French refugees? I seem to remember he was a hero in France,' Jo put in, half her mind on the clutter of burned stones and half on the conversation.

'He also rode hundreds of miles in the pursuit of bettering agriculture. That was his most important function,' Kit said definitely. 'His epitaph.'

'More than his pamphlets and his political papers?' Jo queried, shivering as she took in the import of the tumbled blocks. 'What a fire that must have been. And in so isolated a place. There'd be no one to help put it out.'

'More than that.'

'What happened over there?'

'That, Jo, was a house that belonged to a man called Carter.'

'Carter? I seem to recall the name—'

'Jack Carter ran off with Bran Amberwood's mistress. His wife, Anne, stayed on there, a recluse. She was in the place when it burned down, poor soul.'

'Bran Amberwood? Oh, God, that was not the woman he strangled? The Pengallon woman? Kate?'

'Yes. She went off with Carter but he abandoned her. Then, somehow, the Pengallon child, Bran's daughter, found her mother and I've never really understood what happened but Bran blamed Kate for her death. No one knows the true story, or ever will, now.'

'And Carter's wife? Was she alone at the time of the fire?'

'Quite, with a pack of dogs for protection, so there was no question of foul play. They'd have torn a stranger apart. But she grew careless with drink and they say a coal fell out of the fire while she was asleep.'

'What a horrible place.' Jo hunched her shoulders. 'And has Carter never been back, not even to sell the land?'

'Making merry on his wife's money, they say. But it won't last for ever. Then he'll have to sell. It would be interesting to see who buys it.'

'It's—haunted land,' Jo protested. 'I could never live there.'

'Be comforted,' Gil reassured her. 'We could not afford it. You're quite safe.'

'Don't joke! Not about that. That terrible ruin—'

'But it isn't a joke. We are impecunious, though, unlike Mr Micawber, we are always on the credit side. Just.' Gil laughed as though it did not matter.

'You must come here,' Judith said. 'When you retire from doctoring.'

'You're a kind child. But we're quite happy, aren't we Jo?'

'Quite.' Jo's face showed the truth of her answer.

'That child,' Kit said, 'who's to have Heronbrook after Grandfather because he was born on the right side of the blanket. Have you seen him?'

'A fine little boy,' Jo answered. 'I thought I'd hate him but how can anyone hate a child. One would require to be a monster. And you need not grudge him his dues, Kit Talbot, for Heronbrook could slip out of his children's hands one day, entails being what they are, but this is yours for ever. Father does not mind too much because he was always friendly with Willam and his branch of the family. He used to escape to Berwick at times in order to avoid the attentions of your great-aunts, Judith. Poor old sticks, never a man in their lives, only the sight of my handsome reprobate of a father to give them the dreams that such women need. We are lucky, Judith, you and I, with flesh and blood instead of shadows.'

'There are always women to dream about other women's men!'

'You said that with real feeling.'

'Judith has an over-active imagination,' Kit said, not amused. 'I'm afraid I do not share your maganimity towards—what's the child's name?'

'Nicholas. Nicholas Heron-Maxwell.'

'Heron this! Heron that! Not that your efforts to have me known as Heron-Talbot had much success. I'll always be Kit Ashton to Cramble folk. The truth is there are no Herons now but Richard and Bethel. The rest are all adulterated stock—like watered-down wine.'

'I suppose you are right. Like the

80

Amberwoods. Reduced to that strange creature, Faro.'

Judith compressed her lips. It was obvious she had no liking for the girl. Perhaps the little madam had set her cap at Kit. Amberwoods had always been a fatal weakness for Herons, whether or not they were called Heron or some other quite irrelevant name.

* * * *

As they rode back, Jo lagged behind on the pretext of asking Judith the names of the hills in the far distance.

'You don't look as well as you should,' she said bluntly. 'What's the reason?'

Judith, glad of a confessor, told her of the visit to Dr Bassett and of his unpromising verdict.

'But, if your periods are so infrequent, it's not impossible you could already have conceived without the usual signs becoming apparent?'

'No. I really could not tell. I thought I'd go out of shape. Oh, I don't know what I imagined.'

'You must let Gil have a look at you. He'll know.'

'Would he?'

'He's been doing it for long enough. Examining breeding women, I mean, not helping them to become so.'

Jo thought that Judith would laugh, but she did not.

'We saw the dairy girl,' she went on, 'who did she replace?'

Judith flushed. 'A girl called Broome, daughter of one of the hired men in the cottage nearest the house.'

'Why did she leave?'

'She was—expecting.'

'I see. And no husband.'

'No.'

'How many cottages are there attached to Grey Ghyll?'

'Four. One at approximately each corner of the land. Robbie Dixon has one—he has a wife and three children—well, two are his dead brother's. Then there's Job Hunt and Ethel. They've no children. And the other's occupied by Isaac and Hannah Nisbet and their two sons.'

'How old?'

'Between forty and fifty. Never married, either of them.'

'It looks as if they might have been indulging in an Indian summer. One of them at least,' Jo observed.

Judith looked blank.

'Well, I don't suppose the Broome girl was visited by the devil or got her child under a gooseberry bush.'

'No.' Judith looked away.

'Get—strange, sometimes, bachelors of that age.'

'Her father said it was a married man.'

'Well, that leaves Isaac, Job, and what's the Dixon man called?'

'Robbie. It wouldn't be any of them. Isaac's too old. Job has enough on his hands with Ethel, says she's turned him off women for good. She's a scold.'

'And Robbie?'

'Thinks the world of Janie. She's a bit of an invalid and he does lots of things to make life easier for her. He and Kit get on very well. He'd never want to hurt Janie. You can see how kind a man he is, taking on his brother's girls. It was having his own child damaged Janie.'

'So, she thinks it must have been Kit,' Jo thought, hardly aware of the passing countryside, vast and silent and impressive though it was. 'And now she sees Pan Boswell as another threat. We must get rid of that girl. Gil might have an idea.'

It was not until after lunch that Gil announced that he was going to examine Judith, with Kit's permission.

'If you think it necessary,' Kit said in such a manner that betrayed the fact that he did not.

'Kit,' Jo said when Judith had gone upstairs with Gil. 'Your poor little wife is afraid she cannot give you a child.'

'If she did not give way to certain obsessions, perhaps she'd find it easier.'

'Like you and the Broome girl—you and that hussy in the dairy?'

'Exactly.'

'And has she cause? No, I should not have asked you that,' Jo said. 'Your life is your own and I cannot interfere. But Judith has been told that a difficulty exists. A visit to Dr Bassett, do you recall?'

'She said it was because she feared a chest complication.'

'Women find it difficult to disappoint the men they love. And she is right to think you'd place importance on an heir to all this?'

'Of course I want a son!'

'Where Judith is concerned, there are only rare times when she could conceive.

84

Do you see her problem now?'

'You mean, we might never hit that exact moment?'

'To put it baldly, yes.'

'And I thought—oh, no matter, she's right to feel I'd be disappointed. Only it would be cruel to show it, now you have explained matters. What am I working for, building up this farm, if it is not to pass on to my own flesh and blood?'

'It is possible—'

'But highly improbable.' Kit shrugged. 'I think I'll go over to the byres.'

'Will you not wait?'

He shrugged. 'What for? To see Judith's face when there's nothing wrong with her but spleen?' and he flung himself from the room.

Jo sighed and went to the window to watch him go down the hill. She saw him hesitate and look towards the dairy, then he turned and plunged in the direction of the whitewashed byres.

'Jo?' Judith had come back unnoticed. Jo looked at her tear-wet face and was filled with compassion. She held out her arms. 'You've got years ahead of you. What's six months? Hardly an apprentice-ship, is it?'

'But you don't understand!'

'What—you mean, you *are?* Oh, Judy, that is the answer to all your problems. Kit will be so busy cherishing you after the realisation that it could have been so much more difficult, he won't have time for—distractions.'

'Shall I tell him? Now?'

'No. Choose your moment. Have a bath, dress up. Make him look at you. That's—that's what I would have done.' Jo shivered as though a goose had walked over her grave.

'Then that's what I'll do.' Judith, unnoticing, went upstairs singing.

* * * *

The evening meal was a vastly different occasion from the early and disagreeable lunch. Judith had come down, radiant, her black and white beauty set off by a gown of peony red she had been saving for a special occasion, her eyes so brilliant that the shadows were hardly noticeable.

Kit who was standing with his broad back to the fire, talking to his guests, stared and could not look away. He'd meant to be cool and censorious but this

86

was a Judith he had never seen before and his senses responded to her gaiety, the added dimensions to her undeniable looks. She had always held the suggestion of remoteness with that moonscape colouring, but seeing her in that dress with the bodice cut lower than usual, he was visited by the image of the goatskin rug and of all the totally enjoyable encounters he had enjoyed thereon.

'You look delightful,' Gil said gallantly, raising the glass Kit had just filled. 'To you, Judith. Is there any reason for this evening's splendour?'

'You know there is!' Judith said, the colour racing up her cheeks so that her eyes were brighter than ever. 'Have you not told Kit? I fancied you might.'

'Told Kit what?' Gil parried. 'There are things no intermediary should attempt.'

'What must I be told?' Kit asked, his pulses suddenly pounding.

Jo moved towards the window, wanting, ridiculously, to cry for the babies she had never had, babies who might have inherited Gil's dark, keen looks or her father, Rich's red hair and green eyes. Boys who would have resembled Kit. A touch of her arm showed her Gil, his gaze compassionate. 'Forgive me? I'm being so stupid,' she whispered.

'I feel like doing the same,' he murmured, stroking her wrists gently, taking her hand up to his lips, knowing that nothing he did would be noticed by the two young people at the fireside. 'My poor Jo—'

'Well?' Kit was saying, his hands held out to take Judith's. 'What's the secret?'

'Can you not guess?'

'It's not—a baby?'

She nodded, not trusting herself to speak.

Kit gave a shout and swept her up against him, the red skirts swaying in the draught of the fire. 'I thought Gil must be making mountains of molehills. You clever, adorable girl. It would have been strange had you not fallen, for you've had little enough peace. Eh? My darling Judith—'

'Shall we go?' Gil asked, laughing. Jo had recovered from her moment of regret and was smiling, glad of the reconciliation. Kit's baby would be her first grandchild—as good as any real grandchild.

'We must drink to the bairn. And to

my wife. Madge? Madge! Where's that wine I had put away for Christmas? Fetch it out, woman. Why? Because I'm to be a father. Aye, woman! You heard right. And bring a glass for yourself. What a ridiculous theory that was of yours, Jo, that Judith would have difficulties—'

'This time, it is all right,' Jo tried caution but Kit would have none of it.

'We'll have a quiverful—'

'There may by only this one—'

'What a time to be a Jonah!' Kit scoffed, Judith still held up against his massive chest. 'It's time for a gift, my sweet. What would you like most of all? Today, I'll refuse you nothing.'

'I should like to see the Boswells go. And not come back.' Judith's voice sounded loud and clear in the sudden silence.

Kit set her on her feet and laughed with forced amusement. 'You certainly pick your times to blackmail.'

'That is the only thing I want.' Her voice was a challenge.

'How can I refuse?' He laughed again, awkwardly, and turned away. 'You shall have your wish, little wife. I did promise.'

'You've not asked when it is to be. The

child's birth—'

His face became animated. 'No. I hadn't thought that far ahead. When?'

'April or May. Gil could not say any closer.'

'So—' Kit counted up on his fingers. 'It must have taken me at least two or three months to put you in this interesting condition. One of us is a slowcoach. Do not just stand there, Madge, my love. Come in. This is to celebrate the impending arrival of my son.'

'It may be a girl,' Jo pointed out.

'Never,' Kit said confidently. 'A boy. You'll see. You'll all see.'

* * * *

Pan Boswell, drawn by the lights and sound of laughter, crossed cautiously towards the uncurtained window. She had slipped away from the camp after supper because she had experienced a violent desire to see Kit even though it must be from a distance.

There were several people standing around the table, the red-haired woman and her man, Madge, the housekeeper, and Kit with his wife. Pan almost forgot discretion when she saw Judith's gown, the animation of her face. That beautiful bluish-red, that pale skin and black hair. She watched Kit fondle his wife, tip the glass so that her lips might drink. The lips that had said so many harsh words in the past few weeks. Kit bent to kiss Judith and Pan clenched her hands till her nails pierced her palms, then slid to the ground, her cheek resting against the damp cobbles. She knew the wren had been a bad omen.

It was a witch-bird. Gipsy lore was never wrong.

* * * *

Jo and Gil were to leave at the end of the week. They were not entirely happy about the locum and some of their patients would not go to a stranger no matter how much they might need medical help. Besides, they had done their part in the reconciliation of Kit and his wife and could go with an attendant glow of satisfaction.

Judith sang as she went about the house in an even better humour since Pan Boswell had not put in an appearance this morning. She had sent for Joannie Dixon so that if the girl did come later, she'd find herself redundant. Joannie, clean and rosy as her sister, and decently clad, did not require to be washed in the kitchen like a street arab.

Coming down from the supervision of Betty Dixon who was taking over the bed-making since Judith was not supposed to stretch, she found Jo at the kitchen door, looking down past the byres to the cottage once occupied by the Broomes.

'Kit must find another man if he's dismissing the Boswells today.'

'He'll have no difficulty there. Always plenty of labour.'

'And he's really pleased about the baby?'

Judith, with memories of Kit's more private thanks after they'd gone to bed, smiled.

'He's pleased all right. Is Gil with him?'

'No. Gil wanted to stretch his legs up the hill. Kit went off on his own. I hope Ben Boswell's as good at keeping his family under control as you say he is.'

'He's the only one who can. Perhaps they won't come this way again now Grey

92

Ghyll's changed hands. There's no one to stop them on the Carter land. Why don't they go there?'

'There's water, I presume?'

'Oh yes. Not so abundant, but perfectly adequate.'

'I think I'll go and look for Gil,' Jo decided. 'You seem well organised and we don't often have the chance of a climb together. It's flat in Northumberland apart from the Cheviots and those are too far from Cramble. No, don't you come, Judith. It's too rough. Take a rest on the sofa.'

'I shall find it very irksome. I much prefer to be active.'

Jo, with words of caution, departed in the direction Gil had taken earlier.

Alone, shooed out of the kitchen by Madge, seeing that Betty was coping admirably, Judith was restless. She went down to the byres, already cleaned by the scowling Boswells, and looked at the calves, then drawn by some compulsion, made her way to the Broome cottage.

The rooms were silent with that peculiar, haunted emptiness of abandoned dwellings. Running a finger over the window frames, Judith saw that they needed cleaning. On the bare, scrubbed table that was part of the furnishing of the little, dark house, were lumps of candle-grease that required to be prised off. Neither task was onerous. She'd do it herself since everyone else was busy.

Returning to the kitchen which was now empty, Madge having taken herself off somewhere else, she found a clean cloth, soap, filled a pail with warm water, then took up the sharpest knife she could find to use on the hardened wax. She saw Robbie Dixon in the distance, wearing muddy corduroy trouser legs tied under the knee with leather thongs. A good-looking man in his own way, fresh-complexioned and fair, good inside as well as out, she reflected, balancing the bucket on her hip as any countrywoman would do. Robbie had not seen her, his attention being fixed on some portion of the fence beyond her line of vision.

Judith pushed open the cottage door quietly and set her cleaning materials on the table. A sound from the next room startled her. Perhaps some tramp had wandered in during her absence unnoticed by Robbie. She took up the knife and went to the partly-open door. Not much

94

light came in through the small window, but there was enough to see the two figures on the floor, Kit's humped back. Unmistakable movements—

Kit turned his head to look up at her, alerted by the hoarse, ugly noise she had made and Judith struck out at him. He half-rose, blood pouring from his face onto the naked body of Pan Boswell.

* * * *

She had wandered for ever it seemed. There was blood on her hand and she could no longer remember how it had got there. It was cold for she had gone out without cloak or shawl, and her finger-tips had turned white. She had walked through tall, brown grass, pools of icy water, climbing stiles like an automaton. Mud caked her pattens and came over the tops of her shoes. She waded through a tortuous stream and continued to climb up a bank studded with thin trees that shot up from a carpet of needles and beechmast. The sun was a pale watery red behind a cold void that was no colour at all.

The track became difficult, wet and

slippery, and all of her senses were directed into staying on it and not slithering downwards into even worse conditions. Her numbed mind began, slowly, to rebel against the impossible task.

Voices impinged upon her consciousness but she felt neither alarm nor relief. Every nerve in her body was centred upon staying on this wet, broken path that led to—where did it lead? Away from something she could not face. Away from a knife and candle-wax. Nakedness—She began to whimper.

Somewhere else there was warmth, something red and beautiful, but in this present world, redness was shocking, distorted, something to do with the rusty stains on her hand. She screamed then, the sound high-pitched and ugly, going on and on. She lost her footing and began to slide, faster and faster, until she crashed onto the more level ground of the gipsy camp site. Figures gathered round her, staring down without expression.

All except one. Ben Boswell smiled.

* * * *

Gil had stitched up Kit's cheek. It was the

ugliest wound Jo had ever seen, the jagged cut having barely missed his eye and opening his face to below his mouth, dragging down both eyelid and lip into a travesty of his former looks. Uncharacteristically, she hated Judith for the act of vandalism. Lammeters were trouble and she'd had her own problems with Judith's father, Miles. He hadn't always been a pompous social climber. He'd been a detestable youth who had once tried to take advantage of her. There must be some of his characteristics in Judith.

The anger died slowly as she washed and disinfected the scarred cheek. The soreness in her heart remained, but fairness returned. For Judith, after the magical evening of last night, to find Kit and that gipsy together had been something too dreadful to endure. She had not remembered what she had done. She'd run blindly, oblivious of Robbie's shouts and Pan Boswell's screams. The episode was wiped from her mind.

Kit seized the whisky bottle and took another long swig.

'It's finished,' Jo said miserably, avoiding his eye. 'You should go to bed.'

'How long will it take before the

stitches can be removed?'

'It's hard to tell. I'll stay, of course, to keep an eye on it. Infection—'

'No need. I'll clap whisky on it every day.'

'Oh, Kit. Why *did* you—!'

'Tumble that gipsy? Why does one do anything? Eat, drink, draw breath.' He shrugged.

'That child will go mad when she sees you—'

'I'll tell her it was an accident.'

'She may remember. Sometimes the unpleasantness is blotted out for ever. But now and again it comes back in patches, or even entirety. She may know one day that she did this to you.'

'Well, go back to Cramble and pray she does not.'

'You'll not be cruel to her?'

'How can I answer that?'

'It could be hard not to hurt her. Revenge yourself—I beg you will not.'

'You're too good for this earth, Jo. How does it look? Oh, no need to answer! I'm a monster, aren't I?'

Jo could not reply. Kit crossed the room and stared at himself in the glass.

'No wonder you'd not commit yourself. Will it—ever improve? And don't tell me a pack of lies for I couldn't stomach them!'

'No.' The word was drawn from her in an agony of grief.

He drew a deep, ragged breath. 'Thanks for your honesty, at least.'

'You were not to know she'd react so, but I can understand her feelings. Only a day since, she gave you the promise of a child both of you wanted. She was mad in love with you—'

'Aye! Mad. The operative word.'

'It can hurt to love someone and find that love is not enough.'

'What can you know of that with a husband who'd not look at Helen Troy or the Queen of Sheba?'

'He did, once.'

Kit, bitterness turned temporarily to curiosity, asked 'Who?'

'Your mother.'

'Chris Ashton?'

'It was my own fault. I would not let Gil near me and he was only flesh and blood. So he turned to her. But you have not that excuse.' Jo's tone was unexpectedly hard. 'That child had never refused you, yet you cast her love in

99

her face—'

'I am tired of this conversation.'

'Oh, Kit, I cannot see the end of it. But you'd not jeopardise your child?'

'Oh, dear me no, I'll be as nice as pie till my son is born! No one will be more understanding.'

Jo went out of the room.

* * * *

The Boswells disappeared the following day and when Kit's cheek had knitted together, leaving it more warped and ugly than ever, Jo and Gil left for their neglected practice at Cramble. Madge and Betty ran the household for Judith had turned strange, still recalling nothing of that day she had attacked her husband, not really aware that she carried a child. A child herself, she must be watched and cared for, spending much time in the high bed with the oak poles, her mind turned in on itself.

Sometimes she was clearer in her thoughts, holding more reasonable conversations at supper which was the only time Kit put in an appearance. 'It was an accident,' he would say when she exclaimed over the healing scar. 'I was cutting a rope when the knife flew upwards from my hand.'

'Oh, poor Kit. My poor Kit—' Only with him was she ever a person.

He turned to her in bed, which was inevitable, but there was no longer the love there had been between them, only the need to satisfy the all too human urges of the flesh. Sometimes she did not understand his demands and tried to push him from her but he insisted on his rights. Then Judith cried and Madge looked at Kit accusingly over the breakfast table. She was now mistress of the house, taking advantage of Kit's liking for her.

'She's only a child in her present state,' she'd say disapprovingly.

'She's my wife. And who else will have me now?'

That would silence her, for the scar was the irrefutable proof of his words. There was something terrible about the face he now presented to the world. He avoided going anywhere, and Hodge, his new foreman, installed in the Broome cottage, was delegated more and more into the necessary visits to Keswick to do Kit's business, so sensitive was he about his appearance.

Jo wrote long letters which Kit answered with chilling briefness. The days dragged on through spring towards Judith's inevitable confinement. She had her first pains at supper, her dark eyes dilating with shocked surprise as she clung to the cloth, dragging the dishes towards her in the spasm of agony.

Kit sprang to his feet, cursing, and bellowed for Madge and Betty, who now had a room of her own in the attic. Judith, uncomprehending, had a sudden glimpse of a cow, of two thin, roped legs, the rope stained with blood. She screamed loudly.

'No!' she cried. 'No! Not me—'

'Hush,' Madge said soothingly. 'Be off, Master Kit, for the doctor, if you will. It's your lad. Who's to know what may go wrong, her the way she is?'

'You do think the child will be normal?' Kit reached for his riding-crop.

'Of course. How could the bairn know what's passed between you?' But Madge's tone carried little conviction. Kit pulled on his boots and ran to the stables, thanking God for the stars and the presence of a moon that was almost full.

Up in the bed-chamber, Judith lay, suffering terribly, for she did not know how to help herself. Madge sent Betty for Ethel Hunt. Ethel may be childless, but at least she was a married woman and would be more use than Betty when the child began to appear, if it ever did. The housemaid was despatched to the kitchen to keep plenty of water boiling and to line one of the drawers with bedding for the new arrival, no cot having yet been made. She listened to the distant shrieks and vowed to remain single if that was what marriage brought on you. Then, everything ready, she set to, to make a batch of bread since the child was delayed.

The child had not arrived, hours later, when Kit returned with Dr Bassett, and eventually it had to be taken from her, its face an ugly mess from the forceps, its frail body misshapen. Madge, setting a meal in the dining-room for the doctor, hardly dared look at her master.

'She has made me into a monster,' Kit said, 'and given me another to keep me company.'

'All children delivered with forceps are bound to be ugly to begin with. Mrs Judith did not do it on purpose. You

should pity her for her suffering. And
don't let Dr Bassett hear you!'

'Where is he?'

'Washing his hands.'

'And—my wife?'

'He has given her a draught to make
her sleep.'

'It was not even a boy. And for God's
sake, woman, no platitudes about next
time! There'll be no next time, not ever,'
Kit added grimly.

'Have you thought of a name for the
infant?' the doctor asked, hurrying in.
'You'd best waste no time in having her
baptised.'

'I have not.'

'Then I should think seriously on the
matter.'

'What's your wife's name?'

'My wife?' Dr Bassett looked puzzled.
His long, big-nosed face was lined with
weariness and his snuff-coloured suit
rumpled. But the faded blue eyes bright-
ened at the sight of the food Madge set
out before him. He picked up the knife
and fork.

'I shall call the child after her.'

'Why not after your own?'

'I—we decided we would not have the

same name, nor one in use already in our families.'

'My wife is called Rose.'

Madge shook her head at the incongruity of naming that poor, battered creature after so lovely a thing as a flower, and the doctor looked up just in time to see the gesture.

'She will not always look so,' he said positively.

'She is deformed,' Kit pronounced almost unfeelingly. 'That cannot change. But Rose she shall be. What's in a name? There, that's settled and I'll have the minister call—'

'I will mention it when I return, Talbot. We are neighbours and it will save you a journey. You'll have your hands full enough here.'

'Thank you,' Kit answered. 'Now, I beg you excuse me. I've much to do. If you will tell me your fee, I'll leave it on the table by the door.'

'Very well. And I cannot counsel you sufficiently to avoid—to avoid any further strain upon your wife—'

'There will be none.' Kit clipped off the words savagely. 'Never fear, I'd already decided.'

'Good.' The doctor returned to his bacon and Kit banged his way out into the spring sunshine. Only yesterday, Grey Ghyll had looked fair and smiling, a good place to bring up a strong, healthy little boy. Today is was a graveyard of hopes, of never to be realised dreams. Kit swore and kicked out at the nearest stone but it was firmly embedded and the only result was pain.

* * * *

Judith awoke to a soreness of the body that perplexed her. She had laboured through some terrible nightmare of oppression to find herself aching, the curtains of the bedchamber drawn to shut out the daylight. There were only thin cracks where the hangings did not keep out the sun, and these made pallid lines across the floor and furniture. Dimly, she recalled some vast ordeal that had left her spent and her mind fuzzy.

A sound made her turn her head. A small girl stood near the bed with a bunch of flowers in her hand, a stout, red-cheeked creature with straight, fair hair. A stranger—

106

'Who—are you?' Judith asked, disturbed.

'Mary Hodge, ma'am. My dad works for Mr Talbot. These are for you.'

'That's—kind of you. Have I—been ill?'

'You had a baby. Don't you remember?' The pale blue eyes were shrewd.

Judith put a white hand to her brow. 'My head feels tired—'

Madge came bustling into the room. 'Now, Mary! Who said you could come up here? You should have left those in the kitchen with Betty or me. Hasn't bothered you, ma'am, has she?'

'No—'

'Off you go, Mary. I'll put these in water and it was good of you and Mrs Hodge to send them.'

'I wanted to see Mrs Talbot. Ain't never seen her before—'

'She hasn't been well and she oughtn't to be bothered now. So off you go.'

' 'Bye, Mrs Talbot.' The sturdy form retreated.

'Goodbye—Mary.' Memory was returning in patches. An evening when she wore her best red dress to please Kit. To get him in a good mood to tell him about

107

the baby she was sure she'd never have. And now some strange brat told her there was a child—

'Where is my baby?' Judith asked quite rationally. 'I want to see it.'

'It's asleep, ma'am. A pity to disturb the little thing.'

'But I don't understand.' The muzziness was wearing off a little. 'How could I have it so quickly? April, Gil said, or May.'

'It is April.' Sounded almost sensible, she did, Madge thought. But then, she'd seemed compos mentis before but it never lasted.

'Kit. I must see my husband—'

'I'll tell him, ma'am. Just come back for a cup of chocolate, he has. Would you like one?'

'No. I want my baby and my husband. And I want to know what happened to the autumn and winter and to February and March. Someone has stolen time that is precious to me—' Judith's voice rose dangerously high.

'No one has taken anything, Mrs Judith, ma'am,' Madge said soothingly.

Judith gave a sudden moan. 'Oh, it hurts quite dreadfully. Who has done this

108

to me?'

'Having a baby always hurts, dear. A few days and you'll never know it happened. Dr Bassett left you some medicine. I think you should have some.'

'Let Kit bring it.'

'I'll ask him.'

There was a torment-filled interlude, then Kit was near her in the dimness of the bedchamber. There was something wrong with his face. Something quite terrible. She shrank against the pillow, her mouth dry.

'You did that,' Kit was saying in a whispering voice. 'It was you, Judith. Are you pleased with your handiwork?'

It was as though a fog rolled away from her brain. She saw him with Pan Boswell, the knife there to scrape off the blobs of hardened candle-wax. Blood running over Pan's breasts and down into her navel. Judith was first angry, then appalled.

'It should have been her, the slut!'

'Here is your medicine.' She was made afraid by the coldness of his voice.

'The baby. You'd not keep him from me out of revenge?'

'Her,' the quiet voice corrected hatefully.

'Oh. It should have been a boy. Perhaps you'd have forgiven me, then. I'm sorry to have done this.'

'Do you still want to see her?'

'Of course I wish to see it!'

'Rose. That's her name. I'll fetch her, shall I?' Kit sounded perfectly polite.

Judith struggled back against the bed-head. 'Please.'

She waited, her mind a confusion of hate for Pan Boswell and dread of Kit's attitude towards her for what she had done. But it was six or seven months ago. He'd had time to adjust. Where had she been all that time? She seemed to recall grey labyrinths out of which she had emerged into pockets of brightness, snatches of horror, and moments when she had been a pin-point of nothing. She had been very ill, that much was obvious.

The floorboards creaked and Kit was there again, holding a swathed whiteness.

'There's your baby, Judith.'

He handed her the bundle and waited impassively for the inevitable reaction.

* * * *

Madge watched her mistress narrowly.

110

She looked dreadful. Judith had lost weight and her face was all protruding bones and stark pallor, her hair was neglected, her dress careless. Even her nails were grubby and unkempt. Madge did not like to see her touch the child but it was not her place to forbid Rose's natural mother. Natural! It was not the most appropriate word. If Mrs Jo Talbot knew, she would have been down in a minute but Mr Kit had never mentioned the state of affairs at Grey Ghyll. He couldn't have said anything. When she thought of how they'd been at first, she could have cried. Like two turtle-doves. They'd even imagined she knew nothing of what went on in the room with that fur rug by the hearth. You'd have to be deaf and stupid not to have known of the hanky-panky there behind locked doors. And now he could not bear to be alone with her. She'd heard Mrs Judith begging him to come to her but he would not. He'd flung Dr Basset's directive in her face but Madge knew it was not the real reason he'd not sleep with her. It was because of the spoiled face and the fact that the baby was a girl and a hunchback at that.

111

'I could have been Lady Amberwood!' Judith would scream.

'I wish to Heaven you had been,' Mr Kit would say. Then Judith would cry most dreadfully. It was better, really, when Judith had been out of her mind. That way she was easy as an infant to handle, grateful for small attentions. No one should ever be so set on a man for jealousy was the most destructive of all emotions and it had most surely destroyed the young Talbots.

Little Rose had certainly improved. True, one shoulder would always be higher than the other, poor mite, and she was still small for her age, but the marks of those cruel forceps had faded as the doctor said they would and the child now showed promise of reasonable good looks. Her black hair had fallen out to be replaced by a shade of most unusual dark red and her eyes were grey like her mother's. Madge hoped, sincerely, she would not have Judith's temperament. She'd taken very well to cow's milk since her mama had been too ill to feed her to begin with, and was now able to eat solids. Judith's attitude towards her child veered between a passionate possessiveness and almost total indifference.

'I was not wanted because I was a girl,' she would say. 'I know how it feels.' Then she would show interest in Rose for a day or two, but, after a further rebuff from Mr Kit, she'd leave the child entirely to Madge until her emotions had swung around to a renewal of the maternal instinct. You never knew where you were, Madge thought, and spooned strained vegetables into Rose's waiting mouth. There'd be fireworks one day and no mistaking—

* * * *

Kit was away on one of his rare excursions when the tragedy occurred. Hodge, the foreman, was ill and Kit had to go to arrange the sale of his beef cattle.

Madge and Betty were on edge because of his enforced absence for Judith had shown signs of disturbance and, once Kit had left, she had paced the house, her draggled hair witchlike and her hands unquiet.

It was autumn again, and, though the Boswells had not been near the place this year, Judith had ridden off several times

113

to inspect the copse the gipsies favoured, or had walked the woods in case they reappeared. She had even taken the fowling-piece once or twice and Madge was on edge in case she used it on some unsuspecting vagrant or on that Pan Boswell, who'd been in the dairy last year and was the cause of Mrs Talbot's breakdown, the brazen hussy.

Judith had been especially critical of little Rose and her disability. 'I don't know how I can bear to look at her until I die. All those years—'

'Mrs Talbot!' Madge expostulated. 'You must not talk so. And the child cannot help her infirmity—'

'I suppose I can?' Judith's eyes were large with self-inflicted pain and detestation.

'You need not see her, ma'am. Betty and I would be happy to do what's required for Miss Rose, I'm sure.'

'And I am not fit, not desirable!' Judith burst into a storm of weeping and rushed up to her lonely room.

'Heaven knows how it'll end,' Madge said sombrely to Betty.

Judith seemed calmer that evening and had even made an attempt at regaining some of her old attraction. She had put on the peony red gown and swathed her hair into some sort of order. 'I think Mr Kit will be back. I sense it somehow— Someone is coming.'

'He said not for a few days,' Madge warned, not wanting to see the girl's inevitable disappointment, 'but it's good to see you looking so pretty. It's your favourite soup. Drink it all up. You've got much too thin, ma'am.'

'I do fancy it.'

'And a nice bit of chicken afterwards?'

'Yes. I think I could manage that. How dark it is. I hope he can see his way. There's no moon.'

'Knows every inch of the way, Master Kit. Never fear.'

Madge returned with the chicken and roast potatoes.

'Is Miss Rose crying?' Judith asked, looking agitated. 'I seem to hear a baby somewhere—'

'Fast asleep, the little soul,' Madge assured her. 'I just looked in. But lots o' mothers get that feeling even when there's nothing wrong. Hear their little ones at all sorts of queer times. You eat that up. I'll be back soon.'

She returned to the kitchen to see to the apple pudding, not that her mistress would eat that. It would be a wonder if she ate the middle course. There *was* a sort of wailing sound. It could be cats. Noisy brutes they could be when they were mating. Madge dismissed the noise and went back to the dining-room.

'It *is* a baby!' Judith said, getting up. 'You're lying about Miss Rose.'

'See for yourself,' Madge returned stiffly. 'I think it's cats. You know how they hang about the barn. Or gulls can sound just like crying children—'

'Perhaps they can. But this is neither. You and Betty are neglecting my daughter.' Judith pushed past an outraged Madge to stand at the stair foot.

'It isn't Rose.' Her pale face gleamed uncannily in the light of the candle. Even her head, tilted as she listened, had an unnatural look.

'No, ma'am. Now come and finish your supper.'

'There it is again!' Judith looked quite unbalanced, Madge thought with misgiving.

'Perhaps there is something,' Madge admitted at last. Her hearing wasn't as sharp as it used to be but there was someone crying in the night. 'It'll be that little Hodge girl, maybe.'

'The Broomes' cottage is too far off,' Judith objected, her fingers plucking at the small bows on the bodice of the red gown.

'We'd best go to the door and take a look,' the housekeeper said, lifting the candlestick.

There was a plaited cradle on the step. That much they both saw in the flickering light. Judith gave a gasp and Madge stooped to peep inside. The child cried again, quite loudly. It was a robust sound, quite unlike Rose's wailing. Madge was so still that Judith could not bear the suspense.

'Well?'

'It's a dark child. And there's a message pinned on its shawl.'

'What—does it say?'

'I cannot read, ma'am.'

Judith thrust her aside. 'Hold the candle lower.'

Looking into the cradle, she saw the child's face under the hood. It stared back at her with black, shining eyes out of brown skin. Its hair was dark and it flourished a strong hand as though demanding that it be let into the house. Judith peered harder at the handwritten message. The import of the text struck her like a blow.

''Property of Christopher Talbot'' she read, then in a puzzled, childlike voice she said, 'What does it mean? It's a joke, isn't it Madge? It is, isn't it?'

'Of course it is,' Madge assured her, her heart thudding. 'Mr Kit will get to the bottom of it, I shouldn't be surprised.'

'Shut the door on it,' Judith said unexpectedly.'

'But, I can't, ma'am!' Madge protested aghast, just as the infant set up a lusty howl. 'This mite'll freeze to death. I couldn't do that. We must take it in and look after it till other arrangements are made. You needn't be bothered. I could ask Mrs Hodge—'

'It said, ''property of Christopher Talbot''. It's no business of the Hodges. No, you are quite right. It should stay here at Grey Ghyll. Where it undoubtedly belongs. Don't you see? It's that Boswell girl's or Deborah Broome's—'

'We don't know that, ma'am—'

'Then tell me! What else could it mean?'

Madge, silent under the force of Judith's logic, picked up the cradle and set it on her hip. 'I'll take it to the kitchen and feed it. It looks fair starving.'

'I shall go to my room,' Judith told her. 'Would you send one of the Nisbetts for the minister tomorrow?'

'The minister?' Madge looked up from her contemplation of the now quiet baby.

'It should be named,' the girl said in a hard tone.

'But oughtn't you wait? For—'

'For Kit? No I don't think so. He chose Rose's name after all and I have the perfect one for this child. Goodnight, Madge.'

The housekeeper stared after the retreating figure of her mistress. The red skirts flowed up the staircase, merging imperceptibly with the darkness above. Madge had never experienced such a sense of imminent danger. She'd hide every weapon in sight. The knives, the axe, the fowling-piece. Heaven send Kit back before there was murder done.

* * * *

The newcomer was a boy, beautifully

formed, the skin of his body as brown as that of his face and hands. Madge washed and fed him, pondering on his ancestry. Amy Broome's side of the family were dark skinned, and of course, so were those rascally Boswells. It was difficult to pin-point the child's age. He could be an uncommonly large recent arrival or a small few months old infant. The contrast between its strength and Rose Talbot's weakness was cruel. And both Master Kit's, or so the note implied.

Judith came in to inspect the boy next morning. She was extremely pale but oddly composed as though she had emerged from some massive struggle, passive yet victorious.

'I knew it would be male. It had to be—'

'He's a strong little feller.'

'But the running of the house cannot be set aside because of him.'

'He seems content enough now.'

'Of course. He has a foot over the door. Both feet—'

'Come, ma'am. He'll be fine here by the range. It's warm and he's fed well. He'll sleep.'

All the time, until the minister arrived,

120

Madge or Betty contrived to be beside their mistress or one of them with the cuckoo in the nest, and when Judith and the minister were in the pretty little parlour with the shiny black floorboards and the marigold yellow curtains, and Judith was pronouncing the child's name, they both had an ear to the crack in the door.

Broome Boswell! They could hardly believe that Judith would betray her husband's infidelities so openly. And yet, there was something about the name that suited the swarthy changeling. Staring at one another, they tiptoed away to attend to the chores, and to that pathetic legitimate offspring of the Talbots, pretty, misshapen Rose.

* * * *

They missed Judith later. Madge wished to ask her advice about the following day's luncheon but the big, shadowy bedchamber was empty, curiously hollow-sounding like a room without furniture.

'It's as if she'd flitted,' Madge pronounced uneasily. 'Taken her traps and—gone.'

'She must be out,' Betty agreed. 'I looked everywheres else.'

The children were both attended to, Rose, in white and ribbons in her pretty nursery, Broome Boswell in his wicker cradle in the homely kitchen.

'Should be together, for company,' Madge said. 'Shouldn't be surprised if Master Kit didn't prefer that black little bastard in his heart of hearts.'

Betty looked shocked.

'Little Miss Rose might like him,' Madge went on. 'Better than being an only child—'

'She should never have done that. Called him by that name,' Betty said, 'Cause no end of trouble, that will. Don't know as I'd want to be here when he knows.'

'It's none of our doing. Can't take it out on us.'

'But it wouldn't be right to take it out on a loonie, neither.'

'Betty! We have no call to say Mrs Judith's a—a lunatic. Don't never let me hear you say that again, d'you hear, my girl?'

'There's someone at the door. I'll go, shall I?'

'We'll both go. Things being as they are.'

Mary Hodge stood on the step, her small hands dirty with moss.

'What is it, Mary?'

'I saw Mrs Talbot in the woods,' the child said vacantly, as though she were in shock.

'Did she say anything to you?' Madge asked sharply. 'Hurt you?'

'Never spoke to me, ma'am. Just put out her tongue at me. And her face was a funny colour. Thought I should tell you. She didn't move—and her toes were not on the ground.'

'Oh, my God,' Madge whispered. 'Oh God—God—God—'

PART TWO

FARO

3

Queen Victoria was in the heyday of her married life. True, she'd had her ups and downs with Palmerston, and there were disappointments with Bertie. It was Vicky who had the brains and that was unfortunate, the laws of the succession being what they were. But both she and Albert persevered and the boy had been allowed his own suite and tutor though he was still strictly supervised. The heir to the throne must be properly behaved and educated however difficult or abhorrent the process seemed at the time.

1850 had painful memories. Victoria was struck on the head by a man called Robert Pate, an occurrence that gave rise to unfortunate puns—then two days later she was terribly distressed by the death of Sir Robert Peel from a fall from his horse on Constitution Hill. But Albert's engrossment with the Great Exhibition, and its attendant criticism or adulation, drove the sadness into limbo. Joseph Paxton had done his work well and the glass Palace glittered splendidly, housing living trees and birds and the wonders of the world for the populace to gawp at and discuss. Tennyson dedicated his book of poems to the young Queen and she found a new Chancellor whose name was Disraeli.

The years passed. Wellington died; then Prince Leopold; haemophilia haunted the Royal Families of Europe. The Queen produced another baby, aided by the controversial chloroform, thereby damning those—principally men!—who maintained that a mother could only love her child because of the pain of childbirth. A delightful miniature Swiss Cottage was built for the Royal children at Osborne and copied by the rich.

War was declared against Russia in support of Turkey and as the ally of France. Palmerston was restored and the cruelties of the Crimea produced a national heroine in Florence Nightingale who was later to have tea with the Queen, a signal honour. Napoleon III and the Empress Eugenie brought themselves— and the crinoline—to England and Victoria and Albert visited the Paris Exhibition in the new yacht that bore their names. Sebastopol fell and the following spring a peace treaty was prepared. The Princess Royal married Frederick William of Prussia the year after Albert became Prince Consort. The Prince of Wales acquired a Governor called Robert Bruce. And, quite horribly, after rumblings of discontent in India, came a letter describing the massacre at Cawnpore, of bodies in wells, of sabred women and children.

Bombs were made in England that were intended to blow up the Emperor of France and his beautiful wife, the instigator being a man called Orsini. Life was not dull.

Faro Amberwood laid aside the newssheets pondering on the momentous changes that had taken place since her father died. The breakfast table was frugally set since neither she nor Bender cared about food. Only one end of the long, shining table was ever laid, these days. She had grown sick of card parties that lasted a week with a swarm of opportunists nesting in the now deserted bedrooms. The house had begun, little by little, to decay around her and the glorious freedom of the removal of Carne Amberwood's yoke had turned imperceptibly, to the prison of boredom and loneliness.

Bender had become much more than a manservant. He controlled the house and the staff, who, if they were decent, despised her for taking him as a lover, or, if they did not care, became familiar and took liberties. Her domestics were far from satisfactory, and had been whittled down over the years to only sufficient to keep her in a modicum of comfort. She affected mannish simplicity, despising women's frills. The golden glow dimmed inside and outside Amberwood. The grounds had become neglected and the yellow roses had turned to the hedges that might have encircled the abode of the Sleeping Beauty. She preferred them overgrown to carefully cultivated.

She still attended gaming-clubs and Chamwell had never tired of pursuing her. She had bested him once over a gambling debt and though he had been furious at the time, the anger had turned to admiration and a determination to have her at all costs. The knowledge brought its own satisfaction. She tried to analyse his smile, never sure whether his teeth were real or false. They were so white she was convinced they were made of china, yet they appeared strong and regular. The dark, hawk-like features and satanic brows were striking and many women would have considered themselves fortunate indeed to have captured the attentions of a man who was not only wealthy and conveniently widowed, but presentable into the bargain. A suggestion of the sinister intrigued her.

She was no longer sure of her feelings concerning Bender. At one time, she had been in control of their relationship but of late she suspected that he directed her motives, her every action. She still wanted what he gave her in a physical sense but she resented the usurpation of her powers of discrimination. If he decided she would not be available to a visitor, she would not see the caller, nor, indeed, be informed of the effort to contact her and only an incautious mention by one of the servants would alert her to their endeavour. And this made her angry, reducing her to the status of a cypher in her own household. Few letters came. He would listen to her strictures then take her in his arms and the potency of his personality would eventually overcome her objections to his audacity. But it could not go on indefinitely, she had decided.

It was just at the time that she had come to this decision that restlessness drove her to her London club under the guise of Monsieur Foredor, a fictitious refugee from the French Revolution. Always individual, Faro had adopted the guise of a young man about town for several years, having the right type of figure and mentality for such a masquerade. Chamwell had been the only man to penetrate the disguise, having been a friend of her father's and recognising the golden eyes peculiar to the Amberwoods, a feature passed down from the time of Charles the second, when her ancestress, Fanny, had been one of the royal mistresses, rewarded by the gift of a baronet husband and this house that had recently begun its journey into decadence. The Prince Regent had been a frequent guest, not to mention many minor Cabinet Ministers, soldiers, squires and recently, businessmen, Faro met at her various clubs. Card-play had always been her life, apart from that year she had spent abroad, a period that even now, she did not care to look back on.

The thought of that time brought her to her feet, the news-sheets falling to the floor unnoticed. She would not think of it. Tonight, she would exorcise the hated memory with card games until she was too weary to play any further and Bender would drive her home through the quiet streets, across the heath to the four honey-coloured pillars of the house that was called, appropriately enough, Amber-wood. Her ineffectual mother, Blanche, had presided here, and before her, the strange, remote Savannah Heron who, in turn, followed Lady Josephine West and Mary Brandon. Further than that, lay only conjecture from family letters and documents. But the atmosphere of the house was shadowed by many deaths, by accident, by burning, by hanging. Brandon Amberwood had been hanged by the state. Kit Talbot's wife had hanged by her own hand in a wood in Cumberland.

It was Jack Carter who told Faro, that evening, in the club. She had been placed next to the tall, florid man, careless in his dress but with a presence and a sense of humour not entirely destroyed by an addiction to claret. It was a wonder he had not the gout. The dampness of the Lake District had inoculated him against rheumaticky ailments, he had explained, his bloodshot eyes still handsome, his fine, once blonde head still distinguished. And the mention of the lakes had reminded Faro of Grey Ghyll and her kinsman, Talbot, and his wife, Judith.

The story of Judith's madness and suicide had surprised her. The girl had always seemed so quiet and contained. But it appeared that she was repressed, an entirely different kettle of fish. Repression put out its warped, distinctive roots and dark Judith had woven her own pattern of destruction.

Carter had, apparently, been staying in Keswick to make a preliminary survey of the ruins of his house, preparatory to selling the land. Claret-drinking and card games could not be enjoyed without resources and he needed the money the estate would fetch. She had enquired, rather maliciously, about the Talbots, to find that Judith was long-buried on unconsecrated ground, that Kit lived solitary, Madge and Betty to take care of his own child, Rose, and the foundling on his doorstep.

'The girl is a hunchback,' Jack said without much feeling, his fresh face only beginning to show the traces of dissolution, blue eyes red-rimmed yet not detracting too much from his former looks.

'And the foundling?' Faro's tone betrayed her interest and Jack had been intrigued. Why should an elegant young Frenchie have any reason to be concerned about Kit and his problems?

'Why do you ask?' His fleshy hand stroked the baize surface of the table as the cards fell, face-downwards, in compulsive anonymity.

'Because Talbot visited Amberwood while I was there. I knew that girl. Briefly—'

'I had not realised, Foredor, that you'd any connection, however tenuous, with Cumberland.'

'I only saw it once. Years ago—the foundling. You have not specified the sex of the child.'

'A strong, handsome boy. Dark as a gyppo. They say he's the bastard of a girl employed by Talbot one autumn. Mrs Judith took exception to his interest in the wench and had her dismissed. Later, the girl dropped the infant and left him on the doorstep in a revenge that had far-reaching effects.'

Faro picked up the cards that had designs of golden bulls on their shiny backs. 'It was that caused the Talbot girl's death? The finding of a changeling?'

'I said a foundling. There was nothing supernatural about the child I glimpsed as I passed the house. They were together, heiress and byblow, friendly as you please. The girl is pretty despite her handicap and the boy was protective.'

'And Talbot? Did you see him?' Faro's tone was idle. She shuffled her hand expertly.

'I glimpsed him. He's grown broad and burly. Dislikes company, apart from a house in Keswick he frequents now and again.'

'What sort of house?'

'Need I say?' Carter laughed a fraction coarsely. 'The kind of place we all need to resort to sooner or later when we are widowed. Or a bachelor, as I presume you still to be.'

Faro bent her head over the table, seeing the shadow of the flower she wore in her hat. A yellow flower for luck. Yellow like the rooms at Amberwood, like the roses in the thicket that surrounded the fountain and the bee-skips. 'I'm not wed,' she agreed quietly.

'Then you'll know what I mean.'

'I know.' As Kit Talbot would know. His mother ran a whore-house for long enough in St James's Place. Expensive and select as it had been, Chris Ashton had sold herself time and time again.

'You have a buyer for the land?' she asked when the game ended.

'Land?'

'Your estate in Cumberland.'

Jack Carter frowned. 'I have not as yet. It's too isolated for most.'

'I might be interested.'

'You?'

'I weary of London at times.'

'I'll warn you there's nothing there but a mass of rubble. You'd have to build. And it's cut off in winter. I'd not sell a pig in a poke.'

'I—like solitude.'

134

'Never could abide being lonely,' Jack said gruffly. 'I enjoy life.'

'Solitude is not necessarily loneliness.'

'You'd care to see it?'

'There's no need. I was there—once. I know the district. It would be the question of price.'

'We could meet at my solicitor's office,' Jack suggested, his face brightening.

'We could. When?'

They had just arranged to meet the following day when Chamwell joined them, then Carter left, having lost as much money as he could afford for that night, an angry mistress waiting.

Chamwell was attentive and Faro was more receptive than usual, being occupied with the tragic story of the Talbots and thoughts of owning land at the end of nowhere. It was this pre-occupation that led to her acceptance of an invitation to Chamwell's country house, something she had so far avoided.

'We'll go down after the gaming on Friday,' Chamwell said, his eyes gleaming.

'There's only one condition,' Faro said, aware that she had let slip her customary advantage. 'I must bring my man. He goes everywhere I do.'

'My dear. You do not need to impress me with your facade of masculinity. Why not a maid? I intend you to come as Lady Faro Amberwood, not as Monsieur Foredor. That is, unless you've any violent objection?'

'Will you have any club members there? I don't wish to instil any doubts in their minds.'

'No club members. Only local friends and dignitaries.'

'I should still want Bender. We could encounter footpads. Highwaymen—'

'If it is the only way to get you there.' Chamwell shrugged. 'I agree. Unwillingly—'

'Thank you. I assure you, I'd be lost without him.'

'I look forward to having you as a guest.'

'I've made no promises, mind you—'
'I know that. But I warn you, I intend to be persuasive.'

She stared at him, wondering what he saw in her, slim and sexless in the man's garb she affected for her night excursions, the only concession to femininity, the leonine splendour of her eyes. For the

136

first time she was drawn to him in the physical sense and she knew that Bender had created a breach between them by reason of his arrogance, his high handedness in the matter of turning away those who came to see her. The pillars of her former life were threatened and she was, unexpectedly, disturbed. Chamwell grasped her hand as she was on the point of leaving and the warmth of his touch remained with her on the homeward journey, Bender dark and brooding beside her as though he knew already that his security was in jeopardy. His dark shadow lay over the buttoned interior of the coach like a third occupant, someone silent, malignant, black as the region that led to Hell.

Faro sat still, speechless under the burden of his disapproval. Only a few years ago all would have been different, she issuing orders, he obeying, waiting on her every whim. She had created a monster out of her own servant and she could not decide how to rid herself of him. He would not go. Not unless—her mind shuddered away from the death that would be her only passage to freedom. And it was only half of her that wanted that liberty. The rest accepted, even desired his attentions. It was as though one eye saw his underlying evil, the other recognised only gratification of the senses. And senses were important for most of one's living was through them alone unless one was a saint.

'You are very subdued.' Bender said eventually and his shadow squirmed as he turned his head to look at her pallid reflection in the shifting light of the coach-lamps.

'I am tired.'

'Only tired?'

'That's all.'

'What did Chamwell want?'

'Lord Chamwell invited me to a week-end in the country.'

'Alone?'

'I may take a maid.'

His black brows drew together warn-ingly. 'You'd go without me?'

'I told him I went nowhere without you. But it would be the kind of visit where a maid would be essential. You'd be with the rest of the valets and butlers—'

'I'm no manservant. Not now—'

'How touchy you are!' She moved

away from him. 'You'd best stay behind, if that's how you feel.'

'I'll not have him paw you! You know what these house-parties lead to. Why did you agree after so long keeping him at arms length? You'll not set me aside so easily, my lady.'

Faro took her time about replying. 'I've grown tired of being usurped in my own house.'

'Usurped?' Again the shadow fluttered as he bent towards her like a gaoler.

'You know perfectly well what I mean. I've been informed that callers are not admitted—I rarely receive a letter. It seems they are—intercepted.'

'Who has told you this?'

'Do you turn people away?' she asked directly.

'Sometimes. For your own good. Your own comfort—'

'I would prefer to deal with such situations personally. It's as though you considered me mentally deficient. Or that you wish me to be your prisoner.'

'Nothing of the sort.' His hand caressed her wrist. 'It's only—I'll not have you annoyed.'

'How can you tell what annoys me?'

'After all this time? I can read you—'

'Like a book? That's a cliché, Bender. Like other things—'

The dark-skinned hand stopped caressing and became a fetter. 'I'll not be jettisoned for Chamwell. It's a whim. You've known him for ten years or more. If it were a real emotion, surely it would have surfaced before now?'

'All relationships can change. Can become stronger or wither and die. Like a wreath.'

'And this is our—funeral?'

She was afraid, for the first time in her life, of the brutality of his expression.

'I did not say that—'

'Not in so many words. But your meaning is clear.' His eyes were hard as coal.

'No—'

'I have protected you against life, against your father, Talbot—drunken gamesters.'

'You had not the right!' Her voice had risen. 'I prefer to live my own way!'

'The coachman will hear,' he said contemptuously.

'What can he find out that he does not already know? That I am not mistress of

140

my own house? That you are master? But I rebel against that. I intend to make changes—'

His scowling face terrified her.

'What changes?'

'You—must go.' There, she had said it at last.

'Go? Where?'

'You must decide. I'll give you a reference.'

'For what! Which services?' he sneered.

She slapped his face with all her strength and his eyes blazed.

'I'll not go! There's no one capable of putting me out.'

'I'll think of something. I must be left to live my own way.'

'What way!'

'I will not tell you. But I do have plans.'

'That will not include me?'

'That do not concern you.'

'I see.' How quiet he was now and he'd drawn away to stare out at the darkness of the heath where the coachlamps illuminated, briefly, the straggling branches of trees and made gnarled figures out of the crucified trunks.

141

'I will not need you from Thursday on. I leave for Chamwell's house on Friday with Lettice Hurley. You are free to look for another post. I'll take a maid instead.'

The bravery induced by his silence dissipated, drop by drop, like the rain that fell from the night black foliage.

* * * *

Faro locked her door that night. She had gone upstairs before her normal time to forestall the possibility of Bender getting there ahead of her, bent on revenge. As she brushed her hair before the mirror, she tried to think of other people but all these cogitations led to death. Young Harry Grey, fair and handsome, partner of many an all-night sitting at Hazard, shot to pieces in some engagement of the Crimea; Hubert de Courcy blowing out his brains in an ante-room at Mrs Brand's after losing heavily at Macao. Old Sir Pumphrey struck down with a handful of aces. She could see the cards yet, splayed out on the mulberry carpet, Pumphrey lying there, his face almost the same colour. Ben, the hunchback, stabbed by an unknown gambler who had gone off his head and was dragged away, bloody and screaming. Many a time she had bought a touch of Ben's hump for luck. All these men she had come to know because of her masquerade as Foredor which began as a convenient way to escape the vigilance of her father and his spies and had become as essential as breathing. She had two lives—one as a gambling Frenchman, the other as mistress of Amberwood and near recluse.

The door handle turned slowly. Faro's mouth turned dry. Her arm stopped in mid-stroke.

'Faro. Faro?'

She did not answer.

'Faro!' The voice was ugly. For the first time she wished that her room was not so far from the rest of the household. But she had chosen it for its isolation, because of her need for secrecy. There was only herself to blame. Again she ignored him. There was silence for a minute. Two minutes. She had dreadful images of his mouth set in a soundless snarl, of his pits of eyes, and then the door shuddered under the impact of his shoulder. Shuddered again. The lock was torn away from the painted panel and

Bender was in the room, his head thrust forward, his hands bunched. He kicked the door shut violently.

She did not scream. For one thing it would be useless and she had her pride. The servants were all miles away in the kitchen, supping off the joint and tart their mistress had only toyed with, their mouths greasy, the gobbets of meat washed down with ale, the place filled with noise.

For all that she was half-paralysed with fear, she laid down the brush, very carefully, its chased silver back uppermost, and waited for his advance. The strong hands fastened on her shoulders and she was certain he meant to choke her. Her eyes widened. She swallowed convulsively.

'Shut me out, would you?' he growled.

Unable to reply, she could only go on staring at him, at the fury stamped on his dark features.

'I can say things about you,' he whispered harshly. 'There are secrets between us you'd not like Chamwell to get wind of. Not anyone for that matter. But I'll blab it all to anyone who cares to listen if you cut yourself off from me. There'll be no place left where you can hold up your head. Do you understand?'

Still she did not speak. Fiercely, he shook her until her head rolled from side to side.

'I still-intend-to-go-to-Chamwell's,' she said, hating him as she could never have anticipated only a short time ago. He had been her life. He had been—

He gave vent to a low cry that changed to a howl. Pushing her against the wall he struck her first on one side of her head, then the other. Pain shot through her temples and her ears rang dizzily. She began to struggle against him but the effort was useless. Losing consciousness briefly, she recovered her senses to find him pressing her down on the bed. Her gown hung in rags on the chair-arm.

'No,' she said. 'Please, no—It's finished.'

'Never,' he answered. 'This is to show you your place. Did you really imagine I was some little lap-dog you could lift up and put down at will?'

'You're hurting me.'

'Aye, and I'll hurt you a lot more before I've done. Say you'll not go to Chamwell's.'

She refused.

'He'll be disappointed if he expects to see you beautiful, I warn you.'

'Bender—'

But it was all useless as she had known from the start.

* * * *

She crawled from the bed when he eventually fell into a heavy slumber induced by his foray into the brandy cupboard. Pulling on breeches and shirt, she made her way along the hall that was barred with sharp bands of moonlight. Every part of her was hurt and bruised. She pulled open a drawer in the study where she kept a hip flask and saw in the candlelight, her father's pistol. Carne Amberwood had used it to kill Kit Talbot's mother and now she wanted to go upstairs and blast a hole in Bender. But she'd no desire to end on the gallows. Two hours ago she could have murdered him in hot blood but that fierceness had died to a cold hatred. She could never forgive the man who had so degraded and brutalised her. She must leave before he awoke.

Faro wrote a hasty note for the housekeeper, then struggled into her boots and cloak and went to the stable. She'd not be able to sit her horse but she could manage the driving seat of the small brougham she occasionally used on the heath.

To rouse the groom from his cottage would mean delays and necessary explanations so she saddled the horse herself and fixed him between the shafts, her palms damp with sweat, expecting at every moment that Bender would awake from his black sleep and confront her. Lifting the whip from its place on the wall, she climbed, with infinite care, onto the padded seat. Flicking the whip, she flinched as the black moved out into the moonlit yard. Every part of her protested against the jolting progress over the cobbles. Her nerves screamed out at the resultant clatter. She stared up at the windows, anticipating the glow of a candle at the darkened panes but there was no light, no face pressed to the glass. Small side-lamps flickered as the carriage swayed and moths flew towards them, scraps of thin whiteness, drawn stupidly to their own deaths as the heat of the fat candles reached them. More came, undeterred or uncaring of the fate of the others.

The track through the heath and bilberry shone white. Across the deep chasm of the moor shone the scattered lights of the city, the intermittent loops of the Thames. Tomorrow she was to see Carter about his tract of land in Cumberland. No matter how much it cost her she must have it. She'd tell no one where she was going but her banker and solicitor.

In the evening she was due to meet Captain Brent for cards. He was to leave for the continent the day after. Some war involving the Emperor Franz Joseph and Napoleon III. Napoleon had some bee in the bonnet about freeing Italy from the Austrians and there was a situation in Sardinia. Like all those other men she had come to know as friends, she may never see Brent again. Another of those stark notices in the papers. Died of wounds in some ghastly British outpost or other, or worse still, in the sunshine of a place like Solferino.

But if she kept her appointment, Bender would know where to find her. She must send a message to the captain, either a cancellation or a change of venue; she had not yet decided which.

Weariness struck her like a blow. She felt limp and disjointed like a rag-doll that had leaked its sawdust. She'd have to put off Captain Brent, whether or not he returned from Italy. Faro wondered, not understanding why her thoughts should have taken this uncharacteristic trend, if Brent would have loved her had he known she was a woman. Indeed, if any of those friends would have done so had they known this fact.

She had left the heath and was driving slowly down Well Walk, the avenue pressing down on her in a green shroud. The ghosts of other, sorrowing women rose up and held out supplicating hands. Her mother, grandmother, aunts and great-aunts, Fanny Carne who must have experienced such moments of great sadness, of loss.

Dawn coloured the sky and Faro was glad. The memory of the preceding night appalled her. She wanted it gone and buried for ever. She'd buy Carter's land and build another house, very different from Amberwood. That would be put up for sale and her lawyer instructed to sack all the servants. That, of course, included Bender who would have no option but to go. For a fleeting instant, she wished to respond to the echoes of his dominance, but the impulse vanished. The past years burdened her with their emptiness. Cards and Bender. Being a Frenchie for Harry Gray and Tom Brent. In Cumberland she'd be herself. Too late to renew the ties with Heronbrook. If they had written this last ten years, she'd never received the letters. Jo Talbot would have tried to keep in touch. She was that sort of woman. Unless Judith's untimely death had quenched that loyal spirit. The thought of Jo's vanquishment depressed Faro who had always admired the woman, seen her as a symbol of the age. She should have visited Jo at least.

London was just waking as she drove into the city. She'd gone by Shoreditch instead of by Camden and Bloomsbury, afraid of being pursued by Bender. The squalor oppressed her in her weakened state. Cat's meat shops and rat catchers, crossing-sweepers, busy before the traffic grew too great, night watchman staggering home, their eyes bleared with sleep, scavengers and dustmen and a yard where children and women in filthy gowns and leather aprons sieved dirt. There were dark, cluttered shops with fly-blown mutton or where a broken Dutch clock thrust against murky glass in a medley of second-hand goods. Bone pickers and rag-gatherers searched for waste metal, on their bent backs shapeless bags out of which protruded the leavings of London households, old stockings and shawls and frayed blankets.

The slums had given way to the city out of which the softly hazed dome of St Paul's rose like a benison. Faro, keeping well out of any area she had frequented with Bender, went on until she found a respectable coffee-house, left a link-boy to take charge of the brougham and feed her horse, and sat down wearily to a breakfast she could hardly manage to keep down. But the coffee put life into her. She ordered a paper and pen and wrote an apology to Brent, summoned a messenger and paid him to deliver the note by hand, then wondered where she could spend the time until her appointment with Jack Carter.

Tipping the link boy, she rode on searching for some quiet hotel where she could lie abed for a few hours, and, finding one with a stable-yard, she lay down, every inch of her sore and aching like a bad tooth. When she drifted off to sleep, that slumber was disturbed by nightmares where Bender followed her, his shadow writhing on the cobbles of an alley from which she could not escape. She shuddered upwards, her heart pounding, as he caught her and pounced on her like a beast. The roads outside were noisy now with street-cries and juggernaut wheels. Her mouth tasted of despair.

She washed her discoloured face at the stand and held her wrists in the cold water. The jug had been made for the Exhibition and the faces of Victoria, Albert and their children decorated the inferior china, surrounded by palm leaves and the shapes of elephants and other animals. Faro had attended the Crystal Palace with Bender, then still knowing his place. Shivering, she recalled his new aspect. He reminded her of a strange book by Mary Shelley, the poet's sister, about a doctor called Frankenstein who had created a monster he could no longer control, a creature who eventually destroyed him.

Once outside the shelter of the hotel, hat pulled down, she looked around her, unconvinced that he was not in the vicinity, seeing only hurrying grooms and tavern maids, a baker with a tray of loaves, an old woman with a basket of flowers.

A side road near the address of Carter's solicitor provided a place to leave the brougham, this time in the charge of a nearby stableman, then Faro presented herself, still tired to exhaustion, at the fanlighted door, glad she had remembered all the papers appertaining to Monsieur Jean Foredor. For years now she had banked her winnings under her alias, supplemented by large sums accrued by the Amberwood estate, the proceeds of produce and cattle, sales of silver and valuable paintings, jewellery she had inherited and would never wear, old furniture, indeed anything of worth that remained after her father, Carne's death. All she had left of value were the chandeliers for they were the eyes of Amberwood and the house would have been blind and humbled without them, but there turn would soon come. Amberwood would become a shell for someone else to fill with Victorian monstrosities, antimacassars, what-nots, glass domes filled with dried flowers or stuffed birds and animals, faded daguerreotypes and velvet footstools. Fussiness and stultification—She wondered who would buy it. Some member, perhaps, of the nouveau riche whose money was founded on iron or wool.

The door opened and she was ushered into an office burdened with files and mustiness. Carter was already there, excited, slapping his thigh absent-mindedly with a small crop, intent upon getting the utmost out of the sale. But the solicitor, tall, grey and narrow, had the bleak eyes of the realist, knowing perfectly well that his client's property had been difficult to sell, that the negotiations could stagnate without some bending on Carter's side.

Some of Faro's tiredness and pain left her. She had always enjoyed a gamble and this was much like a game of cards.

They all sat down and wine was poured and Bath olivers produced by the clerk. The lawyer's thin shanks were bonesharp under the grey tweed trousers. A cape of the same material hung on a hook behind the door, topped by a black hat. Faro breathed more easily. The man was conservative, unlikely to deviate from her first opinion of him. Producing her credentials, she began to sip the wine and nibble one of the biscuits, watching the faces of the two men as they inspected the documents. Carter was flushed now, the pupils of his eyes very blue in the network of red veins. A price was mentioned and Faro sat very quiet, betraying no expressions, aware, suddenly, that Carter had not noticed the bruising of her face but that the solicitor had.

She shook her head, annoyed by his discernment. 'Too much for a parcel of ground and no dwelling.'

'It's good land.'

'Maybe, but I've the bother of building and the expense of transporting labour and materials. You said yourself it was the back of beyond.'

'And that is the commodity you wanted most,' Jack reminded, laughing. He was attractive when he was amused and Faro could see what women liked about the man. He'd worn well in spite of his years. He must be near Chamwell's age, the wrong side of fifty.

'I agree. But I could have the choice of the loneliest tracts in the world if I went to the Western Highlands. As I might'. The threat was barely veiled.

'Perhaps the figure is a little high.' The lawyer brushed the crumbs off his narrow, tweed lap and looked warningly at his client.

'Well—' And Jack was set thinking again. And again.

It had taken longer than she had imagined but she'd come out of it well. Her bank must be contacted and certain requirements met, a contract signed, but to all intents and purposes, she, Faro Amberwood, was now the owner of a Cumbrian property and the knowledge was peculiarly satisfying.

'I know there's no longer a house but it must have had a name. What was it?' she asked.

'West Winds,' Jack replied vaguely, his mind obviously taken up with his recently acquired wealth, the effect upon his long suffering mistress, the prospect of still being able to afford his claret and Hazard.

'West Winds?' Faro was satisfied. The name had a rightness.

* * * *

Once that her business was over and she
156

had no motivation, the exhaustion of body and spirit returned. She had no close friends, none that she could call upon for a room and hospitality at a moment's notice. Inventiveness deserted her. She was sick of coffee-houses, skulking about like a criminal, and dubious inns, but she took care that the club she went to was the last Bender was likely to visit in his certain efforts to find her. Eating a predictable meal, she fell asleep in a leather wing chair and half-woke to find herself listening to a conversation about the Queen's grandson by her daughter Vicky. It appeared that the Princess of Prussia had given birth to a deformed child, a boy called William. The child's arm had been dislocated in a painful breech birth and could only wither with time. The story reminded Faro of Kit Talbot's child, Rose. But a hunchbacked girl must fare infinitely worse than a one-armed princeling. Some women found a man's disability irresistible. Few men would find a crooked shoulder attractive. The body was of supreme importance in matters of the senses.

The talk turned to the bitter rivalry between Richard Burton and John Speke over the journey to find the source of the Nile and Faro's interest quickened. She had liked Burton's looks—what women could not?—and his suggestion of wildness. Lord Brougham, judging by the portrait she'd seen of him, had possessed the same type of devilish attraction, and a definite simliarity to Chamwell.

The thought of Chamwell evoked his physical presence. For a moment, they stared at one another, he shocked, she unspeakably glad that, at last, she was not alone with her problems and her all too evident pain. She tried to rise from the slumped position and could not. Chamwell made an angry sound that echoed in her head like the resonance in a sea-shell. She hoped she would not disgrace herself by swooning. A woman had rushed into the club, creating a welcome diversion. Amid the noise of protests, she managed to distribute a few leaflets before being seized by flunkeys to be ignominiously ejected, crying out, "Child murderers! Why does no one act? Act decisively, I mean. We get only half-measures. Half-measures—"

'What is she talking about?' Faro whispered, whitefaced, recognising visiting Members of Parliament.

Chamwell looked at the piece of paper in his fist. 'Godfrey's cordial.'

'What—is that?'

'Some mixture of treacle and opium administered to small children so that their mothers may go out washing bed-linen or whoring, as the case may be. They are dying like flies, according to this tract, if not at once, slowly and painfully. But infants have always been prone to being snuffed out by some disease or other. The poor beget too many and the rich and influential too few. We'll be overrun one of these days, and there'll be the same anarchy that attacked the French. And, speaking of the French my dear Faro, what has happened to you? The self-sufficient—'

'I—was attacked.'

'I saw as much in a single glance. It was one of the stewards pointed you out to me. Your bruises did not pass unnoticed. Tell me the name of the cur and I'll destroy him—'

'You must not become involved. But I must leave London. He'll find me.'

'We'll go to Windsor. That should be safe enough.'

'You said—Friday.'

'To the devil with Friday. The house would have been packed with sycophants and pleasure-seekers. Today, there'll be none but you and me—'

'I made no promise,' she mumbled, then rallied a little with sheer relief at being taken under someone's wing. Chamwell's face shivered before her then became clear. He did have a look of Brougham and Burton about him, even if his teeth were too white and regular. She wished, futilely, that the thought of false teeth did not repel her. Those old hags on the streets with their sunken faces and puckered smiles always reminded her of the irrevocable passage of one's youth.

He put an arm about her shoulders and called loudly for brandy. The paper the woman had thrust at him fell upon the carpet showing Faro an etching of two boys, naked but for breeches, being let down a mine shaft on a chain, and a picture of lucifers with the word phosphorus in huge letters, followed by exclamation marks. It was supposed to cause diseases of the jaw in much the same way as soot from chimneys caused lung rot, she remembered vaguely. The Act of 1840 had not improved these ills.

The brandy was brought, and Chamwell, shielding her from curious stares, poured the liquor down her throat. Her body relaxed as she swam in a sudden haze of near wellbeing. 'Can you stand up?' he asked. The nearest politician picked up the tract and rustled it.

'I think so.'

'My carriage is outside. I'll support you.'

'The brougham I came in—'

'I'll have it follow us, never fear.'

'I drove it myself, from Amberwood. I—left rather suddenly.'

'Then it was that brute, Bender!' He sounded very angry.

'Let us go, please,' she pleaded.

'Very well, but he's not heard the end of the matter, you mark my words.' She was aware of his arm around her waist, then was surprised to find herself on her feet, her legs carrying her weight without too much difficulty. Chamwell had thrust his broad body between her and the rest of the club members so there was little for them to gossip about except the fact that young Monsieur Foredor had bruises and was probably the worse for a minor attack. It would be theft or a drunken argument. They were common enough. She almost heard their conjecturing.

Faro sank back onto the velvet lined interior of Chamwell's coach. The velvet was mulberry coloured, like the carpet where Pumphrey had collapsed, his face purpling and the cards splayed in a fan. The ace of spades had lain uppermost and she had never liked that card. Bad luck. Bad luck. The coach wheels were grinding over the cobbles, taking up the sombre refrain. Her head was placed on Chamwell's shoulder and she was dimly aware of his fingers at the buttons of her coat but she had not the strength to push him away. The hand slid inside but she was already asleep.

She was awake and feeling better when the carriage reached the outskirts of Windsor. Another vehicle was proceeding down the castle ramp and Faro recognised the figures of Victoria and the Prince Consort, both blue-eyed and unmistakably German, alike in the way that close married couples adopted. A child sat on the Queen's knee. There was always a boy or a girl to perch there, radiantly fair, expensively clad. People pressed around for a closer look and the Queen flinched for a moment before she leaned forward smiling and showing a great deal of pink gum. She must always fear another attack, Faro thought, then became aware of her own injuries.

'You slept soundly,' Chamwell said, an odd note in his voice, and she remembered the moment before sleep overtook her. She moved away from him, ashamed of her lapse into dependence, disliking the images that came of his hand on her bare flesh. But she could not blame him for his opportunism. He'd had a long enough wait for the vicarious pleasure.

Everyone cheered and the men waved their tall hats. The Royal coach came close enough for Faro's eyes to meet those of the Queen. The smile had gone, leaving Victoria's face serious and heavy. It was not difficult to see how she would look in ten—twenty years. She'd be an ugly old woman. It was as though the Queen read her thoughts. The blue eyes grew cold, stared ahead as though Faro and Chamwell did not exist. This overt disapproval had the effect of rousing Faro from the remnants of lassitude and self-pity she had experienced ever since the bargain was struck with Carter.

'I'm wide-awake now.'

'So I see. Youth is so resilient.' There was a shade of envy in his tone that touched her briefly. Brevity was the adjective that described most of her emotions except for the long thrall of her liaison with Bender. She blamed her parents. Neither had loved her and those who lacked affection rarely conceived it for others.

'I'm sorry for my foolishness.'

'It was out of character to find you so—helpless,' he told her and patted her hand. She did not object to the touch and his profile pleased her afresh.

'I'll not be so again. I had an unpleasant experience that had a delayed action. Now I am almost my usual self, or will be if I may have a hot bath when we reach the house.'

'You may have exactly what you please.'

She laughed very softly. He'd warned her he would be persuasive and he still had the memory of that furtive petting to bolster his appetites. Her spirits rose still further. She had Chamwell in her pocket and would make him dance to her tune.

A tree-lined drive enclosed them turning the deep red velvet to a dark brown. Chamwell's face had turned to a satyr's. She felt a momentary qualm for her recent self-satisfaction. How could she know how he would behave? There was no one to know she was here. He could do as he pleased and none would gainsay it. The elation evaporated.

They were met by an array of servants of a vastly different calibre to her own. It was evident that Chamwell would stand for no such nonsense as plagued herself. He was master and she suspected that he'd be ruthless should any displease him. It would be funny if she had merely jumped from the frying pan into the fire! But she did not feel like laughing.

He gave orders for bath water to be taken to the main guest room. 'You'll find a change of clothing in the press,' he told Faro and showed his teeth wolfishly. Absurd to find her feelings change so rapidly from attraction to detestation and back again. But it would be foolish to exchange one gaoler for another. She must take care.

All the time she spent in the painted bath, her tired body leaning against the high, rounded back, she worried at the problem of how she should behave towards him. She knew that her long masquerade had not the same satisfaction as when she was ten years younger and Carne Amberwood dictated her behaviour. Or tried to—she'd foxed him, beaten him in a battle of wits, rebelled against feminity. But she had changed, imperceptibly, in the last year. Thoughts of a more settled, more normal way of life had begun to haunt her. Chamwell would cushion her against the outside world if she gave him what he so obviously wanted. The only snag was that he'd know if she cheated. It excited her, suddenly, that she walked a tightrope.

She tugged at the bell-pull and two maids came to replenish the water from great jugs of copper. When she had soaked for long enough, the bruises dark as plums on her white skin, she dried herself on a huge, luxurious towel and turned to the Chinese press Chamwell had mentioned. The red and gold lacquered doors opened to disclose an array of garments obviously made for more than one woman, though it was soon plain that he did not care for the buxom. How many

166

had used that ornate bath with its pictures of clouds and cupids, ridiculous miniature bows and arrows meant to pierce the heart with darts of love? How many had pushed and pulled at the gowns in the oriental cabinets, liking this, discarding that? Anticipating—what?'

Few of the dresses appealed to her, indeed, would not have suited her with her boyish figure, but there was one in the Grecian style—long out-dated but miraculously pure and classic in line, that she suspected might flatter her as the heavier, more waisted Victorian creations never could. And there would be no one to see it but Chamwell who would not have kept the robe had he not liked it well.

There was no sign of underclothing so it was plain she was meant to wear the long white shift next to her skin. A prickle of danger ran along her nerves.

It was the only thing she could have worn, she decided, studying the draped folds and brushing her hair so that it hung straight and smooth past her shoulders. The maids would be reporting on her at this moment. No detail would have escaped them. Her flat bosom, the fact that she had been beaten, her arrival in men's clothing, all would be grist to the mill, not that they'd dare repeat the titillating gossip with Chamwell in charge.

A discreet knock at the door made her start. 'Have you found something to your taste, my dear?'

Chamwell's voice, low and disturbing. 'Yes.'

'Let me guess. I should say the white with the Greek Key band around the hem.'

'You must be a warlock.'

'No. But I know women. Are you ready to go down to supper?'

'Quite ready.' She opened the door. The wolfish eyes devoured her. He smiled.

'How are the aches and pains?'

'Not so bad but still there.'

The smile turned a fraction cold. He knew what that meant. If there was any thought of taking her to bed tonight he was doomed to disappointment. 'I can wait,' he told her, and stared at her breast where the chill of the passage had made the nipples stand out against the white material.

'Can you?'

'I have just said so.' His fingers were

on her back, propelling her gently in the direction of the staircase. He let his hand slide downwards over the firm smoothness of her hip, then go further. She slapped at his wrist, but not too hard.

'I'd not give a fig for your will-power,' she said, and laughed with a resurgence of the surety of her hold over him.

'It is your own fault for being so distractingly beautiful.'

'Even with these?' She pointed out the dark patches on arm and neck, on her face.

'Even with those.' His hand was busy again, touching, investigating, rousing her in spite of her previous disinclination.

'What if we meet some footman?'

'My servants are all blind and dumb.'

'Would that mine were.'

'You still have not told me why he assaulted you. Your man Bender.'

'Because I tried to rid myself of him and his hold over Amberwood. And he would not accept the fact.'

'It's a mistake to allow underlings overmuch power. You are not the first to discover that.'

'I was left in charge of a sizeable estate when I was very young. Inexperienced—'

'I might have helped if you had let me. Warned you that your tactics were bound to fail.'

'How could I know who I might trust? You were not always so open in your dealings. When I was once in debt to you, you made it quite plain you'd take advantage if I let you, only I managed to raise the amount, remember? You were so angry!' Faro, forgetting her bruises, laughed at Chamwell. 'It was the narrowest of escapes.'

'Perhaps it was not the best way to go about gaining your confidence. But I wanted you then as I do now.'

'And no woman in between?'

'I make no pretensions to being a saint. We both know there were other women. Transient beings. Expedience. You, I have stalked untiringly.'

'And now think you have me inside bars?'

He studied her, serious now, and she became wary. 'I think we should discuss the matter over food and wine. Come, Faro.'

Two flunkeys in red and white stood by an open door leading to an intimate room where a small table was laid for two. A leaping fire made the chamber very warm. The flowers in the centre piece were already wilted.

'Could we not have the window open?' Faro asked, 'Or the garden door?'

Chamwell nodded and one of the footmen went to obey. The resulting current of air was delicious.

'You will not be too cold?' Chamwell looked dubious. Faro shook her head.

'I cannot abide stuffiness. I never sleep with the window closed.'

'I'm glad you have warned me.'

'So long as you know what to expect.'

'And when may I—expect?'

'I will tell you when the moment seems right or, I should emphasise, *if*—'

'What if I am not content to wait?'

'You said you would! Not ten minutes ago.'

'I dare say I will stay at heel.' He motioned her to sit down with her back to the windows while he took the seat nearer the fire. 'If I am allowed small liberties meanwhile. They, surely, can hurt no one.'

'I dare say that could be managed.' She breathed more easily at his apparent acceptance.

The supper was begun and the food delicious. Her glass was refilled as soon as it was empty. Whenever she looked at it, there it was, miraculously replenished like the milk jug in the Greek legend of the kind old couple who invited a god to share their frugal fare. Not that there was anything cheese-paring about the meal she ate with Chamwell. Fish, meat, fowl, all appeared in enticing guises, baked or glazed or in rich sauces, but she ate only a little of each, noting that he did the same.

'A sweet?' he asked. 'I never eat them but they are there if you wish—'

'Then that is why your teeth are so good.' She wondered if he'd admit it if they were not real.

'I've taken excellent care of them. There, feel for yourself.' He lifted her hand and nibbled at one of the fingers as though it had been a drumstick. She watched him carefully, or as attentively as she could considering all the wine she had drunk. His teeth had not moved. They seemed deeply rooted. And then the sensation of having her finger gently bitten became pleasurable and she found herself laughing again. Everything seemed subtly accentuated, the intimacy of the supper-room—so much less intimidating than a huge dining-room might have been—the scent of the reviving flowers, the memory of the palatable meats, the fruit and the board where cheese was displayed, cheeses that neither she nor Chamwell had wanted. There was a slight echo in her skull and her thoughts seemed unnaturally clear. Chamwell looked more devilish than ever.

'I also dislike sweets,' she pronounced carefully.

'You look very different from this morning.'

'I confess I feel it. Last night was—not agreeable.'

'It could not have been. I mean to seek him out. It is not right that you cannot return to your own house—'

'It does not matter. I've bought land a long way from London. I'll sell Amberwood to the first industrialist with the necessary money—'

'When did you do that?' he asked sharply. 'Buy the land?'

'This morning. Before you saw me in the club—'

'Then you must sell it again.'

'Why?' Some of the candles must have

been extinguished for the room seemed perceptibly darker. There were only two now, one in front of each, and the fire had been allowed to burn lower. She could feel the air playing on her shoulder-blades like a touch from cool finger-tips.

'I thought I'd never marry again. The first time was not a success and I've kept clear of it. But this time—I mean to have you for wife so you cannot take yourself off where I cannot see you. Do you understand? I want you to be Lady Chamwell. Sell Amberwood if you must, but forget the parcel of ground. Or put some factor on it and take a holiday there from time to time.'

'Marry?'

'Marry. Wed. I know I'm old enough to be your father but there's life in me still. I've been told my looks have not entirely gone. And I know how to please a woman. I've had enough practice in my time! I'd look after you. Protect you—'

Great Heaven, she thought. He sounds just like Bender. And he'd want more than a nibble at her knuckles before he committed himself. A man in his position always wanted a taste of the fruit before buying it and she was not promiscuous.

She'd been faithful to Bender for years.

'I don't know that I wish to be—owned.'

'Oh, come, Faro! You see where your much vaunted independence has got you. A thrashing from a servant. Flight from your own house, not a great deal of happiness—' Chamwell dug into his coat pocket and produced a long leather box which he proceeded to open. 'I have come armed. This was to be your betrothal gift. See?' The hands, filmed with fine, dark hairs, lifted up a rope of pearls. Their size and quality took Faro's breath away. So it was not merely an affair Chamwell required.

'You mean it, then?'

'Don't these prove anything?' The pearls clinked against a wine-glass. She had never cared for intricacies of metal and precious stone but these silky, sea-born treasures were different. Faro would not care to hazard a guess as to how much they had cost him. The thought humbled her. All of her life she had been conscious of being lacking, of not meeting the standards that had been set for her, but this token made her see the strength of Chamwell's obsession. She realised already the physical attraction she possessed for him. He could not keep his hands off her. He was not too old, reasonably good-looking, and he wanted to care for her. He must already have been in possession of the magnificent gift for they had not been out of one another's company since they met so unexpectedly in the club. Obviously the proposal was to have been made at the weekend. He must have been reasonably sure of her once she consented to come.

'Well?' Chamwell asked and dropped the pearls onto the starched linen cloth.

'I will marry you.' Faro was as surprised as he at the speedy capitulation.

The white smile flashed as Chamwell rose to his feet. 'Come,' he said, and held out his arms. Then, his expression changed to one of horror. Faro's skin crept.

'What is it?' she whispered.

Chamwell shook his head and put out a restraining hand. There was a bang that rattled every object in the room and half of Chamwell's face disappeared. His teeth had been real enough, Faro thought, numbed. Fragments of bone splinter and human molars had fallen to mingle with the soft glow of the pearls and pools of bright blood.

People were running, Chamwell's body, that sickening half head, swayed and fell to the floor, out of sight behind the table. The wall behind was marked with black chips.

She turned mechanically, to see Bender in the gap of the french window.

'Murder!' a flunkey was shouting, his voice high with fear. 'Murder! The master—' The voice broke as the man slumped, retching against Chamwell's handsome wallpaper. And then the room was filled with other servants with red and white livery. Loud cries—

Bender hesitated, the fowling-piece clattering at his feet, then disappeared as suddenly as he had arrived, leaving the space dark and empty.

Faro became aware that some of the pellets that had destroyed Chamwell had pierced her flesh. She was conscious of burning pains, of small rivulets of red that coursed down her arm, her breast, marking the Greek gown like watercourses on a map. She felt her mind swimming, her body refuse to obey her orders. Slowly, she slumped over the table.

PART THREE

THE FRENCHMAN

4

The Frenchman had come again. Kit had seen the slight, black-clad figure riding along the track to West Winds, from the upper pasture. The children had seen him too, and had shouted, waving their arms, but the face had not turned, nor had the black horse slowed its pace. The funereal figure had begun to disturb him. What use was a neighbour who did not acknowledge one's presence? Who was but a shadow on a skyline.

'Time for your lessons!' he shouted to Broome, knowing how the summons would annoy him. He swithered in his feelings concerning the boy. There was pride in the strong, dark body, the fierce good looks. But there was bitterness, too, that the child was not Judith's. Broome was like himself, base-born, his mother a gipsy. Local folk gossiped that the foundling was Deborah Broome's, but this at least Kit could refute. He'd had no dealings with the girl, though she'd encouraged him. Jim, her father, had told Kit who was responsible for the pregnancy. The disclosure had surprised Kit at first and then he had realised its inevitability. Robbie Dixon adored his Janie but could have no relations with her for fear she'd fall for a baby, and Deborah, ignored by Kit, had made herself available. Proximity, seduction and human need had brought about the situation. It was a story old as the hills.

'The Frenchie,' Broome panted, reaching Kit. 'He won't look at us. Well, never at me. Sometimes at Rose.'

The old, familiar pain swept over Kit Talbot. He was used to people looking at his daughter with her rare beauty of face and deformed body. If he could have taken that hump on to himself, he would. When he drove her into Keswick, folks stared and made remarks. ''Beauty and the Beast'' one man had said, noting Kit's disfigured face and not seeing Rose's affliction because she was wrapped in furs. 'Can the child be safe with him?' And Kit had whipped the horses so that the man had to jump for his life from the path of the trap, taking with him the memory of a red-headed giant whose face was sown together where it was once cut open by a jealous woman's knife.

'Get inside,' Kit ordered. 'Mr Henry arrived ten minutes past and you are not so clever that you can afford to skimp your lessons. In fact, I should call you stupid.'

Broome's eyes flashed.

'Now! Not tomorrow!' Kit gave him a push in the direction of Grey Ghyll.

The boy glared, then ran, ducking his head as though he had tears in his eyes but Kit knew that any tears there might be were only those of rage and not contrition.

Rose came more slowly, eyes anxious. 'You are not cross with me, Father?'

'How could I be?' he replied gently, lifting the frail body and setting her on his massive shoulder. 'But you must not allow Broome to distract you from more important things. It is only good manners to be there when your tutor comes. It is not as though you did not enjoy your work.'

'I love learning. But Broome is my brother—'

'Half-brother,' he corrected swiftly.

'And I love him too.'

'That is only natural,' Kit agreed stiffly, striding down the track, half his mind on the appearance of his cows and the other concerned with the feelings he entertained for his boy. 'But one must never lose sight of one's obligations. Of elementary good manners—'

'No, Father.'

She was no heavier than a bird on his shoulder. Bitterness seeped into his being. Rose should not have been so afflicted. It was Judith's fault that the girl was spoilt for life. She had left her mark on them both and he could not find it in him to forgive her. Depositing Rose on the doorstep, Kit began his business about the farm. Jo had taken the little girl to Heronbrook once and had introduced Rose to the Lammeters, Judith's parents.

'Why, she's a cripple,' Una Lammeter said, drawing back with repugnance.

'She's what I could have expected of

such a union,' Miles pronounced coldly.

Even so long afterwards, Kit clenched his great fists as though he would pound them both to jellies. If he ever set eyes on them again, he'd not be able to keep his hands from them. Pettifogging poseurs, he told himself as he examined and shifted and probed. Thank God Rose was not small-minded. She accepted her disability with equanimity. Not that she would always feel so. There was bound to come a time when she would question, rebel, when she would want to know about her mother.

'I'll meet that when it comes' Kit thought, and knelt in the muck to feel the udders of a cow who was not giving the milk she should. There was a slight hardness there as though a teat had become blocked. Perhaps he should call the horse doctor from Gillerthwaite. He was due to ride over to Peg's tomorrow. He'd go first to Clarke's.

The though of Peg, if it did not bring him undue excitement, brought its own satisfaction. He was not the only caller there but undoubtedly the most welcome. She was comely and good-natured, not possessive, the perfect antidote to his dead wife.

The memory of Judith brought back the main reason for her death. He'd not seen Pan Boswell since, though there were reports that the gipsies now used the old Carter property infrequently. They passed in the night for sometimes the dogs would bark for half an hour or more and in the morning there would be marks in the mud of the track. Once he had risen and run down to the gate but saw nothing but the distant bulk of a wagon swaying, then gone in an instant round the bend of the road as though he had only dreamed the occurrence.

The image of Pan aroused an itch he had imagined long forgotten, obliterating the more homely picture of Peg in her cottage bed, smelling of lavender and other men, of animal warmth. If he saw Pan again, he'd not hold it against her that she'd left her brat on his step. It would be Ben's doing. Ben Boswell was proud. He'd have no mixed blood in his encampment. Kit stood for a minute, uncharacteristically, dreaming, the vision of the gipsy girl tantalising him as she had done in real life. But, and he shrugged, they'd not come to these parts again now that the Frenchie was there, building his grey house behind the spinney. He'd seen the foundations laid, the carts of stone and wooden props, the sacks of nails and plaster, the workmen themselves with their stoves and tarpaulins, ride past on the wild path to West Winds. No place now for the Boswell tribe. They'd be forced back to the common land, to law and order and the dreaded magistrates.

Unaccountably, he sighed, then went back to his chosen work.

* * * *

'I want to see the Frenchie,' Broome told Rose. The rain was sweeping down from the hills, sighing against the greenish pane like soft voices. 'I never wanted anything more.'

'How can we? He never comes near enough. And we are not allowed to go to West Winds because Madge and Father say the labourers are rough and would swear at us, or be drunk and quarrelsome. We'll never set eyes on him.'

'I shall think of a way.'

'Will you always be so determined?'

'Always.'

184

The rain went on whimpering. 'Play something that I would like,' Rose coaxed, holding out transparent hands to the fire behind the big brass guard. 'Adeline Bassett and her sister do—'

'The doctor's daughters are good little girls and very dull,' Broome retorted, squashing a fly against the glass and wiping the sticky residue onto his trousers. 'I'll not play "Puss in the corner" again, nor "Teapot", nor "Dumb Crambo", and I am sick of "Hunt the Ring"—'

'You only play "King of the Castle" because I can't pull you off. Ever—'

'And we need several children for "Russian Scandal" or "Oranges and Lemons". And it's too wet to do anything outside.' All of Broome's frustration and boredom showed in his expression, his hunched, strong shoulders, his voice which had become disagreeable in the way Rose secretly feared.

'We could play "I love my love with an A," he suggested, turning from the grey-green world outside. 'I've thought of a good one. "I love my love with an H".'

'An H?' Rose repeated, disturbed by the glitter of his black gaze.

'Because she has a hump,' Broome said

185

cruelly, then was knocked flying by a blow from Kit's fist. Neither had heard him come into the play-room. Broome, lying sick and dizzy on the floor saw him horridly foreshortened, his green eyes blazing with fury. A boot kicked him in the side. Prudently, he stayed where he was, his eyes closed.

'He didn't mean it,' Rose told her father. 'I'm sure he didn't. Is Broome dead?'

'Broome is very much alive,' Kit answered, 'And if he doesn't get his backside out of here and into his own room, I will thrash him until my arm is tired.'

The boy crawled towards the door, helped by Kit's toe, then disappeared in a crash of heavy foot falls that brought Madge up and onto the landing. 'Mercy! I do believe we've a plague of elephants in the house.'

'Broome is not to have supper until he has apologised both to Rose and to me,' Kit announced curtly.

'What has he done?' Madge was understandably curious.

'Nothing I care to repeat.'

'It was not a lie,' Rose insisted. 'He

does love me. And I do have a hump.'

Kit uttered a strangled exclamation, then pushed his way past the housekeeper and down the stairs. The outer door closed with a dull thump.

'You should not say that to your father,' Madge said uncomfortably. 'You know how it upsets him.'

'But it is the truth. And it was only a game.'

'I'm sorry! Sorry! Sorry! Broome bawled along the passage. 'If that's what he wants, then I'm sorry. Do you hear?' His door banged so loudly that the pictures hung crooked on the wall. Madge cast her eyes Heavenwards. It was bad enough when the boy was small. Only God knew how things would be when he was older. She took Rose's hand. 'Come, sweetheart. We'll make pastries in the kitchen and you shall spoon in the jam. Would you like that?'

'But Broome—'

'You heard what your father said. I cannot interfere.'

'He has apologised.'

'Not to your dada. Broome must stay where he is till Mr Kit returns. You know that as well as I do. You must not get it into your head that the boy can do no wrong. He can be a cruel little beast when he likes. He's been the cause of more trouble in this house than I care to mention. Come, Miss Rose.' They began to descend the wall-papered staircase. Madge had thought the dark purple with the flowery branches would not show the dirt of children's hands but the whole effect was of overpowering gloom. Rose's spirits flagged.

Broome, crouched in the furthest corner, heard their retreating footsteps and hated them equally.

* * * *

Kit had forgotten the fair. Keswick was noisy with it, the inns full to bursting, the sound of voices, scraping fiddles, screams, cries to try this or that, to see the sideshows that usually displayed fat women, two-headed calves or some other such monstrosity, or a moth-eaten bear with eyes that pleaded for freedom. There'd be cock-fighting in most suitable yards or barns, and it was diplomatic to keep away from lanes and dark alleys if one did not wish to become separated from one's purse.

The fairground itself, lit by flares and lanterns, seemed to ply good trade against a background of red and gold caravans with the black chimneys silhouetted against the night sky. He'd buy some gingerbread men with raisin eyes and currant coat-buttons for Rose. Kit found himself hardening his heart against Broome. 'I love my love with an H.' In that one sentence was the essence of cruelty. He'd found excuses for the boy in the past but he'd not do it again. The young whelp should go to school and only come in the holidays, preferably a hard place that would teach him manners and discipline.

Kit pushed his way past a man with a string of dubious horses for sale and went into the "Lamb and Fleece". It was full of dalesmen and farmers, a smattering of gipsies, none of whom he recognised as Boswells. Dirty and shiftless, he thought contemptuously, then dismissed them from his mind. Perhaps he should buy a fairing for Peg. It was the sort of appreciation she was likely to value.

Finished with his drinking, he thrust his way out of the overheated atmosphere

189

into the comparative rawness of the night air. The horse-trader had gone and the street was quiet though the distant tumult of the fair smote against his ears with renewed vigour, as if, during his sojourn at the "Lamb" a new spirit of vitality had entered the cramped confines of the field that housed the tents and booths, the stalls and caravans.

He went towards the sound, his tensions eased by the liquor, conditioned now to enjoy the infrequent experience. One was never so conspicuous in a crowd and with his hat brim pulled down, the worst of his scars would not be so noticeable. Not that they had put off Peg. If anything, the marks of Judith's knife had made Peg fancy him more. Would that it were so in poor Rose's case.

"I love my love with an H".

Kit cursed and ploughed a relentless track through giggling dairymaids and bucolic ploughmen, the gipsy woman who promised entrancing futures by the cross of a silver coin in the palm. The smell of the bear was carried on the breeze, rank and dangerous. There'd be pandemonium if the beast broke free of its chain as had happened the first year he'd been at Grey

Ghyll, not long after Judith had hanged herself and he'd ridden for Keswick as though to sanctuary. A girl had been mauled to death, two youths had been savaged and left near dying before the animal was despatched. Kit still had a vivid picture of a disembowelled dog, its dull eyes filled with agony. He had wrung its neck himself rather than let it suffer.

Buying the bag of gingerbread men, he thrust them into a capacious pocket, felt for his purse to reassure himself that he'd not been robbed, then made his way in the general direction of Peg's cottage, kicking aside orange peel and nut-shells, the usual litter left in the wake of the gathering. He had reached a barn on the outskirts of the field when he remembered the fairing. It had slipped his mind that he'd intended to purchase a bit of ribbon or a trinket. He halted, irresolute.

Something moved inside the barn. There was a thud, a suggestion of a partly-suppressed scream, a thrashing in the loose straw. It was none of his business, Kit decided, if someone's passions had got the better of them. Any woman who accompanied a man into a barn knew perfectly well the risk she ran.

A fair induced excitement, a loosening of the morals. A man spent money on a partner and expected some return for the generosity. And yet—

Another scrabble, a low moan, then a man's voice. 'Be still, you bitch.'

'Who's there?' Kit challenged. If the wench had changed her mind there was still time for her to break free.

Again, a snatch of a cry, a curse from the man. Kit had the impression now that there were more than two people in the shadows of the building, and that seemed ugly. Feeling around the entry to the barn, he picked up a stave of wood that had come off the side. Standing in the doorway, he waited to allow his eyes to become used to the darkness, but almost immediately, he was attacked. A great, bunched fist swung out. Kit moved his head more by good luck than judgement and the fist crashed against the door-frame. The man bellowed with rage.

'Please,' the woman was pleading. 'Please—'

Kit side-stepped and struck out with the stave. The wood snapped with a soft crack leaving him with the stump of the plank. Catching sight of the glitter of steel, he thrust the jagged fragment forward to where his opponent's face should be. The man screamed and dropped the knife. Kit bent swiftly and picked it up. The burly figure had staggered out into the dim glow reflected from the fairground, groaning fearsomely.

'You'd best get out while you can,' Kit said. 'or you'll fare as your friend did.'

The woman's breath caught a gasp. 'Leave me be, you pig,' she insisted and now there was a kind of triumph in her voice. The voice, Kit thought, with a sudden conviction, reminded him of something long past, something he had pushed into a cupboard of the mind and then turned the key in the lock. He heard the man rise from the straw, the retreating movements of the woman. Outside, the injured man groaned and kept his hands to his face.

'I'll treat you the same way if you don't go now,' Kit threatened. 'Not so brave when you're alone! And I do have his knife.'

There was a long pause, a whispered curse, a sloping shadow, then silence.

'You can come out now,' Kit said. 'They've gone.'

'You sure they ain't waiting?'

'I can see them, half-way back to the fairground. Perhaps you should have the knife they left behind.'

'How did you know I was here?'

'I didn't. I stopped because I'd forgotten something and couldn't decide whether to go on or go back.' He could hear her adjusting her clothing, brushing off the straws that clung to her garments. The sounds titillated his senses. The thought of Peg receded.

'Lucky you did.'

'Why take such a chance?'

'Didn't. I was grabbed and didn't 'ave no choice in the matter.' She had still not tidied herself to her own satisfaction and he was impatient to see her.

'You'd best let me escort you to a safer place. It really would be advisable.'

'Live in Keswick, do you?'

He recognised a similar curiosity in her as afflicted himself. 'No, I just came to spend the night with—a friend.'

She laughed unexpectedly. 'You're keeping 'er waiting, then.'

'I will see you to safety first,' he repeated stubbornly.

'Well, seems you're set on my company. 'Ope *she* don't mind.'

'She won't mind. She has too much sense.'

'I feel that—I knows you.' The woman put into words his own sense of familiarity.

'Come outside and the doubts will be resolved.'

'I do know. It was the way you said that—'

'Then you must be—Pan. Pan Boswell.'

'You don't sound too pleased.'

'A nice load of trouble you created but I need not remind you of that!' he said sharply.

'What trouble?'

'Look, those men may come back with their cronies. We'll go to some eating-house and take supper. Why did you never return to Grey Ghyll?'

'Ben would not let me. Never came this way again till two years gone, then it was at Carter's we stopped, only this year we found it being built on. Some Frenchie whose father had his head chopped off in the Revolution they said.'

He heard her feet scuffling in the dry straw, then she was beside him, the air

195

suddenly vibrant with her warmth and vitality.

'Did you know those men?'

'Never clapped eyes on them before. One asked for directions, then, when I was showing 'im, t'other got 'old of me an' they 'ad me in the barn afore I knew it. I'm glad you forgot whatever it was an' stopped to think. 'Ow can we 'ave supper though, if you've got a woman to see?'

He could make out her face now, dimly, the womanly shape of her body. Whatever else she had lost, there was still that aura of sexuality. Then he remembered Broome and the viciousness of the "game" he played with Rose and was conscious of a flicker of anger. It was Pan who had left problems that had far-reaching consequences. But he had played the greater part in the debacle. He should have known better and it would be Ben who had insisted the child be taken from its mother, who had stayed away from the Keswick area.

Kit sighed and Pan took this as a sign that he regretted his suggestion that they go for a meal.

'Don't *'ave* to sup wi' me! I'll take

myself off. And thanks—' She moved away. Kit grabbed her arm. 'Oh, no you don't. There are things we have to talk about, as well you know. Peg will understand. It's not the first time I have not appeared when I was expected. Some emergency on the farm.'

'You said you were going to spend the night wi' her.'

'Well?' They began to walk in the opposite direction from the fairground.

'Then where do you intend to sleep?'

'I've not yet decided.'

'You mean, it depends on what we talk about?'

'I suppose so. We'll make for that corner there. I seem to remember a chophouse a few doors down.'

'You been drinking,' Pan observed. 'I can smell it on your breath.'

'What's it to you?'

'You didn't much years back.'

'We all change. Don't tell me you haven't.' The light from a window played over her and Kit pulled her to a standstill. She smiled wryly. 'You can see 'ow right you are. 'Ave, 'aven't I? Don't mind if you says it. Fleshed out a bit and my hair can't look too good after rolling about in the barn.'

Kit stared his fill. She was like some disorderly Ceres, full of the bounties of the earth. Nothing, not even time, would alter the dramatic bone-structure. Pan was tall enough to carry the extra weight, not that there was too much of that for his taste.

'Oh, God!' Pan cried suddenly. 'Lost me basket. I 'ave! Dropped it when those pigs caught me. Supposed to sell all those things, I was. I should go back. Look for it—'

'I think that would be to invite trouble. I still maintain your abductors could return with reinforcements.'

'He'll beat me, then. Always beating me he is, Ben. Nearly killed me after I'd been with you. Couldn't walk for a sennight.'

'No one will beat you while you are in my company. Look. There's the chop-house. We'd be safer there. If those men are seeking you, or me, they'll come here. But the chop-house has a back room with oak settles. Private places where you'd not be observed by anyone trying to look inside. Come, Pan.'

' 'Asn't put you off, then, taking a

closer look at me?'

'You know perfectly well that I find you eminently pleasing—'

'Don't rightly know what you mean.' Pan allowed herself to be directed into the doorway of the eating-place, her long nose wrinkling up in anticipation of the cooking meat. The savoury smell was delicious. She ran her tongue over her lips.

'I mean,' Kit said, aware of falling a second time into the same trap, 'that I find you attractive as ever.' He elbowed her into one of the alcoves and almost pushed her onto the leather covered bench behind the oaken screen.

'Christ Jesus, but I'm hungry.' Pan strove, unsuccesfully, to tidy her abundant hair. Straws fell from it onto the table-cloth and the stained carpet. Kit laughed, intercepting the pot-man's knowing look.

Most of the other recesses were occupied by couples but none of the women were as arresting as the gipsy in her tartan kirtle—some trophy of a foray over the Border—and the bodice that strained over her splendid breasts. Kit was aware that they were noted, she for that animal attraction, he for his disfigurement. It no longer troubled him.

'What of me?' he asked, signalling to a slovenly serving-maid. 'We've not had an encounter since my wife left me bleeding like a pig in the Broome's cottage.' Even after the passage of time it was still known as Broome's cottage—always would be.

'Ben couldn't help knowing what 'appened, me brothers being up there. That was when 'e thrashed me.' She shivered.

'I'm sorry you had to suffer on my account.'

'As you did on mine. 'Urt each other we 'ave, 'aven't we, Mr Kit?'

'Mine was the major blame. I should have left well alone. We want chops, young missie! And baked potatoes. Pease-pudding?'

'Yes, please.' Pan's face took on a look of near ecstasy. ' 'Aven't eaten since s'morning.'

'You don't look starved.'

'Some days the food ain't so easy to find. I could eat that girl, never mind our supper! Always been one for me food.'

'Was it your idea, or Ben's, to leave the child at Grey Ghyll?'

200

'Child?' Her look of stupefaction was well contrived.

'There's no real mystery, not to me,' Kit said. 'The child was my property, so the label said. And you were the only person with whom I'd had relations. So the boy is yours and whether or not you or Ben left him there, that fact remains unchangeable.'

Pan said nothing but her expression showed a brief cunning.

'Well?'

'I ain't saying. And you can't make me.'

'Nevertheless, between us, we made a boy, yet you show no curiosity? Ask nothing about him? How he looks? Behaves? What his future holds?'

'O'course, I'm curious!' she burst out. 'But you know as well as I do that po-faced Madge won't want the likes o' me around, giving myself airs above my station. Not after Mrs Judith—'

'So you know about my wife's action?' Kit's face became grim.

'Didn't till two years back. I already told you we kept away—'

'I can well imagine why! You might have got your bastard back again!'

'Don't you mean—our bastard?' she asked quietly.

'Don't bandy words with me, woman.'

She reached across the table. 'I would like to see the boy. He favours you, I 's'pect?'

'He resembles me not at all. He's black as the Earl of Hell's waistcoat. And a tongue as dark as his looks.' Kit frowned, remembering his displeasure. 'A gipsy.'

'Is he now? And Mrs Judith's girl, she's a cripple, I'm told.' Pan shrank back from the violence in Kit's features. 'That's what they said, those workmen at the Carter place. O'course, I'll be glad if it ain't true.'

'She has a—weakness,' Kit admitted stiffly. 'Thank God. Here comes the chops. They'll keep you quiet for long enough for me to assemble my thoughts. Would they look for you should you not return with your basket of pegs or whatever it was you hawked round the doors?'

'I dare say they would. But they'd not go to Grey Ghyll. Leaving these parts, Ben said, for good, now the Carter's place is sold. Would never go back to your copse, not after your wife hanged

202

herself from that tree—Bad, dreadful luck—'

'Be quiet,' Kit said shortly and watched her attack the hot food, then applied himself to his own belated meal. Peg must have given him up by now. He should by rights have gone in person to tell her the affair was over but he couldn't do it in cold blood. It might hurt her less if he wrote to her, then he remembered, she could not read. The thought nagged at him as though some important fact had escaped him. The only thing that was certain was his intention to take Pan Boswell back to the Ghyll.

* * * *

Madge had not troubled to conceal her dismay at the reappearance of the Boswell creature.

'Trouble she was last time,' she muttered grimly, 'and trouble she'll be again. There's no knowing how it will end, and her mother of that Broome. It stands to reason, don't it, if he's fond of the boy— and he is, of course, however much he'll try to deny it—and she's got her hooks into him again, he could easily wed her.

Never had much time for the local gentry
did Mr Kit so he won't care that they are
bound to disapprove. Oh, why did he
have to go to Keswick that particular
night?'

'T'is fate,' Betty opined. 'You can't
fight what's mapped out.'

Madge looked at her pityingly. 'What's
fate got to do with it? What *is* fate come
to that!'

'She'm—bold-looking. Do you really
think Mr Kit will marry her?'

'The signs is all there. Dropped Peg
Booker, he has, not that that's a bad
thing, but her he'd *never* have brought
home. Can't say that I fancy that Jezebel
with the household keys. It was all
because of her that poor Mrs Judith went
off her head and I'm surprised Mr Kit
hasn't remembered that.'

'Maybe he does and the back-bed-
room's as far as she'll get. But it ain't
right with them children in the house,'
and Betty slapped the rolling pin down
on the pastry with unnecessary force.

They lapsed into an uneasy silence.

* * * *

'You haven't been to see the Frenchie,' Rose said, kneeling to pick buttercups.

'How do you know that?' Broome asked, rolling off his back and propping himself on his elbows to watch her.

'You wouldn't go without me?'

'Why should I take you? Kit wouldn't like it, anyway, I'd have to go away to school.'

'I shall tell him he can't do that to you.'

'He likes you better than me. Oh, yes, he does! People should like their children equally.'

'He does love you. I think he's ashamed of me. I suppose I'm like a pot that didn't come out right. You could never admire it as much as one that was perfect.'

'It's a wonder you are so sensible. The Bassetts would spend all their time crying,' Broome observed. 'I hate cry babies.'

'They are kinder to me than you are. Why is that, Broome?' She raised her pale, oval face and fixed huge grey eyes on him. Her hair was the colour of the mahogany press Madge loved to polish. His heart jumped queerly.

'They're girls. Soft as butter,' he said arrogantly.

'I heard Madge say that woman is your mother. Mistress Boswell. You do have the same name.'

'She's not! How could she be? She's only just come. I don't want her to be my mother.'

'We do not always get what we want.' Rose spoke with feeling.

'I'd know it if I saw my real mother. I'd feel—she was different.'

'I do not remember mine at all.'

'She's dead. Dead people can't catch out at you and tell you—'

'Tell you what?'

'That you—belong.'

'You do look like her,' Rose observed.

'I don't!'

They stared at one another over a chasm. It was Broome who looked away first.

'I saw the Frenchie this morning,' Rose said, struggling back onto her feet. 'He rode by very early as though he left Keswick during the night. I waved from my window but he was not looking. He appeared very sinister—'

'Such big words we are using!' Broome mocked. 'It means left-handed, according to our worthy tutor.'

206

'And unlucky. Disastrous. Corrupt.'

'No wonder you are teacher's pet! Father's pet. Everyone's pet. Except mine.' Broome got up and began to move away.

'Yours, too,' Rose said quietly. 'Let's go to the Frenchie's place. I'll say it was my idea.'

'Who'll believe that! Anyway, how do we get there? I could go on my pony, or walk if need be. You could do neither.'

'We could go on a horse. You first, then you could pull me up and I'd hold on to you.'

'You have it all thought out, haven't you?'

'I like you to be able to do the things you want to do. And I'm just as interested in the Frenchie.'

'When shall we go?'

'Robbie goes to Keswick on Wednesday. I heard him say so. There'd be no one in the stables.'

'Are you sure?'

'Quite sure.'

'What if the Frenchie doesn't want to see us?'

'He does,' Rose said, lifting up the buttercups to look into their shining centres.

'How do you know?' Broome asked curiously.

'I just know.'

'Then we'll go on Wednesday.' He walked off, whistling.

* * * *

'I was thinking,' Kit said in the wax-scented darkness.

'Were you?' Pan sounded lazy and replete. 'What about?'

'It might cause less heart-burning if you had some regular duties while you are here.'

'Thought I 'ad!' Pan laughed and snuggled further into his embrace.

'Household duties, I meant.'

'I like these better. And I do stop you 'aving to ride to Keswick whenever the urge do come on you.'

'I mean it, Pan.'

'Don't send me back to the dairy, please. 'Ated that cold place, I did. Always 'aving to take baths in the mornings. Chapped 'ands—like a morgue, it were.'

'You could do with another bath,' Kit

said frankly. 'I'll not come tomorrow if you've neglected to take one. You know where the bathroom is, where to find the hot water?'

'Oh. I'm not expected to use the kitchen, like before.'

'Not now. About those other duties. I think you should be responsible for the children. It would take some chores from the shoulders of Betty and Madge. And it might bring you closer to Broome. You've not taken much notice of him so far.'

' 'E doesn't like me. I can tell.'

'Perhaps it hurts him to think he was left on a doorstep, like a—cabbage.'

'Don't know anything about children. Never 'ad any—but the boy. And you know Ben and 'is ways. Cruel 'ard Ben is. Didn't even let me hold the baby once.'

'Then Broome must take after him.'

'What should I need to do? I never really cared for the baby at all. Scarcely saw it.'

'See that they are clean and well-dressed. Arrive punctually to meals, and are there when their tutor comes. Taken for walks when he's not there, supervised in the nursery—'

'Supervised?' She stroked his back contentedly.

'Looked after.'

'Rather whittle pegs or snare rabbits. Tell the Tarot cards,' she grumbled.

'Pan. You must forget those ways if you are to stay here. You do enjoy being at Grey Ghyll?'

'Mostly. Don't care for them women, much. No more than they likes me.'

'But you like me, don't you.'

' 'Course I do.'

'Even with—my face the way it is?'

'Don't make no difference. Looks can be a snare—'

'I had them once. I do not—repel you?'

'If you did I'd not be 'ere, would I?' The stroking became more urgent.

'I suppose not.'

'You'll never be really sure, will you? Of nobody.'

'Never.'

'That seems a shame. A fine upstanding man like yourself.' Pan laughed softly, as at some secret joke.

His hold on her tightened. The smell of wax was peculiarly haunting. A wind came down from the mountains and moaned down the chimneys. Twigs thrashed against the pane. The night was suddenly unquiet, thoughts of sleep

210

banished.

'But you'll do as I want?' he asked.

'I suppose so. Always do, don't I?' Pan murmured and stretched out so that he could avail himself the better of those privileges he thought of so highly.

* * * *

It was after early lunch and Broome saddled the roan with careful fingers. Kit would never forgive him if he placed the mount in danger. The buckles fastened, the boy looked around for Rose. She had not yet come though he had tapped quietly on her door. But it took her so long to put on her outdoor things, though it was not her fault. Poor Rose.

He heard her light footstep. Her shadow darkened the doorway, thin and hunched. Broome swallowed hard. The sudden tenderness unmanned him. He thrust it away.

'Hurry!' he commanded crossly. 'Must you take all day?'

'I'm sorry.'

'I've bread and cheese and apples from the kitchen. We'll eat later.'

'I'm ready.'

Broome swung himself up onto the strong equine back by way of the mounting block and sat astride competently. He had shortened the stirrups so that his feet would go into them. Too much danger of falling off otherwise, not only himself but Kit's precious daughter. He bent, reaching out his hand, pulling her onto the big grey stone, then lifting her quite easily, to sit close behind him. The feather-light arms encircled his chest. He could see the thin white fingers linked, the blue veins branched like small rivers. Why did she always make him feel so coarse, so—stifled?

'For Heaven's sake sit still and don't let go,' he admonished curtly.

'I won't.'

Broome took the horse out quietly. The sun and clouds made patches of light and dark over the fields and hill flanks. The track to West Winds lay, inviting.

'*She'll* wonder where we are,' Rose said when they were away from the house and the roan trotted strongly along the river bank, kicking up a pungency of leaf mould.

'I don't s'pose she'll notice. Not straight away.'

'She was in Dada's bedroom trying on those dresses in the big press.'

'You mean—your mother's?'

'Yes. I saw her standing just in her shift and drawers, humming a tune I did not know.'

'Some gipsy nonsense,' Broome growled, disapproving.

'She's—very handsome. He thinks so. I've seen him look at her at supper.'

'You think she means to stay?' he asked, disturbed. 'For ever?'

'Madge says gipsies don't ever stay long. Always needing to be on the move.'

Like me, Broome thought, the realisation bitter as gall. He did not want to be linked with the comely, slatternly woman Kit had brought back from Keswick. The woman Kit visited after the household was in bed. Broome had heard them talking, then the bed moving, the gipsy laughing. Madge and Betty whispered together about his father and the colourful stranger.

'You know the idiot boy we sometimes saw in Keswick?' Rose said. 'They say he's been sent to work in a mill. Somewhere a long way off. He's to be a piecer.'

213

'What ever's that?'

'He must join broken threads on the spinning machines. And put fresh bobbins in when the previous ones become empty. Will he mind, do you think, that he is shut away? May never see Cumberland again? Must work till he falls down with tiredness?'

'Why was he sent? It sounds awful.'

'His mother died and there was no one left to care for him. He was a strong, big boy and it was decided he must work for his living. I think no one cared sufficiently for him. Terrible things happen to people when they are not loved or wanted.'

A great spasm of dread overcame Broome. He had heard of the lot of workers in mills and factories just as Rose had, from Kit who had those Radical leanings from the folk who brought him up, the Talbots from Cramble. This escapade could turn Kit against him permanently. Perhaps he'd not bother to find him a school. He was a big strong boy like the idiot and could work his passage through life. Broome realised in that swamping moment just how pleasant his conditions were.

'It won't happen to me!' he asserted boldly.

'Of course not. Your mother wouldn't allow it.'

'Be quiet about her! I've told you she's not my mother. Look. There's a rabbit over there.'

'Where?'

'Too late now, stupid. You'll be too late for everything. Always. You're too slow.'

There was a hurt silence, then Rose said, 'The stone cart's been this way. See that fresh bit by the rut on the track?'

'Yes. I think I heard it yesterday when we were out with—the gipsy.'

'She thinks wrens are bad luck. She calls them witchbirds.'

'Superstitious mumbo-jumbo.'

'Now who's using big words!'

They bickered their way through the wilderness, then Rose grew quiet and Broome began to worry. 'Are you all right?'

'I'm—tired. And my back and arms are hurting. I don't think I can go back.'

'But we must!'

'It's the motion of the horse. It joggles all my bones.'

215

'I knew it was a mistake to bring you,' Broome said contemptuously.

'Please stop. You said there was bread and cheese.'

'That was for the way back.'

'You must stop,' Rose whispered and Broome saw that the small fingers were sliding away. He pulled at the bit, but it was too late. Rose had fallen already and lay by the track, her small white face up-turned towards the sky.

* * * *

Kit washed his hands, thrust away the towel, and went in search of Pan. He mounted the stairs quietly for such a big man. Years ago, he'd come in search of Judith at odd hours of the day when one task was done and another not quite ready. Madge and Betty were in the kitchen, sulking, presumably because Pan had been put in charge of the children. Kit had affected not to notice. He liked Madge but he was master in his own house and Pan was more essential to him than any housekeeper. She did not ask where he was going, where he had been, turn her back on him when he needed her

216

most. There was a generosity in her, a simplicity he found refreshing and even when she was old there'd be a grandeur about it. A pity there was that suggestion of discord between her and Broome, but he knew, from experience, how it felt to be abandoned. Strange how his own problems had become those of his son. Pride struggled with regret as he thought of the boy.

The door of the bed-chamber was not quite closed. Through the gap he saw a glimpse of red, had an impression of dusky hair and gleaming arms. Stepping inside, he shut the door with a decisive sound. In the shadows, she made him think of Judith. That was the gown his wife had worn the evening she told him she was expecting his child in spite of all Dr Bassett's gloomy prognostications. It had been a very happy evening. Gil and Jo were there and they'd all ended up wildly gay. Kit was surprised to find that he was angry.

'What do you think you are doing?'

Pan turned to stare at him with the beginnings of alarm. 'I'd no nice dresses and there wasn't no one using these. I thought you'd be—pleased. 'Ain't never 'ad no pretty clothes—always what no one else be wanting. Not nice always to be wearing some woman's cast-offs—' Her voice trailed away.

'Did it not occur to you to ask? To tell me what you felt? I would always listen.'

'Never thought you'd mind. If you didn't want no one wearing these, why'd you not give 'em away? Burn 'em. They're nobbut gathering moths and damp.'

'I don't have to account to you for my actions. Take that off. It's too tight for you—'

Pan crossed her arms in front of her breasts, defensively. 'But it's so pretty,' she said coaxingly and revolved slowly between Kit and the mirror so that he'd appreciate how the garment became her. 'Always wanted this gown, I did—'

'You've seen it before?'

She became still. 'Saw *her* in it one night when I came to take a look at you unbeknownst. All laughing and clinking glasses you were. I were—proper jealous.' She let her arms fall to hang by her sides, leaving her defenceless.

'All the more reason for you to have picked something else,' he said curtly and

218

threw open the door of the press. 'There,' he went on, flinging first a blue dress and then a green across the room to pool the carpet. 'And another and another. Take them all, but not the red.'

'T'is the only one I like.'

'Then we'll buy another in Keswick that's to your taste. Take that off. I'll dispose of it some way. I do not want to see it on you.'

'I'm not good enough, is that it?' She was angry now, her strong fingers plucking at the small buttons, pulling one off in her agitation.

'You know that's not the reason.'

'Then—you still love *her*. T'ain't healthy to go on loving the dead.' Another button flew across the carpet. 'Not so long after.'

'My feelings are my own business. But it was the occasion that has good memories for me. One night out of our married life when everything was right. I don't want that spoiled. Now do you understand?'

'That's as good as saying I'm a dirty, slovenly nobody, who ain't fit to be in your 'ouse. Didn't think so much of 'er then, did you? Fine time we 'ad round this place afore she came on us in the cottage that day!'

'Pan—'

'It were plain as the nose on your face, you an' she weren't 'appy.' The red gown was undone at last and slid from the voluptuous body to form a shining lake around her bare feet. 'But now it pleases you to make me feel like summat that came out from under a stone.'

'I agree we were not always in tune. But if I cannot preserve those memories that were pleasant and meaningful then Judith might as well have never lived. And I'll not snuff out her existence just to please another woman who has her own place—'

'You mean—if ought 'appened to me, you'd think on times we was 'appy?'

'How could I not?'

She bent to retrieve the gown and he saw most of her breasts exposed inside the neck of the shift, firm and warm, the cleft between them deep and dark. 'There,' she said, holding the red folds out to him. 'Best put it away then, 'adn't you? Don't want to rob you of anything that matters. Now what was it you came for?'

'What is it that I usually come for?' His voice had thickened and somehow the

touch of Judith's dress became an aphro-
disiac. As if the splendid bitch didn't
know how she looked in those peculiarly
virginal calico monstrosities she'd affected since her return.

'Can't think what you mean, sir,' she
teased. Thank God, he thought, as he
stuffed the gown into a drawer, that
Pan's jealousies were quickly over, that
it was possible to reason with her.

'Something you do better than anyone
I've ever known.'

'Truly?' The black eyes widened with
mock innocence.

'What on earth do you want to wear
these things for?' He was busy with hooks
and eyes, fingers clumsy. 'You never used
to, apart from the dairy.'

'Acause ladies wear them.'

'And you think you're a lady now?'
The top half of her was bare and he
turned his attentions to her waist fasten-
ings. 'You need to improve your speech
if you want to be thought that, my girl.
And I suspect you're too lazy to try.'

'You'll teach me, won't you.' Her arms
were around his neck, her breath on his
cheek.

'All you have to do is listen. Ask the
221

meaning of anything you don't understand.' The frilled drawers went the same way as the tantalising shift with its narrow ribbons. He lifted her against him.

'You'm just a great beast,' Pan whispered, 'in need of servicing. That's all. No gentleman!'

It occurred to him later that she had not only filched Judith's dress but his dead wife's own description of him.

* * * *

It was not until afterwards, when he was on his way downstairs, that he noticed the quietness of the house. Making his way to the kitchen, he put his head round the door. 'No children?'

Madge looked up from the jam pots she was covering, the big pan still sticky beside her. 'Why should they be here? They're none o' my business.'

'That's unfair. They're everybody's concern.'

'You made them that gipsy's business if I remember aright.' She looped a piece of string round the neck of the jar and tied a painstaking knot. 'Maybe you'd better ask her where they are. Not seen

222

them, myself, since lunch, but Master Broome had a look in his eye I recognised. Not that Mistress Boswell can be in two places at once.' Madge went on trying the jam pot covers, her gaze everywhere but on Kit.

'Would they be with Betty?' He decided to ignore her last remark.

'She's gone to have a word with Joannie in the dairy.'

Kit frowned, then tramped round to Joannie's domain but neither maid had seen either Broome or Rose. He returned to the house after a search round the farm and byres and a quick scan of the fields and the nearby slopes. Calling several times, he received no answer.

'Pan!' he shouted from the foot of the stair. 'Come down here, you lazy slut!' She came down wearing the green gown that fitted her better than it ever had Judith.

'Do you like it?' she enunciated carefully.

'No games,' he said sharply. 'We decided the children were your responsibility.'

'You decided.'

He made himself remember the recent

satisfactory encounter to prevent his anger from bursting into anything more explosive.

'When did you last see them?'

' 'Aving—Having their dinners. I said would they like to go for a walk but Master Broome said no-thank-you-very-much and a look on his face that would turn milk sour. Ain't no use trying to get near that boy, Kit.' She came close to him and put a hand on his arm. 'You do like the dress, don't you?'

'Yes.'

'It's special-like, for you.'

'Rose. Did Rose say what she intended?'

'Didn't say nothing—anything—at all. They'll be 'iding in some secret place. All children 'as—has—their own hidey-holes.'

'Must you try so damned hard to put on airs just at this time?'

Pan looked injured. 'I thought that was what you wanted?'

'Well, so it is! Only—can't you see I'm worried? I wish I'd never delegated the responsibility now. Madge always knew where they were.'

'I can't be both looking out for your

little 'uns and taking care of you at the same time, can I? Stands to reason. They'll be fine, you mark my words.'

'Help me look for them, then. You go to the copse—'

'Couldn't go there, Kit. Not after *she*—'

'You'll go to the copse or you can get out. I'll try the stable. If Master Broome's pony's gone, at least I'll know he's out riding, though he is supposed to ask permission first—'

'Perhaps he did try to get permission, only you were otherwise occupied,' she retorted.

'Go to the wood,' he repeated curtly, trying to subdue his feelings of guilt, running up to the children's rooms only to find them still empty. Returning to the kitchen, he said to Madge, 'Try to remember what the children have talked of lately.'

Madge, seeing his expression, became her old self. 'All sorts o' things. Broome did tease Miss Rose for using such grown-up words and then he told her the Bassett girls were namby-pamby. Which they do seem to be—'

'Yes. But they are better than no company for Rose. And they study her—her affliction.'

'Kind enough, I'll allow you. Oh, yes, I recall they never stop talking o' that Frenchie. The one over at Carters'. Made him into a proper old mystery, has Master Broome.'

'Thank you, Madge.'

Kit clattered over to the stable, seeing, just before he plunged into its gloom, the green-clad figure of Pan climbing towards the fringe of the trees. Then he was hurrying past the shadowy stalls, bumping into the saddles that hung on the wall, shifting a fallen horseshoe that clinked against the stone work.

Broome's pony was there, but, and Kit was conscious of a burning anger, his own roan was not. There could be only one reason for Broome to take the roan. He was up to some mad caper involving Rose who should not be subjected to such exercise. Dr Bassett had impressed this upon Kit, though, to do Broome justice, he had not thought it necessary to warn the boy that riding could further harm his sister.

Kit saddled the mare and took her out, jumping the gates and setting off at a smart pace along the track to West

Winds. There were fresh hoof-marks in the soft ground and the bitter resentment against his son was exacerbated, though tempered with real worry for Rose. She was so readily influenced by Broome.

The cloud shadows shifted constantly, so that Kit received the impression that he raced ghostly horsemen who disappeared as suddenly as they came. The air was fresh and damp against his face. A small lake grew and went again as though it had been only a mirage.

Kit's eyes narrowed. There was another horse ahead of him. The roan, with a humped bundle on his back. Spurring the mare, he decreased the distance between the two mounts. Two heads, one black, the other undoubtedly Rose's with that strange colouring.

It was in that moment of recognition that it happened. Rose slid sideways and was thrown off as though she had been a doll, to lie very still on the rough grass of the verge.

'Broome!' he yelled. 'Broome! What have you done?'

The boy looked over his shoulder, his face set in a mask of horror that turned swiftly to fear. Then he kicked at the roan's sides deliberately and sped on, paying no attention to Kit's furious shouts. Horse and boy dwindled rapidly into ditance. Kit slid to the ground and knelt beside the unconscious girl.

5

Broome dragged at the reins and stared at the scene of activity before him. There were tents of tarpaulin and small wood cabins obviously put up as a temporary measure. Smoke rose from makeshift chimneys. He noted lengths of trimmed wood, blocks of rough or dressed stone. A clink of hammers, the sound of sawing, the walls, half made, with gaps for windows. Men everywhere, carrying fetching, sawing, banging with hammers.

It was fascinating. He looked at the grey walls that ended incongruously in a space of trees and sky and saw the shape of the house that would eventually stand there, not large, yet not small, a compact building with wings not unlike those of

Grey Ghyll that enclosed a square containing a fountain in the middle, and bright flower beds.

He could not see the Frenchie anywhere and disappointment filled him. He'd risked a great deal for a sight of the man. Some of the stone-masons and labourers were now aware of his presence and muttered among themselves. 'What you want, boy?' one of them shouted. He was an older man and by his showing, a foreman.

'Nothing. I'm just—looking.' The boy shrugged.

'Well, don't get in the way. Where you from?' A calloused hand scratched a grizzled head.

'Grey Ghyll.'

'Keep your distance, then. Don't want no accidents.'

Broome hesitated, recalling Kit's unexpected appearance. He could not go back, yet here it was plain his company was unwelcome. He caught sight of a track that wound away past the trees and began to trot away in that direction, but had not gone very far before he heard faint shouts behind him. He set his heels in the roan's flanks and galloped on before anyone could stop him, noticing the hoof-marks in the soft earth and how the ground fell to a small hollow ringed with birch and alder, over which the bare hills crouched like predatory beasts.

Smoke rose thinly from the dell. Broome's mouth dried, understanding the meaning of the workmen's cries. It had not occurred to him that there might be an estate cottage where the mysterious stranger lived while he watched his house being built. But one could not expect a gentleman to live in a temporary shack.

Curiosity drove the boy on. He stopped at the top of the rise, his gaze fixed on the small dwelling below. It had creeper growing on it and a roof of blue, shiny slates. The garden had long since gone wild and contained little but rosebay willow herb and marigolds. And then, the Frenchman was there, long and slender, as always in black. He had come from the side of the cottage, a riding-switch in his hand. Seeing Broome, he was suddenly still. A blue butterfly wavered past the boy's nose. The long moments passed.

'Who are you and what do you want?' The man asked, his voice faintly accented. It was an attractive sound, Broome thought. Foreignness was exciting.

'I'm from the house down the road to Keswick.'

'You mean—Talbot's place?'

'Yes.'

'You have a message for me perhaps?'

'No.'

'Why, then?' The man lifted his shoulders, spread out thin fingers.

'I suppose I am just curious. We have seen you go past Grey Ghyll.'

'Well, since you have come all this way, may I offer you some refreshment?'

'If it's any trouble—'

'If it had been, I would not have asked.'

Broome dismounted, with some difficulty, since he had not the aid of the block, and said, 'Where shall I leave the roan?'

'Tether him to that tree. He'll do no harm there.' That done, Broome went, a little hesitantly, towards the cottage door.

'Is he not a trifle large for you?'

'He belongs to my father. I borrowed him.'

'You manage him very well for a boy of your age. How old are you?'

'Eleven, but everyone thinks I look older.'

'So you do, I should have said thirteen or fourteen.'

'Really?' Broome was pleased.

'I never say things I do not mean. Come inside, then. I expect you will be hungry.'

The room was small and dim with logs burning in the deep, narrow fireplace. Other logs lay in a basket and Broome was reminded of Will Smith at the village with his lapboard, bodkins, mauls and knives, making shoppers and fruit carriers and fish-kiddles for the fisherman over by the Solway. The little table was set with a cloth and a decanter and glasses, tiny biscuits with icing and small pictures on them.

'Not the sort of thing a boy wants,' the Frenchman said, by now a mere shape in the gloom, sombre and vaguely frightening.

'They will do very well.' Broome had begun, with misgiving, to remember Rose and his father's anger.

'You are not at ease.'

'I should not stay long. I had not permission to come.'

'A rebel, eh?' Again that totally foreign gesture. It was fascinating.

'They don't understand—'

'Parents never do. You must be yourself. Are you allowed wine?'

'Not usually.'

'In France it is the custom and consequently one hardly ever sees anyone really the worse for drink. There you are. Sip it, don't rush it down like lemonade! Now, what is wrong at home?'

Broome took refuge in his glass, watching, covertly, the way the Frenchman sniffed delicately at the wine, then partook of just a little, seeming to rinse it round his mouth. He did the same and was rewarded by a pleasant fragrance, followed by the same taste on his palate.

'To the manner born.' His host sounded amused. 'If you remember to follow those rules you'll always enjoy just a little wine. I hate to see men swill like pigs.' He stretched out long, booted legs until they almost reached the hearth. Fire-light played on everything but his face. Broome admired the black velvet waistcoat with the crystal buttons. Kit would consider him merely a dandy. He went on sniffing and sipping till the glass was empty.

'Are you ready to tell me now? Why

you are at loggerheads with Mr Kit Talbot?'

The wine was taking effect and Broome felt very self-assured, very loquacious. He could hear his voice talking from some little echo-chamber while his body stayed in the chair to which he'd been directed. It was the oddest sensation. But even though he spoke of his frustration, his detestation of the gipsy, he said nothing of Rose and her fall from the roan. It was not until he had eaten several of the biscuits with their pictures of soldiers, animals and crinolined ladies on the iced tops, that he confessed he could not bring himself to go home.

'Cannot rebels return to discipline and order? When necessary.'

'It's not like that.' And then the story of Rose came rushing out like an avalanche.

'That was a mistake. I can well imagine your father's fury but you must not lose sight of the fact that in this instance, he has cause. But I will ride back with you.'

'There's no need.'

'Oh, it is only that I require exercise and not because I am chivalrous. You need no nursemaid.'

'Father may be angry with you.'

'I think he'd only be relieved to see you. He's probably worried, looking for you.'

'He only worries about Rose. I don't think he likes me.'

'You've listened to too many servants. I'm sure he never said that.'

'He does not need to.'

'Come, Master Boswell. I insist upon accompanying you. Are you ready?'

'It seems unnecessary. You could take your exercise nearer home.'

'Then, I will use your own excuse. Perhaps I too, am curious.'

That seemed, to Broome, to make more sense than a desire for his own company.

'You are not afraid of a beating?' the Frenchman went on quietly. 'It seems the least you could expect.'

'No. Not of a thrashing—'

'Then, what?'

'Father threatens me with some severe school where I will have bread and water and much caning but I'd rather that than be sent away for good like the idiot!'

'Which imbecile?'

Broome, the exhilaration of discovering both the mysterious stranger and the pleasures of wine having dissipated, repeated the sad story of the orphaned boy.

'And you think that, because you are your father's natural child, and with no legal claim on him, he can give you away like an unwanted gift should he be so inclined, after the accident to Rose?'

'Yes. He's given me board and teaching since I was a baby but not his name. He cannot be sure I am his son.'

'But that gipsy bears out the story. She was at Grey Ghyll around the time of your conception. She says now that you are Mr Talbot's child, a fact recorded on your person when you are discovered on the step. He cannot really doubt that.'

'How did you know? about the piece of paper pinned on my shawl? I said nothing.'

The Frenchman laughed. 'Some of the workmen are local. I've heard every story there is, connected with Grey Ghyll and West Winds, how the two households were interrelated. Country folk have long memories. And what they are not told, they are very good at contriving.'

'I heard Father say that I was a strong,

well-grown infant. That I might have been older than folk imagined.'

'My dear boy, babies have been born weighing thirteen and fourteen pounds, complete with a set of teeth! And a lusty gipsy girl would be expected to bear strong children. Your father is, himself, of considerable size. I'm sure he has his own sense of responsibility that would not allow him to set you aside lightly.'

'I hope you are right. I know that sometimes I want nothing more than to be as troublesome as I can, but I could be much more difficult if I were without family or home. The problem is that I do not always know what I want, or even feel!'

'You are not unique.'

'I must go back. The longer I wait, the worse it will be.'

'Wait a moment while I saddle up.'

'Very well.'

Broome waited in the dimness, listening to the crash of a log, the ticking of the clock. He felt a little sick and the palms of his hands were damp. The wild escape, the queer sojourn in this secretive room—anyone who chose to live out here, must be secretive!—had receded to leave the stark realisation that he'd been incredibly stupid. He should have come alone. All his instincts had told him so and they'd been right. It was the last time he'd give in to the pleading of a girl, even Rose.

The Frenchman called him and he emerged, blinking in the light, to untie the reins and mount from a convenient tree-stump. Through the fog of self-recrimination and apprehension, on Rose's behalf, not his own, he noticed how well the man rode, the elegance of his appearance.

The foreman rushed forward angrily as they reached the work site. 'I could not stop him, Monsieur Foredor.'

'It's nothing. Master Boswell will be welcome should he care to call. You will not impede him.'

'No—sir. But your orders *were* "no strangers".'

'Except for Master Broome, that still stands.'

'Very well—sir.' The man touched his cap but the look he shot the boy was unfriendly.

They rode almost in silence, yet not constrained. Broome found himself entertaining the incredible thought that he might have preferred this man to be his father in place of Kit. He didn't mean it, of course. It was just that he still must pay for what he had done and the imagining was always worse than reality.

The shadows were long on the lake and the hills were not so sharply defined. It was disconcerting, too, how the Monsieur's shadow lay across him, cutting off warmth. Almost as though he were some symbol of darkness or evil. Nonsense, Broome told himself stoutly. If his father were riding there, the sense of coldness would have been as great. There could be no difference.

Grey Ghyll came into view, small and remote, then growing with every pace of the roan. Broome braced himself for coming unpleasantness.

* * * *

'I still say you should of told the boy he mustn't take Miss Rose riding,' Pan said for the umpteenth time.

'There's no need for you to call her Miss Rose. Rose will do in your case.'

'I can't change my habits all in a

minute. Ain't—aren't you going to fetch Broome back? He'll be scared to see you—'

'He should have thought of that earlier,' Kit responded curtly.

'But if he didn't know—'

'Perhaps I should have told him,' he conceded coldly.

'And she can twist him round her little finger. Like she can you.'

'I feel that the world owes her an extra kindness.'

'Tis a shame the poor mite is so—delicate, that's true. But it ain't—aren't the boy's fault e's—he's—so well-set. You can't punish him for that.'

'It is his fault that he is the cause of Rose being bedridden for some time. And only chance that Dr Bassett came this way today to prescribe for her. But, you've changed your tune, haven't you. Pan? Never had a good word to say for Broome. Always complaining that he dislikes you, repudiates your claim to be his mother, which is ridiculous when we both know to the contrary—'

'It's just, I never liked seeing an animal at bay. Couldn't look at a rabbit in a trap. All becos of my brother. Remember, I told you he were caught in a man-trap while he were poaching—'

'Was poaching.'

'Was, then. I never saw a horrider sight, and after, I couldn't bring myself to see anything helpless—or dead.'

'I can understand that.'

'He's nobbut a child, however you looks at it. And your only son, though—'

'What is it, Pan?' Something in her voice alerted Kit.

She rose and went to the window. 'You—you ain't been living like a monk, 'ave you, Kit. And it's only to be expected you'd be fathering something on me, sooner or later. It seems to be sooner.'

Incredulity was mixed with images of Pan in the big bed upstairs, her face half-hidden by swathes of dark hair, of warmth and comfort, the smell of her body. The sense of freedom that would surely go if he had to marry the girl. He should have been more careful but that meant withholding oneself and possession of Pan was not conducive with losing that final, delightful subjugation. Would it be so pleasant if he were shackled, only performing a husband's duty?

'You ain't pleased, are you.' Pan's

241

voice was flat. 'Didn't think you would be. It might be a girl, anyways, and that wouldn't be worth marrying for. But it's for certain it wouldn't be spoiled like poor Miss Rose. Broome's sturdy enough for any man, ain't 'e?'

'How do I know you are telling the truth?'

'How do you know any woman is telling the truth? But it'll show itself afore long, in plenty o' time for any deciding you have to do. I ain't in any hurry to be tied down, any more than you, so don't think you'd be doing me any favour! It's just that I can't see no future for that girl and neither can you if you'd face up to the fact. She could never have a child. But there's still Broome and the one that's coming. You'd want *someone* to leave this big, fine house to, stands to reason: maybe you got a woman in mind already, for wife.' She moved close to him, laying a hand on his arm, yet it did not seem an appropriation but an offer of assurance. She was kind, obliging, good-natured, and gave him all he wanted in the physical sense. But he had sworn, after the debacle of his union with Judith, that he'd not go through that sort

242

of trauma again.

'I've no one in mind. Yet—'

'Hope you don't mind me telling you, but you've got a right to know. If I'd wished to set a trap for you, don't you think I couldn't a' done it years ago?'

'You could and you chose not to. I respect you for that.'

The dark eyes enmeshed him in a confusion of desire and repulsion. No matter how he tried, she would always remind him of those black memories of Judith's self-inflicted death and of her reasons for suicide. Broome Boswell was one of them. Forget all that. Wed the girl to give his brat a name. If it was his child. The circumstances of his reunion with Pan came back to him, suddenly significant. Two men in the barn, both of them intent on one thing. How was he to decide if that were not the start of the child in her body? Another cuckoo in the nest. Broome had never seemed this, whatever that label had claimed.

'There's the boy back again,' Pan whispered.

The sound of hoof beats grew louder, stopped.

'Don't be too hard on 'im,' she coaxed.

'Not 'is fault 'e were born out of wedlock.'

'Don't you think I don't tell myself that every time I think of him?'

'And never feel you owe nothing to me. I'd manage if you wanted me to go. We always do, gipsies. Born to take care on ourselves.'

Kit pushed her hand away. If he stayed any longer he'd weaken, tell the girl it was all inevitable, and he was not ready for that capitulation. 'I'll see to Broome. He'll be afraid to show his face.'

'Don't strike him. Not till you've thought it over,' she called after him.

The boy was in the stable, wiping down the roan, when he got there.

'Well?' Kit said.

'I'm sorry about Rose. We wanted to see the Frenchman and I thought she'd be all right. Only she got tired and she fell off before I could stop. If I'd known she couldn't stay mounted, I'd have told her she mustn't come. You take her to Keswick in the trap. I thought it would be the same.'

'Well, it isn't the same.' Kit controlled the urge to take down the riding-crop.

'I know that now.'

244

'Where have you been all this time?'

'At the Frenchman's place. He rode back with me.'

Kit went back to the stable door and stared down the track. The Frenchman was riding away, slim and straight on his black horse. A mourning figure.

'It was decent of him to take the trouble.'

'Are you going to beat me, Father? If you are, I'd rather get it over and done with.'

'No. I'm not going to beat you.'

'Well, what are you going to do?'

'I—don't—know—'

'You don't mean to send me away for ever, do you? To some factory?'

The boy looked like a cornered animal, Kit thought, like Pan's brother with his thigh caught in a trap, his life's blood ooozing away. No one coming to free him.

'Why on earth should I send you there? You know perfectly well what I think of mills and factories.'

'Rose said—terrible things happen to boys when they are—not wanted.'

'She said that?'

'Yes. It made me feel very unhappy.'

'I see. Perhaps you have received the wrong impression of your place here. You were never intended to feel that I had no interest in you. You had better come in and have tea.'

'I had something at Monsieur Foredor's. He says I may go back if I want.'

'A generous gesture. Perhaps he could be good for your languages.'

'And—Rose?'

Kit turned away. 'She must stay in bed until she is better. Dr Bassett has seen her.'

'But she is all right?' The boy sounded genuinely anxious.

'As well as she will ever be.'

'May I see her?'

Kit shook his head. 'She is asleep and must be left alone for a few days. Her strength was over-taxed. But I must share the responsibility. I did not tell you she should not embark on horse-riding. Perhaps I expected too much when I took it for granted you'd understand that for yourself.'

'I shall never make the same mistake.'

Kit clapped Broome on the shoulder. If it had not been for Pan and her revelation he'd have thrashed the boy to near insensibility and where would that have got either of them? It had been the disclosure of the coming child that had softened him.

They emerged from the stable and Kit's gaze returned to the path to West Winds. The Frenchman was far away now, a tiny black shape, moving fast, growing ever smaller. If Broome had come straight to the house they could have invited the man in for some refreshment. Another time—

He must talk again with Pan about the result of their liaison. Soon.

* * * *

Faro got up and paced the small room restlessly. That boy's visit had unsettled her. She had known who he was at once, and though, by rights, she should have resented him, it had been impossible to dislike the child. It had not even mattered that her essential privacy had been invaded.

She had lived in fear since she recovered her senses after Chamwell's death. Her terror of Bender assumed the proportions of an obsession. Any sighting of a dark man of his height and breadth, or general cast of features, reduced her to panic. Not that she showed it, but it took all of her will-power to control the incipient shaking of her hands.

There had been much questioning but she had never divulged what she knew. Some of the loyalty connected with their long association remained, enough for her to describe the man she had seen at Chamwell's, yet not put a name to him. It had been concluded that Bender was a would-be thief who had taken fright when Lord Chamwell had seen him at the open french-window. Bender in the dock could have given many reasons for his action, all of them stripping off the veils of secrecy with which she had surrounded herself. Her nature would not allow her to envisage such revelations made public. And yet, because of her refusal to name him, she was put into a constant state of apprehension, only partially allayed by the seclusion of her whereabouts and the knowledge that Bender might find it impossible to trace her movements after the fatal shooting. He'd have hidden himself at first, expecting her to betray him and, by the time he'd regained his courage she had gone, and Amberwood was sold almost immediately, giving him nowhere to which he could return. As she had forecast, the house had been bought by a rich industrialist with a large family as popularised by the Queen with her ever-growing brood, a man who made his money out of mills and factories and shares in the big railway companies. Amberwood must have come to life since it changed hands. Boys' boots would clatter on the stairs. Girls would accompany one another on the piano and sing sentimental ballads and German lieder. The house had probably never been so normal.

When she went to Grey Ghyll with Broome Boswell she'd had every intention of staying until she saw Kit, but had shirked the meeting at the last moment, telling Broome she had done all that was required of her and that her presence could only complicate matters. But curiosity gnawed at her all the way home. Had he changed? Would he see through the masculine disguise that seemed even more to her liking since the death of the man she had promised to marry? The brief desire to revert to femininity had gone after Chamwell's demise, leaving her irrevocably tied to her male alter ego. It was as though that one, shocking act had cut the ties of her heterosexuality. She possessed nothing but men's clothing, wore her hair dressed as a man's, had the sexless good looks of an angel.

Eleven years was a long time. Kit could not really connect Monsieur Foredor with his effortless French accent and Gallic gestures with Faro Amberwood. She had changed enormously. Only her eyes might give her away in a strong light—under a hat-brim, or in a dimly-lit room she would have little fear of discovery. Her features had sharpened.

She picked up the letter that had lain on the table since breakfast. The sheet of paper was black-edged and from Brent's sister, telling Faro that the young captain was killed, as she had feared, at Solferino. A musket ball had taken off his left leg and he had bled to death before the army surgeon could attend to him. He had mentioned Jean Foredor many times and had asked for news of him to be sent via Faro's lawyer. After Chamwell, Brent had been the last of her gambling comrades. She'd be missed from the London scene only because she was an eccentric, not for any lingering warmth of feeling in her acquaintances. Would it have made any difference had she kept her appointment with him? Told him the tale that she'd been attacked in an alley? Or even the truth? Might that have in some way altered the sequence of events that led to his death? She would never know, but she doubted it.

Smoothing the letter she had crumpled in that first spasm of horrified rejection, she placed it in her escritoire, one of the few pieces of furniture she'd had sent ahead of the rest so that the cottage would seem more home-like. It did not go very well with the log basket she had inherited from the previous, long-departed occupant who had probably been dismissed at the time of the fire in which Carter's wife had died, but this was not its final place.

Restless and unhappy, she put on her coat and riding-hat, picked up the crop and let herself out. Once on the road to the Talbot house, she questioned the wisdom of her action. She had come here to cut herself off from society, but at the first overtures of friendliness from that brat, she was irresistibly drawn by a compulsion to see Kit. She'd make Rose

Talbot her excuse.

But when she was in sight of Grey Ghyll she caught a glimpse of a woman in a green gown she took to be the gipsy who occupied Kit's leisure time, then a girl in maid's dress who scurried across the quadrangle made by the back-jutting wings of the house. She saw cows and calves in a nearby field, a scatter of reddish-brown hens. It looked very peaceful but it had not always been so.

She followed the course of the stream though she knew she must be trespassing on Talbot land. Not that there would be any trouble. Hadn't she taken Broome home after his escapade?

The tiny track was soon swallowed up in a mist of shrouded branches. She thought the copse sinister but that might just have been because she knew the story of what had taken place there. A branch creaked, jarring upon her senses, and all the shadows stirred. A wren flew from the lowermost branches of a tree, startling her, then perched above her head as though it had been sent to spy upon her actions. Where was it that Judith had hanged herself? The branch yawed, evoking a swinging shadow in the gloom.

Faro wrenched the horse's head sharply and turned to see a man watching her. He looked seven feet tall though that must be due to some exaggeration of the obscurity that enfolded them. His bare head was covered with thick red hair and he'd grown a beard to match. Not that it covered the scar on his cheek that dragged down the corner of one green eye so that it appeared half-shut in perpetual drowsiness. The other was very much livelier and contained a certain annoyance.

'What are you doing here?'

He must know who she was. Black horse, black coat and tall hat, white shirt, breeches, long black boots; she could only be the Frenchman.

'That was the tree where it happened.' He gestured towards it accusingly. 'It was the reason for your visit, was it not? To see where my wife—'

She made a disclaiming motion. 'Do not distress yourself. I admit I heard tales but one is always interested in one's neighbours, particularly when one has so few. I meant to go to the house, to ask how the little girl was after the fall, but I renaiged at the last moment and decided to follow the stream. It does run through both our territories.'

'This stretch is not your concern, Monsieur. But it was kind of you to ask about Rose. She is a little better, and I can now thank you for your care for Broome and for bringing him back.'

'I could hardly do less. You must have been worried. He was afraid—'

'Afraid of what?' His features became set.

'That he would be beaten, but it did not stop him from returning.'

'He is not a coward, whatever else his faults.'

'Did he speak of his visit?'

'Only to say that he did not stay long but that you were hospitable.'

The tree Kit had pointed out obtruded into her line of vision, one branch sagging as though some weight still pulled it down. She quivered. A goose over her grave—

'You must let him come again. The foreman will not prevent him.'

'I doubt if you'll see him in the next months. He is to start as a boarder at a school in Yorkshire. The holidays are short. It is all settled.'

'Oh. It was not because of his disobedience? That he is sent away?'

Kit's face betrayed coldness. 'It *is* my affair, but no, it has been in my mind for some time. He needs discipline.'

'I see. Tell him he may write to me if he wishes.'

'Why should he want to do that?'

She smiled faintly. 'He thinks foreigners romantic, that his visit was an adventure. It would do no harm. I swear I do not mean to corrupt him.'

'No one suggested—'

'No? He mentioned perhaps that I taught him the rudiments of wine-tasting?'

'I heard him tell my housekeeper. I did not think it advisable to give him such licence so early. Young men learn bad habits soon enough.'

'Did you never kick over the traces?'

Kit did not smile. 'If I did, then that's my own affair, Monsieur.'

'I have been indiscreet. I realise that the stream, the boy, yourself and your wife's death have nothing to do with me, and I apologise. I should not have allowed my curiosity to get the better of me. In France it is different—'

255

'Good-day, Monsieur.' Kit pulled aside the foliage and stepped back the way he had come. She could hear his boots grinding over tree roots and stones.

No one could say the encounter had been a success. Kit had turned into a bear, surly and blinkered, seeing only the goads of life. How terribly changed he was. And yet he had far more force of personality than when she first knew him. If she had met him anywhere but on his own land she'd not have recognised him any more than he had known her. That scarred face possessed a curious, warped attraction.

The wren swooped back to the hanging-tree and the black horse shied, almost unseating her. Thoughtfully, she allowed it to amble back the way she had come.

* * * *

Broome had gone, complete with chest and portmanteaux, to his school near York. Rose, recuperating, missed him horribly, but Adeline Bassett had come for a stay and they got on well enough. Kit, to his annoyance, also found himself missing the boy and wondered if he'd done right. Pan seemed relieved, but as she had explained, she was not allowed to keep the child and had barely looked at him before he was whisked away by her father and brothers. She was always disinclined to talk of Broome and Kit had given up questioning her.

He thought continually of the child she carried. It had not been a lie. She could no longer squeeze into Judith's gowns and he had sent her to the dressmaker in Keswick to be measured for maternity wear. It had not surprised him that she chose bright colours and that one garment was the same red as the dress she had always coveted.

Madge was still dry as a rotten stick and Betty, easily influenced by the older woman, followed suit. They always had their heads together, not that Pan seemed downcast by their barely concealed disapproval. She kept her head high and her smile fixed but the state of affairs was not satisfactory and Kit knew that sooner or later he must come to a decision concerning the gipsy and her child. He wanted her, he admired her spirit, Pan was making strides with her self-improvement, but he shied away from permanent involvement. Women grew possessive when the wedding-band was slipped over their finger. But there was the coming infant. He did not want a second bastard son. Indeed, even a girl would have the greatest disadvantages when she grew to a marriageable age. However much he tried to shelve the problem, it was always there.

The Frenchman's house was growing rapidly. He would want the roof in place before the winter and extra workmen had been sent for and waggon loads of slates had trundled by. Kit had ridden out to inspect the place from the shelter of the copse but had not visited the recluse. Something about the man had aroused feelings of mistrust and a disquieting sense of familarity. It disturbed Kit that he had gone to the wood where the Boswells used to camp but the Frenchman was by no means the first person to be drawn by the hanging-tree. Sudden death had its own macabre fascination.

Kit still entertained feelings of guilt over Judith's suicide which had been directly attributable to his infidelity. But she had wronged him in the first instance. If she had not turned against him over Deborah Broome, he might never have directed his attentions towards the gipsy.

Nearing the stable-yard of Grey Ghyll, Kit became aware of voices. One was familiar. Jo's voice, reminding him of the bond between them. He listened for the sound of Gil's amused drawl but it did not come. 'Come into the parlour, ma'am,' Madge was saying. 'The master will not be long.'

'I think I will wait here. I'll walk round the courtyard. It makes one stiff to sit for so long.'

'Are you sure you want to, ma'am? You look real peaky if you don't mind me saying so.'

'I don't mind. I know I must look—neglected—' Her voice was sad, lifeless.

'Not to be wondered at. Would you like me to come with you, Mrs Talbot?'

'No, thank you. I'd rather be alone.'

'I'm putting the kettle on,' Betty said. 'You'll feel better after a cup of tea.'

Kit hurried, filled with misgiving. Jo went nowhere without Gil, just as the doctor would never be separated from his wife. They were devoted to one another, eternal lovers.

He was just in time to see maid and housekeeper vanish inside the door and Jo's tall figure turn the corner of the quadrangle. She was dressed in black. Kit ran, his hands clenched.

Jo heard his footfalls and turned to greet him. He was shocked by her appearance. Her face was pale and thin and the gown and cape hung on her reduced frame as if meant for someone else. Her hands twisted nervously.

'Jo—'

'Kit! Oh, Kit.' She was in his arms, her shoulders hunched as from some blow. He stroked her hair and, gradually, the tautness went out of her body and she lay against him with a sigh.

'When?' He asked, knowing everything.

'Two weeks past. There was no warning so I could not prepare you. He had not told me that he'd developed a heart condition. He hid it from me very well. One moment he was alive and the next—' She shuddered then was still.

'As I would want to go. As any man would prefer to die. No being bedridden—'

'All you say is perfectly true. But I must live without him and I fear I cannot do it, Kit. As soon as I could, I began the journey to you. There seemed no one else.'

'Rich and Bethel—They are your parents. Were they no comfort?'

'They are old and wrapped up in one another. It hurt to look at them. And I suppose my distress made them see their own future. We cannot arrange our own deaths to coincide—it was obvious they realised this.'

'You did right to come. We'll care for you. Rose will be delighted to see you, I know.'

'And the boy?'

'I told you he was to go to school and he has.'

'Rose must miss him.'

'She has one of the Bassett girls to stay. The pretty one.'

'I remember.'

'I'll send a message over to Robbie to take over my chores this evening. We'll sit in the parlour and chat. I've not had an intelligent conversation since I last saw you.'

'That,' Jo said with the ghost of her old cheerfulness, 'is intended to be a compliment?'

'There was never anyone else with whom I was so consistently at one.'

Jo put her arm through his. 'I feel

better already. I think I could go in now and make small talk and do all that's expected of me.'

The parlour was filled with leaping firelight and the curtains glowed warm orange. Madge and Betty had laid the table and the silver tea-kettle steamed invitingly over its small flame. 'It reminds me of Phyllis's days,' Jo said, then gave a small sound of distress as she remembered all she had lost.

'Try not to think of Cramble.'

'No. I mustn't,' she agreed, taking off her bonnet and cape and pushing her abundant hair back into shape. It was still red apart from a thick streak of white at the parting. It reminded Kit of the band on a magpie's wing. 'Let me pour the tea. I must busy myself. It will be best. Are we to be alone?'

'Madge will have told the children you are to have time to recover from your journey.'

'She's a good woman and you need her about the place,' Jo agreed.

'I need a woman, that's true, but Madge and I do not always see eye to eye these days.'

'Oh. Is there any specific reason?' Jo

took up one of the delicate cups that were so rarely used and studied the design of orange leaves and gold edging.

'I'm afraid she disapproves of me and encourages Betty to do likewise. They begin to get on my nerves. I was thinking of making a change.'

'Disapproves?' Jo's brows rose.

'Because I have a mistress.'

'Could you not have found another wife?'

'Judith did not make it easy to contemplate a second bite of that cake.'

'Poor child. There was too much insecurity in her upbringing and, I fear, some instability on her mother's side. The woman's neurotic.'

'I was partly to blame.'

'Perhaps. But I cannot bring myself to be civil to Miles and Una. To think that we once laughed at the Lammeters, all those pitiable spinsters who loved my father so hopelessly.'

'The best thing my brother ever did was to thrash Miles.' Jo put down the cup with a clatter. 'There was something else he did. I think Gil knew he would die suddenly because he confessed to me one evening that he knew how

Mark Hepburn came to be buried under the cottage floor.'

Kit stared at her in disbelief. Mark Hepburn had been the miner's leader at Jingling Cat and had once engineered a strike against poor wages and conditions. No one would have argued that there was not a case to answer but Mark had helped to kidnap Jo as a hostage in order to force her father's hand, and then had assaulted her brutally. Rich Heron had been mad with anger. Blain, her brother, and Gil must also have hated the man equally. Rich gave up management of the mine as a result and it had fallen into disrepair; the cottages deserted and crumbling. Mark had disappeared and no trace was found until Jo went into the Hepburns' cottage after some flooding to find a skeletal hand protruding from the eroded soil. It was the talk of Cramble for years and Heronbrook had been under cloud that was never dispelled. Jo's father was suspected by most people in the district and also by the authorities, but Blain was hot-tempered and the fisher-folk laid bets that he'd killed Mark, while the local gentry looked to Jo's doctor husband for elucidation. No proof had ever been forthcoming and so the mystery remained unsolved. Until this moment—

Jo swallowed. 'Gil was riding home after a late call at the Lammeters' and was almost on a level with the mine when he saw a wink of light. All the pit folk had gone by then and we never could get a night-watchman to stay after the mine was flooded and the day-shift drowned. Gil dismounted and went between the cottages to seek for the source of the light. He bumped into Blain almost immediately. Blain whispered that he'd been coming up from the beach. The tide was out and he'd walked from one point to another. We always loved beach-walking.

'Blain pointed to the Hepburns' house and there was a crack of light between the strips of curtain. The place was still furnished after a fashion after Mrs Hepburn died and Mark vanished. Gil said it seemed a pity to disturb a tramp who could do little harm since the building was abandoned but Blain told him he'd seen a shadow on the window and that was of a very large man. Mark was—enormous.

'I must admit that at this point I begged Gil not to say any more but he told me that what happened that night had always troubled him. He had almost told me once before, when I went into the place and saw the remains of the hand, but he thought I'd not stand up to the ensuing questioning and so kept his silence. He'd imagined Mark buried for ever.

'They tiptoed to the window and looked through the narrow gap. Mark had come back, probably sick of skulking in caves and woods. He was dirty and covered in a mat of beard, and, when they opened the door, engaged in trying to heat water over a small fire. He sprang up when he recognised them, taking up a cudgel that lay beside him. Blain was beside himself with rage, cursing Mark and threatening to kill him for his treatment of me. Mark said I had asked for all I got, and that got Gil on the raw. Then Mark began to lay about with the cudgel in an effort to get his back to the door and clear the way for an escape. He struck Gil who went flying into the corner, half stupid from the blow, then menaced Blain. Blain had noticed a plank from one of the other cottages lying there, ready to feed the fire, so he grabbed hold of that and swung it round his head. It struck Mark and he fell heavily, striking his head on the edge of the fireplace. I suppose his skull was cracked. When Gil came properly to his senses, Mark was beyond help. They—they considered I had been subjected to enough unpleasantness and decided to bury the body so that the whole sordid matter would remain in abeyance. In time, of course, the hunt for Mark died down and so did most of the gossip. Blain and Gil kept their silence and I kept my new peace of mind. Mark had threatened to say that I had—encouraged his attentions, and there's always someone to listen, to place the worse possible interpretation—'

'The Lammeters would have had a field day. It doesn't surprise me that it was my brother. I think I always knew that it *must* be someone from Heronbrook, ever since you wrote to me about the discovery. Judith said she had often gone there, never dreaming what lay under her feet. I said she must not think of it but I'm sure she did. To think it was just—an accident. That's what it was.'

'I have never forgotten that happy evening we had, when Judith wore a peony red gown and you looked as if you'd be in love for ever.'

'But we were not,' Kit said sombrely.

'And now she's dead and you have a mistress. Is she here at Grey Ghyll?'

'Yes. I could put her into a little house in Keswick but where's the comfort in that? A cold bed all week and a tiring week-end making up for lost time.'

'I can see why Madge and Betty disapprove. For the children's sake, you should marry, Kit. They'll see how things are. Put two and two together. They notice more than you think.'

'Every now and again I tell myself the same thing, then old ghosts rise to haunt me.'

'Some balanced, mature woman—'

'Jo, they are not the ones to attract me. And, face up to it, I'm too much of a brigand to draw respectability since Judith tried her knife on me.'

'Tell me about your mistress.'

Kit opened his mouth to seek for words to describe Pan but the effort was not required. The door of the parlour opened and Pan stood there, dressed in red, her body thrust forward so that the small, betraying bulge was unmistakable.

The two women surveyed one another
268

in a grim silence.

* * * *

'She's bad luck,' Pan said later that night. 'She makes bad things happen. I knew so last time. And I was right.'

'She's the woman who brought me up. Her husband's dead and she needs me.'

'I got your child in me and I need you too.'

'It is my child? Sometimes I remember those men in the barn—'

'Well, you can forget them again! Never really got anywhere, thanks to you.'

'Would you swear on the bible?'

'Swear on a 'undred if it'd please you. Honest, Kit. Wouldn't fool you.'

'I wish you'd worn anything but that red gown.'

'Never thought she'd remember. All those years back.'

'Aren't you sorry for her? Gil was her life.'

'And now she'll make you that and there won't be room for me.'

'If you do not accept her presence, you'll be the one to go,' he threatened.

'But, she don't—doesn't like me. Even you must have noticed.'

'Aye, I'll give you that. But I'll try to change her attitude if you'll promise to alter yours.'

'You never could make folk like you if they're not inclined.'

'You must try. Would it help if—if we were wed? Could you get on with her, then, knowing you were mistress here?' Oh God, why had he said that? Expediency—

'Mistress! Kit Talbot! You'd not hear me complain about noth—anything.' She flung her arms around his neck in a transport of delight.

'I might even try to have Broome's name changed to mine.'

She drew away from him. 'Oh, I don't know if you should trouble—'

'I want to. I think that's half of the problem where he's concerned.'

'This one'll have your name? Ain't—isn't that enough?'

'They are all equally entitled, surely? You'd not deny the lad his right?'

'No. Not if that's what you want. It's just, if the little 'un's a boy and we really man and wife, he's being—cheated of

270

his place.'

'I will never understand women.' Kit sounded vexed.

'You mean, you might change your mind?'

'I don't know. You are so generous in every other way, yet you'd exclude Broome.'

'I can't feel motherly about him, Kit. He's like a stranger.'

'It's not his fault.'

'We mustn't quarrel over him. Please, I got no one but you.' Echoes of Jo, Kit thought, pulled in two different directions, but there was no other woman he wanted and she was pregnant. She was not likely to turn cold because she had a ring on her finger. She'd be so tickled she might even turn into something of a triumph.

Now that he'd made up his mind they'd best regularise the union as soon as possible. He reached out and pulled her back beside him. Love-making solved most things.

6

Jo had not thought she would stay at Grey Ghyll once she found out that the gipsy had her claws into Kit a second time. But Adeline Bassett had returned home and Rose was lonely. Jo, passionately attached to the child, remained for her sake. Pan was feckless and would have no time for Judith's daughter once her own baby came.

It was a great pity that Kit had encountered the girl again. Surely, the fact that Pan was responsible in a great measure for Judith's death should have influenced Kit? The finding of Broome had turned his wife's mind, and the boy could not have existed without Pan. She must have set her cap at Kit.

It was hard for Jo to conceal her dislike for the catalyst in Kit's home, but the girl had borne him a son and was now to produce another infant, so she must make the best of the situation. Kit had always been a fool where the opposite sex was concerned. The gipsy had better make him happy or she'd have Jo Talbot to reckon with!

Madge was talking of taking a post in the next valley so there would be a valid reason for remaining. And Broome had written, telling Jo that he hoped to see her on his next holiday. He also mentioned his friend, Monsieur Foredor, and asked how West Winds was progressing. Broome intended to write to the Frenchman at Christmas. There would not be time to travel home but he was to spend the festival day with a pupil who'd become his best friend. His name was Rennie Falconer and he was even bigger for his age than Broome and as fair as he was dark. 'He looks like a Viking,' Broome wrote. Jo was cheered by the epistle which showed the boy as being happy as he'd never been at Grey Ghyll. He'd needed boys' company.

Kit had seemed disappointed that his own letter from his son had been much more stilted and unfeeling and Jo told him that Broome had every right to consider himself rejected, then advised Kit to make a fuss of the boy in the spring.

It was then that Kit told her he was going to marry Pan Boswell as quickly as it could be arranged. Her expression must have shown her doubts for he hastened to remind Jo that she recommended that he wed his mistress.

'That was before I knew who she was,' she'd protested.

'It's unlike you to be unfair, Jo.'

'You realise that she could get up and leave you one day? It's in her blood—'

'She would not. I think she loves me.'

'If you can call that love!'

'If by "that", you mean having a satisfactory physical relationship, isn't that one of the things that kept your own marriage so durable?'

Jo had remained silent for a time, then she replied, 'there was more.'

'And how do you know that I will not find the same? No one can prophesy what may be at this stage. Bear with her, Jo, for my sake. I need both of you. Things will be better once Madge leaves. She casts a gloom on the house. And to think we were once friends!'

'That girl will lose you others.'

'But not you, Jo? You're the one who matters. Damn the rest.'

'I doubt if the Bassetts will be allowed to come if you persist in this ill-advised wedding.'

'There will be the baby for Rose to help with.'

'The gap will be too great.' And Jo had taken herself off to play pinochle with Kit's daughter.

The conversation achieved nothing, for the travelling parson was sent for to perform the belated ceremony in the drawing-room of Grey Ghyll. Madge had left two days before as a token of her disapproval, and none of the more well-connected neighbours, who had been invited, took the trouble to attend. Robbie Dixon came, and the two Hunts, chiefly because Edith was incurably nosy, and Isaac and Hannah Nisbett. Their two sons were busy on the farm and sent their regrets over their non-appearance. The Hodges were present, with Mary, who had been "strange in the head" since she discovered Judith hanging in the copse. Though only fifteen, she was well-developed and her mother watched her closely in case she was taken advantage of because of her simple mindedness. It was dangerous to have a woman's body and the mind of a child. Men took liberties and she'd not realise what was being done to her. Jo, seeing the pretty, vacant face, was made sad. It seemed that Broome's Cottage was indeed, unlucky, as local people believed. No one had tried to tamper with the name in case the bad fortune extended to them also.

Betty, removed from Madge's influence, was less surly, and responding to Jo's ministrations satisfactorily. Between them, the wedding breakfast was prepared, the big room made clean and festive, and trestle tables set up against the wall. Joannie was brought in from the dairy to assist.

But there was no real impression that a marriage was being solemnised. The farm hands and their families were stiff and awkward, the parson only slightly the worse for drink though he kept control of the simple service. Rose was resentful and Jo, in her black widow's weeds, quenched what little gaiety might have existed.

Pan, pale and quiet, was awed by the occasion until she had been pressed to drink a glass of port, after which, her finely-boned face had taken on colour and her eyes a sparkle that transformed her to a rare beauty. The blue gown was suitable for the ceremony, and less gaudy than the others she'd chosen. Jo silently deplored the girl's taste as a rule, but seeing her dance with Kit when the parson had gone and the carpets and chairs were pushed back to leave the floor-boards exposed, she had to admit that they made a striking pair. He looked pleased enough and that was, after all, what mattered most.

Later, when everyone had gone and Rose was settled down, she could not face supping with the newly-weds; the suggestion of intimacy as they sat in the candle-light with the sound of rain on the windows.

In her own room, she took off the mourning clothes and lay on the bed, dry-eyed, trying to recall the details of her marriage to Gil but the only night that came to mind was the one on which he'd come up to her attic bedroom with a copy of Bryon's poetry and a salver laden with champagne and crystal glasses. He'd been wearing a silk robe she gave him as a wedding gift and looked dark and splendid. He'd been very understanding about her experience with Mark Hepburn, and, though she repulsed him initially, they had come together in a relationship that had never lost its wonder and perfection. Her dry eyes burned, were suddenly wet with tears she had imagined were for ever denied her. Rolling over she buried her face in the pillow to stifle the sobs that tore at her body, making her writhe with anguish.

The rain hissed against the glass but she was not aware of it. But later, the worst of the pain washed into her pillowcase, she did hear Kit and his bride come up the stairs and the floor-boards creak at the doorway to his room. Then the door was shut leaving her to her own drugged thoughts.

* * * *

Christmas promised to be unexpectedly pleasant. Pan had gone singing about the house, every now and again, lifting her hand to admire the glint of gold on her finger, revelling in the sound of Betty's 'Mrs Talbot, ma'am,' and Joannie's new deference. Dixon and Hodge raised their caps to her and Mrs Nisbett curtsied when she had occasion to call.

Kit had brought home a tree to decorate after the style of the ones initiated by Prince Albert and Rose was set to cutting out decorations and gilding fruit and nuts to hang in its branches. There were silvered metal clips to hold the candles in position.

The Frenchman's roof was on and the stone masons and labourers had left West Winds to the plasterers and joiners, the glaziers and painters. Pan, staring out of the window, Jo at her side, had seen the dark form of the Frenchman riding in a toss of thin snow-flakes, a lonely figure swiftly vanished in a plethora of grey and white.

A smell of spice and Christmas cake spread through the passages and fires roared up every chimney. Jo sat at the piano and taught Rose to sing "Oh, Christmas Tree, Oh Christmas Tree, how lovely are your branches", and "Silent Night". They saved stockings for the apples and mandarins and sugared almonds. Kit ordered Chinese figs and boxes of dates and the largest goose was hung in the outhouse, ready for the great day. He had been sorry Broome was not there to share in the excitement but Pan could not pretend to feel likewise. His presence would have been a reproach, spoiling her anticipation.

Since the wedding-night, Jo had changed. The cold misery had gone out of her, the taut face had relaxed as though she had found ease. Pan, who had dreaded the fact that they'd be continually thrown together by Kit's dependence on them both, found Jo gradually thawing towards her, and she, in return, tried to humour the older woman, listening to her suggestions and advice. Occasionally, Jo unbent sufficiently to roar with laughter at some joke Pan made, either consciously or otherwise, and Kit, hearing their amusement, would be well-pleased.

Pan was too wise to imagine that all was perfect, but things were better and looked as if they would keep on improving if they both set their minds to the task. And she was happier with Kit than she had ever dreamed. Some important new quality had entered into their intimacy, something she could not explain, yet which heightened their pleasure in one another. She knew she must never harbour suspicions or mistrust him for that was what had poisoned Judith's peace of mind and turned Kit against her. She worked hard at her deficiencies of speech and would usually recognise an impending mistake and rephrase the sentence in time. If she sometimes felt the pull of the wide-open spaces, the secret corners of the woods, she pushed away the impulse for she must never lose what she had. She must remember cold and hunger, Ben Boswell's wrath, children whimpering, the constant need for uprooting oneself, the unpopularity of gipsies, man-traps and marsh-fever. This settled life was infinitely more desirable.

She exulted in the child that grew in her. It would be as legitimate as that poor, puny Rose and ten times more bonny. Kit had never been able to use his father's name and she was determined that their child would do so. Heron would be as suitable for a girl as for a boy, not that it *would* be a girl. It must be a son, to push Broome's nose out of joint. Broome. He was the real fly in the ointment. Everything could have been faultless but for him. He was a millstone round her neck.

And then, it was as though some ill-dream had come true. The door opened on a flurry of sleet and the boy stood there, his back against the weather, staring at her with those eyes that reminded her of bits of coal. Changeling's eyes—

Rose gave a little scream of joy and dropped her scissors. Limped to greet him. There was a wren on the doorstep. It flittered across the gap and was gone like Pan's own contentment.

* * * *

Everything was spoiled. Right from the moment Broome put his foot across the threshold. The tenuous links with Rose were immediately broken. Jo, though surely that must be her imagination, had seemed more distant. Kit had been taken up with the boy to the exclusion of all else, including herself. The shadow of the witch-bird lay heavily over Pan's spirits.

There had been an epidemic at the boys' school and those who had not succumbed were shipped home to escape the infection. Broome had travelled in care of another boy and his parents as far as Keswick and from there in Dr Bassett's trap. The doctor had been going on to West Winds to attend the Frenchman who had taken ill, and could not call on Kit as he had not the time to spare from his duties.

'It's because o' me,' Pan thought miserably. 'He'd have come otherwise, I know.' She began to feel vaguely unwell, though up till now she'd felt splendid. The tree that had seemed so enchanting had lost its charm, the gold and silver trimming subtly tarnished.

Broome was looking at her, his gaze encompassing her figure. He'd known what was wrong with her. Boys talked together, taught one another the facts of life.

'I'm Kit's wife,' she said suddenly. 'We got wed.'

There was a silence that was like the grave and beyond. Kit had told her he'd not write the news in a letter, that it would come better in a face to face chat. Later.

'Why?' Broome asked, his voice high. 'Why did you?'

'Because we wanted to,' Kit said evenly, 'and it cannot be undone to please you.'

'She's not my mother,' Broome muttered. 'You didn't have to—'

'Now, that's no way to talk,' Kit said sharply. 'Apologise to your mother. For that's what she is now and always will be. You are old enough to accept what it is not possible to change.'

He made her sound like prison bars, Pan thought, and a flicker of pain showed in her face. Kit saw it but he did not come to her as she wished he would.

'There's no call to make him say he's sorry,' Pan told her husband, realising he blamed her for the premature disclosure. 'I should have let you tell him. It wasn't my place, was it?'

'I'd have preferred that you'd left it to me,' Kit agreed.

'What difference does it make?' Broome said. 'I'd have felt just the same tonight, tomorrow.'

Pan ran from the room, for the first time full aware of her growing body and the weight of the child. Almost tripping on the stair, gasping with distress, she fell across the bed and longed to die.

Kit did not follow straight away and she knew that he was taking Broome to task. It was no good. Whatever she did would be wrong in that boy's eyes. He despised her as much as the entire

284

household put together. He had that facility for making her acutely conscious of her low origins, her almost total ignorance.

She lay, her spirits heavy as her body, regretting her cessation of those happy days so recently spent in enjoyable preparations for what was to be the highlight of the year. She'd never participated in a real Christmas before and had taken a childlike pleasure in the ever increasing ritual. The holly picked one day, the gilding done another. The cutting out, the bringing down of the ornaments from the boxes in the attics, shining swans so delicate that one was afraid of touching them overmuch, the glittering orbs of candy pink and soft gold, of peppermint green and silver. Blues and lilacs. Chinese red—Relics of Judith's day.

'Pan? Are you all right?'

He did not sound too censorious. She raised her head, wishing that her eyes were not swollen with weeping, that her hair was not unkempt with the abandonment of her grief.

'I do feel a bit out o' sorts.'

'He should not have said what he did.'

'I never done—did anything to harm Broome.'

'It is his fault. You need not reproach yourself. Hush! No more tears or you may harm our child.' He set down the candle and sat on the edge of the bed. The mattress sagged under his weight.

'Our child?'

'Of course it's ours, I believe you. Say no more about that.' But there was an edge to his voice. Broome always made trouble. There was a badness in him.

'I was—happy afore—before he came.'

'We all were.' Kit stroked her hair clumsily and Pan snatched at his hand and pressed her lips to it violently. 'We will be again.'

'I never asked you, Kit. It seemed too much like trying to hold you, but—do you love me?'

'I suppose I do—in my own fashion. But you, yourself pointed out that I'll never be absolutely sure of anything. There's no one else, if that's troubling you.'

'I know there's not. You'd not have time for another woman! T'wouldn't be possible.'

'Well then?'

'I told you a lie, Kit, and you know what they say. Chickens allus come home to roost.'

'What lie?' He had drawn back and was staring down at her with the beginnings of disturbance.

She did not answer and he took hold of her shoulders and shook her. 'What lie! I take it you mean the goings on at the fair in Keswick?'

'Not that. That was true enough.'

'What, then?'

'About Broome—'

'What about him? For God's sake, woman!'

'He ain't—isn't mine.'

'Not yours! Then who the devil *is* he?' he shouted.

'I don't know any more than you do.'

'But you said—'

'T'was *you* said and I saw that it could be—' she stopped seeing his furious expression.

'To your advantage to pretend your father and brothers had left your fictitious child out of revenge?'

'Yes, Kit. I knew it were—was wrong of me, but set on you, I was, and I couldn't help myself. Kit?'

287

'God help me, I don't know what to think.'

'It couldn't have been the Boswells.'

'Why not?'

'None of 'em ever wrote more than a cross in their lives. Not eddicated. I was sure you'd think of that, but you never did. We couldn't have written "property of Christopher Talbot" on no label on the child's shawl. You do see?'

Kit stood up and paced the floor. 'I do see,' he said after a time, 'but why do you tell me this now?'

'Because I want you to understand why I can't take to that boy any more than he can to me. He's none o' mind. This one is, and it's yours for certain.' She clasped her hands over her stomach protectively. 'But that Broome Boswell's been foisted onto you, Kit, by someone as hates you, I'd say.'

She rose awkwardly and went to him. 'Do you know anyone who'd detest you that much?' She put her arms around him but he detached himself and went to the window where the thin snow whirled by, sliding down the pane where it came to rest, making soft puddles on the sill.

'That dairymaid, Kit, who was there

afore me? Deborah Broome. Could it 'a been her?'

The snow kept swirling and glissading against the glass.

'You don't—hate me, Kit? Do you?'

'I don't hate you, Pan. Just go away, like a good girl, and leave me alone.'

'Kit?'

'Please!'

She turned and left him with the night and the increasing blizzard.

* * * *

The world was beautiful next morning. It had grown colder in the small hours and the snow had crisped into a white blanket, not thick, but sufficient to cover the earth's bare bones. The sky was clear and blue.

Kit had gone out early and Jo and Betty supervised the children's breakfasts.

'Can I go out on my pony?' Broome asked. 'It's so long since I saw him.'

'It does seem settled,' Jo replied with a look at the weather. 'Where did you plan to go?'

'Not far.'

'To West Winds, I suppose. To your

friend.'

'Yes.'

'Well why not say so?'

'Father does not seem to want me to go there.'

'You had better let him know your intentions, then. And Broome—'

'Yes?'

'I hope you do not intend to spoil Christmas for the rest of the household?'

'Not purposely.'

'It would please everyone if you were nicer to your father's wife. If you are not, then I can see no solution to the present situation. It will only result in—'

'Being sent to a mill or a factory? I don't care. I'll be too tired to care.'

'That would never happen. Whatever put that into your head? Anyway, I am fond of you and would say what I thought of any such plan! But if you are not pleasant when you do come, you will be forced to stay away over the school holidays and that could be lonely.'

'It wouldn't. I'd go to Rennie Falconer's. He was disappointed I was sent home.'

'You make it sound as though you came against your will.'

290

'I did.'

'Don't you care for Kit or Rose any more?'

'Yes. I like you too. But I hate *her*.'

'It hurts me that you are so unkind.'

'You don't like her, either.'

'At least I have persevered and I found it was not so difficult to take her. She tries hard—'

'It's no good. I will just have to keep out of her way. That's why I thought I'd go out on the pony.'

'Go and look for Kit, then, and take care, Broome.'

'All right. I like you better in green.'

'Widows must wear black. For a time, at least.'

'Promise you'll wear it again one day?'

'Perhaps I shall.'

Jo sighed when he had gone. 'Finish your breakfast, Rose.'

'I do not want any more. Grand-mother?'

'Yes, child?'

'Do you think anyone will ever want to marry me?'

'You are very pretty, Rose,' she said, but not quickly enough.

'That means you don't think so. I don't

either. I think I'll go and cut out shapes in the hall. I want to make some more icy crystals.'

Jo looked after her. Fate invented some cruel traps. A lovely face and misshapen body. Pain stirred in her like an ever-present ghost.

* * * *

'Of course you may go to West Winds,' Kit said curtly.

'Thank you, Father.'

Kit turned his back and Broome was uneasy. It was unlike his father to hold a grudge for so long. The gipsy had been wailing and complaining, that was evident. All the time he saddled the pony, he worried about Kit's unfriendliness. He seemed no longer to care for him. It was all that woman's fault with her flashy good looks and her gaudy dresses. He'd like to hurt her! Really hurt her—

Even when he rode off, Kit never looked his way. Broome burned with anxiety. Perhaps he'd run away after he'd visited the Frenchman. No one wanted him, whatever Jo had said over breakfast. He rubbed his eyes furtively.

292

After a time, the white countryside with its blue shadows laid a spell on him. The bad feelings evaporated. He felt clean and fresh as the winter world. The sun bounced off white hillsides so that he could hardly bear to look at them. They were great moulds of icing sugar spun into occasional burdened trees. The stream was grey as Rose's eyes. Broome thought of her with the usual mixture of irritation and tenderness.

He seemed to reach the Frenchman's copse very quickly. The house was quiet, looking almost perfect with the roof covering the finished walls. But some of the window spaces were blocked with boards to keep out the rain and the wind.

Broome pressed on along the narrow trail, his heart leaping when he saw the plume of smoke rising above the birches. The Monsieur could so easily have gone away to spend Christmas in some city. Paris, perhaps. The Revolution had been over for long enough. The pony half-stumbled on the slope, precipitating the boy into a snowdrift. Broome rose, breathless and wheezing, to see the Frenchman's black figure in the door-way. He was laughing and coming towards him, his long boots deep in the whiteness.

'Hurry, Broome! The snow will infiltrate the cottage.'

The boy began to run awkwardly, dragging the reluctant pony with him.

The Frenchman snatched up the reins. 'Go inside. I'll be with you soon. Shut the door to keep in the heat.'

The room looked much as it had last time. There was a larger fire, more logs in the basket, wine and glasses on the small table. He'd not noticed the paintings on his previous visit. There were half a dozen, all of people with lion-like eyes and cruel faces. Monsieur Foredor had eyes like that. No, the portraits had not previously been there, he decided.

A book lay beside the decanter. Broome picked it up. It was entitled ''Vanity Fair'' and was written by a man called Thackeray. It looked rather dull, so he set it down again. One might have expected the Frenchman to have chosen something different. It seemed more the kind of thing Jo would have enjoyed.

Foredor came in, stamping his boots, holding out his thin hands to the flames. He had lost weight since Broome saw him last and there were bruises around his eyes. It could be easy to imagine how his skull would look. A log shuddered into the fire.

'Are you better?' the boy asked.

'What do you know about that?' The man's voice had changed, lost its friendliness.

'Dr Bassett said he was to visit you. I was sent home because of illness at school and it was a choice of pack-ponies or the doctor's trap at Keswick. I chose the trap as the weather was poor.'

'Yes, I do feel better. He left some unpleasant remedy I suppose I must take.'

The Frenchman picked up the decanter. 'A glass for you. I should tell you that Mr Talbot was not over-pleased to find I'd initiated you into the habit.'

'I didn't tell him!'

'He heard you boast it to the house-keeper. It *was* a boast, wasn't it?'

'Yes.'

'I'm glad you did not deny it. I prefer the truth between us, even if it should hurt. Shall I pour you some wine?'

'Of course. I do not want my father to take my decisions, now or ever.'

The slender hand held out the glass. There were winks of red in the shining surface. 'Have you quarrelled with him?'

'Over her. The gipsy. He's married her.' In spite of all his efforts, Broome's voice shook.

'Oh?' The man raised his head suddenly and the same red glints were in his eyes, giving them the look of Satan. 'Dr Bassett did not mention it.'

'He didn't approve. No one does.'

'Why did he marry the woman? It was common knowledge she was his mistress but they rarely become wives.'

'He wouldn't want two bastards!' Broome raised the glass and set it to his lips defiantly.

'No. Not yet. You have forgotten the bouquet.'

Broome sniffed obediently. 'This is different,' he said surprised and inhaled it again.

'Well done. Most people would not have noticed. I think you give promise of being a connoisseur, young Broome.' He slumped in his chair as he'd done last time, his legs extended, his face in shadow. It was odd, but Broome had never had a clear look at the Monsieur.

There was always something to obscure his features, a hat brim, the dimness of this room, the impression of illness that eroded the flesh from the bone.

They drank the wine slowly and a pool of sunlight came in to lie pale and ob- trusive on the floor. 'So,' Foredor said. 'She is to present Kit with a child. He really should have lived in Arabia.'

'Arabia?'

'Everyone takes numerous wives and concubines and no one bats an eyelid. That might have suited Kit admirably.'

It occurred to Broome that the man knew Kit better than he'd suspected.

The Frenchman sat up and put down the glass with a clatter on the silver tray. 'What was that?' he asked sharply.

'I heard nothing.'

'I did.'

'Snow sliding off the roof or the bran- ches in the copse?' Broome suggested, in- fected by the Monsieur's uneasiness. The Frenchman rose and as he did so, his shirt sleeve was dragged up an inch or two to reveal two small deep scars above the nar- row wrist. Like little black holes—

'It could be. I heard a dull thud—'

'Then it would be the snow.'

The man stared out of first one window, then the other. He pushed home the bolt on the stout door as though to shut out some enemy.

'Why do you do that?' Once more the wine had taken hold of Broome's senses and he was in the same echo-chamber where his own words rebounded tinnily. All his thoughts seemed supernaturally clear.

'Because—I'm afraid,' Foredor whispered, his back against the oak panels.

'Afraid of what?'

'Someone who follows me like the Hound of Heaven.'

'But who could find you here?'

'That's what I thought. Perhaps it was a mistake to return to a place I once knew—'

'You—knew?'

'Oh, yes. Briefly. But he also knows—'

'Why does he follow you? Whoever he is.'

'An old score to settle. A grudge.' The Frenchman moved away, his fears allayed. 'It must have been the shifting snow. But if ever I should be found—dead—it will not be by my own hand but his—'

'Whose hand?' Broome, fascinated,

298

barely breathed the question.

The Frenchman laughed a little discordantly. 'No one who need concern you. It's my problem and I'd rather not hoist it onto your shoulders. I'll see no one over Christmas. Will you eat luncheon with me, Master Broome? You seem to be the only friend I possess.'

'Do not put yourself out—'

'But I wish to be hospitable. You'd not deny me that?'

'No.' It seemed right and generous to agree.

'Good. And a game of cards afterwards?'

'We have not played cards at home.'

'Then I'll teach you. I warrant you've done little but indulge in Up Jenkins and Tirza where you've been?'

'They are more sophisticated at school.' Broome grinned, the dark memory of the Frenchman's fear dispelled, the anticipation of the festive meal accentuated.

'We cannot have you young-missish because you've been long in the company of a girl cripple—'

'It's not Rose's fault!' Broome was impelled to defend her.

'No. It's no one's fault that they are not what their parents envisaged. I should not have said that, knowing what I do. But, come, forget family disagreements and disappointments. I'm in the mood for company and the house is empty until the interior workmen arrive. I confess it would have been cheerless. There's a side of ham. I take it you like ham? Capital. And oranges and Brazil nuts. A hunk of fruit cake and pickles. A cooked capon. We'll need but two plates and the necessary cutlery—' He slumped at the last word and hung over the back of a chair, his face distorted. It seemed an eternity before he straightened.

'What is it?' Broome asked, distressed.

'Oh—just a pain that comes on me, then goes again.' His lips were thin and white. 'Nothing that need worry you. There, it's gone. Will you help, young Broome?'

'I'll help.' Broome followed him, took the handsome plates, the silver forks and spoons.

There was a distant rumbling noise but he told himself it was only the snow. Just melting snow—nothing else.

* * * *

Rose was awake first on Christmas morning. There was a curious emptiness where excitement once lived. There had been too many changes. Broome away at school and now that he was back he seemed to have put up a barrier so that no one could go close to him any more. She missed Madge in spite of enjoying Jo's presence. Adeline was no longer allowed to visit and that seemed worst as they had just begun to talk freely to one another. Pan took up much of Father's attention. Often, when he would once have been in Rose's room he was in his own with the new Mrs Talbot.

Worst of all, Rose had awakened to the full implications of her disability. Her physical ability was limited and no matter how special collars and sleeves were arranged on her gowns, or lacy pillows contrived, nothing would ever take away the stigma of her deformity. She might forget it for an hour, or two hours or a whole afternoon, but as soon as she passed a mirror, there it was, totally distasteful and obtrusive. She was expected to ignore it, disregard the covert stares of strangers—even the pleasure of riding into Keswick was spoiled now that she realised the hump was there to stay. Nothing could ever remove it. She had come to detest her own image. Like the ill-fated Lady of Shalott, a mirror could have the power to destroy her.

The snow was still there, mocking her with its beauty. She lifted up the mirror and dropped it on the linoleum. It cracked like a web in a thorn bush, winking, distorting her further. She would be scolded and reminded that it would mean seven years bad luck. Only it wasn't just seven, or seventeen. It was for the rest of her life. She heard the echo of Broome's voice "I love my love with an H".

She could not even cry.

* * * *

Jo woke next. Some unaccustomed sound had disturbed her for she was still drowsy. She wished she had not been aroused for she did not want to think about the coming day. Her hand slid over the pillow beside her own. It felt cold and unused. No evocation of Gil as there sometimes was. They'd never had lavish Christmases and Gil had always needed to go out to attend to a patient or two, often with the snow two or three feet deep. But it was wonderful when he came back. She'd have the fire blazing and soup on the hob. Chestnuts roasting. Apples in hot ale. And after, they'd go to bed early, drawing the blue hangings so that the draughts would be kept at bay.

'Gil?' she whispered. 'Gil?'

But he did not come.

* * * *

Kit had looked forward to the holiday. He rarely took time off from the daily round of the farm. But now, alive to every slightest sound, he wished himself outside so that he could think of everyday matters instead of brooding on the boy he had accepted as his son. Pan had been telling the truth, he was certain. Earlier, when he'd mentioned giving Broome his own name, she had tried to dissuade him.

Part of him was still angry at her deception but he had kept the fact to himself. Broome's coldness had upset her enough and there was the child to think of. He saw her bare shoulder protrude from the covers, a mass of dark hair across the pillow. Gently, he covered the bare flesh.

They had had a new dress made for Rose. The dressmaker in Keswick was used to allowing for that unfortunate disability. Pan stirred and turned towards him and somehow her face was that of Judith, smiling at the misery she had left in her wake.

He shifted back in revulsion.

* * * *

Pan recognised the action. She had shown her pleasure at seeing Kit beside her instead of the usual empty place, and he had repudiated her. She knew he was suffering because of her need to tell the truth about Broome but she had not imagined he'd hurt her so deliberately.

'I'm sorry, Kit,' she said. 'Don't keep on punishing me. You've every right, though, after what I did.'

'I'm not punishing you.'

'Then why look as if you hated me?'

'Not you.'

'We aint'—'asn't got anyone else in

here beside us.'

'Haven't.'

'Haven't, then. I do my best, Kit.'

'I know you do. I feel restless as a cat. There's a clock inside me says I should be up and about.'

'Pretend it's stopped. Kiss me?'

'Not before breakfast.'

'Once it was any old time, Kit, I'm afraid! It's all disappearing and just because I couldn't live a lie no longer.'

'How am I supposed to feel? For nearly eleven years I accept the boy as mine and then you destroy the illusion in a sentence or two and I'm expected to applaud your honesty! Give me time to think. Get used to the idea.'

'Will you tell him?'

'I don't know. It could be a bad thing—'

'Anything that makes him free of me would be good in his eyes.'

'Don't you dare tell him! Haven't you done enough?'

She lay rigid, swallowing the painful lump in her throat. If that's what you got for telling the truth, it'd be better to go on lying and there were one or two things she hadn't told her husband. Prudence kept her quiet.

* * * *

Broome yawned. He was still tired from
yesterday's exertions. In spite of the fact
that he had not reached home till dusk,
no one had questioned him. Stimulated
by the cold ride and the Frenchman's
wine, he could have been garrulous. The
impromptu meal had been splendid, only
marred here and there by the soft crump
of the snow dropping from the eaves and
sending his host up in the chair with that
watchful look that betrayed fear. He'd be
even more nervous today, alone. Not that
he'd dare say he wanted to go back to
West Winds, and Kit with that dangerous
quiet. He must open his stocking as usual,
play "Christmas Bag" with Rose who
would squeal with delight as they, blind-
folded, beat the paper bag about and
waited for it to split, disgorging its
treasures of biscuits and comfits and
small toys. Rennie would sneer if he saw
him.

It would have been much better at the
Falconers. They were to have numerous
uncles and aunts, all eccentric and wildly

entertaining. But then he would have missed Christmas Eve at West Winds, the heart-thudding moments as the Frenchman admitted his apprehension, had seen his enemy in every shadow. When he had gone for Broome's pony he had taken a cocked pistol. It had been thrilling.

He had stopped at the unfinished house and shown Broome the soaring roof beams, yet to be covered, the skeletons of floors and staircases, the yawning caverns of fireplaces. It felt like a cathedral, all echoes and sharp footfalls quickly silenced as the Frenchman looked behind him at every slight sound.

It would be a beautiful house with moulded plaster ceilings and chandeliers that were at present, in store. 'It will be all yellow and white' the Frenchman said, his voice reverberating in the roof timbers.

Broome got out of bed and stared in the direction of the Carter land. It was a wilderness of white and dim blue. Somewhere in the quiet wastes a dog howled, or a wolf. Out there, anything could happen.

* * * *

Betty, bringing in mince-pies smothered in cream, was aware of the undercurrents. Miss Rose hadn't laughed once when she and that boy hit at the Christmas Bag and the floor was showered with little gifts and treats. The new dress was pretty, in the tartan material the Queen favoured at Balmoral, trimmed with narrow lace and velvet bows and sash, but the girl might as well have worn a hessian sack.

The maid set down the plate on a pie-crust table and went to fetch the short-bread. Old Mrs Talbot looked like a duchess in her black. Mr Kit could have been a pirate instead of a farmer, and as for that gipsy! Betty had still not entirely lost her contempt for Pan. She remembered vividly, Pan Boswell's sojourn here when Mrs Judith was alive. A downright sloven she was. Didn't even wear under-clothes till she had them forced on her. A queer, prickly heat affected Betty as she arranged the sugary fingers onto one of the ceremonial plates only brought out for such occasions. Naked bodies were shameful and only God knew what the master and mistress got up to in that room of theirs. It made her all funny to think of it, all that heaving and humping about. She wasn't ever going to get married, even if someone did ask her one of these days. Marriage was what had turned her ma into an invalid, not that it seemed to have done that for Mr Kit's wife. She had bloomed, except for the last two days, since Master Broome arrived. Like the wicked fairy at a christening, that boy was. He was going to be handsome, though in a dark, dissolute sort of way, probably get girls into trouble in the same fashion as his father. Uncle Robbie had told aunt Janie that Mr Kit was the reason for Deborah Broome's fall from grace. He and the master'd had a heart to heart chat and Mr Kit had let it slip. Not that anyone was surprised! A hussy, Deb had proved to be.

They were all sitting there when she went back, trying to look as if they were enjoying themselves. But she knew quite well they weren't. Mr Kit all tight-lipped and Mrs Pan sitting up straight so that the baby wouldn't show too much. Disgraceful they were and only wed for a few days. Miss Rose pale and looking as if she wanted to cry but who wouldn't, with that monstrosity sitting on her shoulder?

Broome, with the devil looking out of his eyes—

The tree was a shining ghost, a skeleton at the feast, its baubles turning ever so slightly as the wind crept under the door.

7

Rose had been asking Jo about her kinsman, Nicholas Heron-Maxwell and Jo had answered her as well as she was able. Master Nicholas still lived in Berwick and attended the Corporation Academy in Golden Square. Pleased by the name of the square, Rose had elicited the information that the town also boasted a Silver Street that was close to the Palace. Nicholas must be nearing twelve or thirteen, Jo could not recall which, and was of average height, had brown hair and hazel eyes.

'He sounds very ordinary.'

'I did not mean to give that impression.' Jo bent to pick up a rag doll with woollen plaits from the bit of Turkey carpet that lay by the bed. 'Nicholas has character.'

'He doesn't sound as interesting as Broome.'

'Broome's downright wild.'

'When does he come home?'

'Three weeks or so.'

'The baby will be here by then, won't it?'

'Well before then,' Jo said carefully. The child was actually on its way already and it was her task to keep Rose away from the bedchamber where Pan lay twisted with pain. Dr Bassett should arrive soon, that was a blessing. Hannah Nisbett was with Pan. She'd given birth to two sons and though old, was capable. Jo felt that she should have been attending Kit's wife but Rose did not like Hannah and would have suspected what was going on. As it was, some hours had passed without the child's curiosity being aroused or the sounds of Pan's labours reaching this distant room.

'What should you like it to be?' Rose was asking.

'I expect your father'd like a boy, but a girl would be nice for you—'

'Why should I care? It's *her* baby.

Nothing to do with us.'

'It has *everything* to do with this family. This house. It belongs here just as much as you do or Broome.'

Rose craned her neck. 'Is that the sound of a trap?'

Jo breathed a silent thanks. 'I heard nothing. Now shall we play the Drawing Game?'

'It's not so much fun with two.'

'It can be done.'

'Word making?' Rose suggested.

'If you like.'

'Or we could do some French.'

'Your lessons are over for today. Wouldn't you rather play?' Jo was surprised.

'I love French. It doesn't seem work. If I can speak languages I can travel.'

'Yes, my dear.' Jo thought, privately, that travel would be altogether exhausting. And much attention would be paid to the child, most of it directed towards her infirmity.

'I do think there is someone here, Grandmother.' A courtesy title that gave Jo a pleasure she had not expected. 'There were foot-steps on the stair.'

'Betty, I expect, doing something she
312

forgot this morning. Where are your books?'

'On the bottom shelf.'

Jo's ears tingled. She was certain she had heard a scream, cut off by the closing of a door. 'Which one do you want?'

'Pierre à l'école.'

'Ah, yes. Shall we start at the beginning?'

'Please—'

The door opened and Betty was there, red of face, hands twisting. 'You'm needed, ma'am. I'll take Miss Rose down to the kitchen to help with the baking.'

'Why?' Rose asked.

'Don't ask questions,' Jo said crisply. 'No one does anything here without good reason.'

'Come on,' Betty urged, shepherding Rose towards the servants' stair.

The child's suspicions would be fully aroused but it could not be helped. Jo turned the knob of Kit's bedchamber door and saw him standing, pale and frowning by the hangings.

'What is it?' she asked.

Pan moaned. Hannah moved in the shadows. 'There, there—' she soothed.

'Bassett had another confinement,

damn him. There was no one else.'

'I'll do what I can. Is that a clean apron?'

'Yes.'

'Ask Betty to heat some more water. Take Rose out. I can manage, I think. I helped Gil often enough.' Jo could see Pan now. She was drenched with sweat. 'Hannah, could you go and make some tea?'

'Yes'm.' Hannah bobbed and left the room.

'Please go, Kit.'

'Very well. Be brave, Pan.' He was inclined to linger.

'Go away!'

Jo turned her attentions to the girl on the bed. She concluded her examination in a thoughtful silence. The gipsy had not previously borne a child and that was disquieting to say the least. But all that was Kit's business and his wife's. Yet, all the time she worked and encouraged, all through the girl's gasps and screams she thought of Broome and the horror that had attended his appearance. Had Kit lied about Deborah Broome? It seemed all too possible.

Hannah brought the tea and Pan

managed to keep a mouthful or two down in between the pains that came faster and sharper. They changed the sheets again and Jo wiped the girl's forehead with a cool, damp cloth. Unnoticed, the daylight had faded and the dusk turned to darkness.

The child's head was emerging and Jo saw that the hair was red. She was reminded of the birth of Kit. Chrissie Ashton had not had the trouble Pan was experiencing but her child was a lusty redheaded boy. The rest of the child followed, slippery and blue-skinned. Pan closed her eyes on an exhausted cry.

This baby was a girl. Jo picked her up and wiped her clean, slapped her bottom. Her cry was loud. By the time Kit had rushed upstairs, the cord was tied and Jo had the child in a shawl while Hannah dealt with Pan behind the screen.

'There's your daughter,' she said, swallowing a lump that rose to her throat.

He took the infant from her. 'It's—like you,' he whispered.

'It's a Heron all right.'

'Mrs Talbot do be ready,' Hannah called. 'She'd like to see the baby.'

The screen was set aside. Pan, propped

up now against a fresh pillow, was dreadfully pale. Jo was concerned by her looks.

'A little girl', she said, 'and the spit-
ting image of Kit. There, see for yourself.'

Pan stared at the swaddled infant, then
burst into tears. 'Oh, thank God—'

'Pan?'

'I meant, thank God it was over and
it's all right.'

'I'm sorry you had to suffer so,' he said
gently.

'It's your fault,' Jo said. 'You are a
very large man. It's your fate to sire
giants.'

'Are you sad you didn't get the boy you
were set on?' Kit asked his wife.

'A little. But she looks a strong little
thing. And I can still call her Heron, can't
I? Heron Talbot.'

'I don't see why not. Now I think you'd
better sleep. You've done well.' He kissed
her.

It was after he had gone downstairs to
open a bottle in celebration that he
remembered the tears and the way she had
said "Thank God". Was it really a reaction to her pain and relief that the child
was born perfect? Or was it perhaps that
she had feared the child was not his and

might live under the same shadow that lay over Broome? She needn't have worried.

Heron was unmistakably his, whole, perfect and beautiful, his child in a way that the others had never been. He must be careful that his feelings for her never amounted to an obsession. Kit sank back into a chair with a sigh of satisfaction and raised the glass to his lips.

* * * *

Broome came again at Easter. He regarded the new Talbot jealously. No one seemed aware of anything else. Kit doted on little Heron, holding her, playing with the child as though she were the sun in the firmament. Betty was all silly coos and pointing fingers stuck in the baby's stomach to make it smile and gurgle. Pan and Jo were equally besotted.

Rose had meant to stand aloof but the newcomer was pretty for an infant—some did have an unfortunately rat-like appearance—and although she did not overstep the mark, she was drawn to watch it being bathed and fed, an interesting process, though she'd hate to do it herself. It was so—unprivate.

No one paid any attention to Broome after the initial greeting from Jo, a flash of dark eyes from his step-mother—he'd never accept her as his real mother—an odd, critical stare from Kit, and not a great deal of warmth from Rose who seemed to have become self-castigating and shrewish.

The only occasion of any interest was the visit to the back door of the packman. He was not one of the more ordinary pedlars who arrived on foot with articles in a woven basket suspended from a yoke. This man had his own horse with panniers strapped to its sides and traded in buttons and ribbons and fringes with which to trim the countrywomen's plain gowns.

Then the post-horn had sounded and there were letters delivered, one of them, the letter he had written announcing his arrival! Apart from these excitements, there had only been glimpses of Robbie and the Nisbetts with their corduroys tied under the knees and their hobnailed boots, Mrs Hodge in her faded sun-bonnet, leading Mary by the hand.

It was time to visit Monsieur Foredor. Plainly, no one here would miss him. He did take the precaution of telling Jo in

Kit's absence. She was walking the quadrangle with Heron in her arms, her bony face upraised to the sun.

'Take care and do not be late for supper.' She did not look away from the child.

'I believe they'd not notice if I said I was to throw myself in the stream,' he thought resentfully, noticing how the sunlight outlined the baby's hair, accentuating its redness. Rose's was far more unusual and not so showy. Heron would be as flashy as her gipsy mother. Rose had quality.

He stood there, hating the child. Kit came from the corner of the quadrangle, wiping his hands on a handkerchief, smiling at his tiny daughter with such pleasure that a knife turned in Broome's heart. 'Let me hold her for a moment,' he said quickly and Jo stared at him in surprise. He'd never shown any interest in Heron.

'Are you sure you know how? You must support her back very carefully, and her head.' She sounded doubtful.

'I can do what you are doing. Give her to me.' He heard Kit's feet coming over the cobbles, his voice very gentle, saying 'little sweetheart, little darling.'

'Very well. But do mind what you're doing.' Jo bent to place the white-wrapped bundle in Broome's arms. In one brief, shocking moment, he knew what he was going to do. He would drop her onto all those hard, shiny stones and then he'd have revenged himself on Pan Boswell for ever. Babies' heads were soft. His arms relaxed their hold deliberately and the child swayed perilously, like a flower on a stalk. Kit gave a howl of rage and swooped just in time. He scooped up the baby who gasped and gave vent to a frightened cry, then nestled against him.

'You young bastard!' Kit ground out. 'Get out of my sight! Before I do you some mischief I'll have good reason to regret. Get out! You'd be well-advised to do as I say.'

'But, Kit—' Jo protested.

'You heard me,' Kit persisted, his one good eye fixed on the white-faced boy. 'It was no accident, was it, Broome, so don't bother to lie. You intended harm, and nothing you or Jo say will ever make me believe different. Take yourself off. You're no son of mine. I know that now. Whatever devil spawned you is welcome to you.'

320

'Oh, Kit!' Jo was deeply distressed.

Kit marched off with the baby held close against his chest. Broome, sick with realisation that Kit was right, appalled by the sense of rejection, hesitated only for a moment, then lunged off in the direction of the stable.

'He doesn't mean it!' Jo shouted but Broome paid no heed. He took out the pony and was soon on the track to the west, the sun on the hills that were not yet green but grey or dun-coloured, showing harsh bones and strong bullies. There were daffodils by the small lake but he ignored their promise of spring.

He rode hard, his feet kicking at the pony's sides, his hands tugging at the bit, never slackening until he saw the copse in the waste of pale boulders, the thin branches fuzzed with fresh leaves, the shape of the new house beyond. There was a sound of hammering from inside it, blurs of faces and moving figures beyond the windows. Someone laughed. The temporary huts and caravans had their doors open to let the breeze blow through and a cage, containing a canary, hung from a nearby tree. The bird was singing.

The Frenchman was at his door, a fowling-piece under his arm, his stance threatening. 'Oh, it's you, boy. I heard you coming.'

'Did you think it was the man who follows you?'

'I thought it might be.'

'I had to come.'

'Had to?' The lion's eyes were watchful.

'I was going to do something dreadful.'

'And what was that?'

'I wanted to kill the gipsy's baby. My father knew.'

'And?'

'He said I was no son of his and that whatever devil spawned me, can have me, as far as he is concerned.'

'Did he indeed!'

'And now I have nowhere to go.'

'So you thought of me.' The Frenchman put back his fine-drawn head and laughed a little discordantly. 'Why, Broome Boswell?'

'I thought we were friends. I'd do anything you wanted. Perhaps you need a servant about the house. I could split logs and wash pots, trap rabbits. There are all sorts of things I could do.'

'Come inside and we'll think of it over a glass of wine. We'll see if you can decide whether the bouquet is different this time. I suspect, however, that Mr Talbot or your grandmother will be over, post-haste, to ask for your return.'

The dimness of the room with its burden of portraits enclosed the boy like a womb. He felt safe here. The cruel faces approved him as one of themselves. He was a near-murderer who could demand his own kind of respect. It was almost as if they smiled and whispered, "Welcome to our ranks".

The Frenchman looked tired. As he poured the wine, his hand shook so that the pale gold-liquid spilled onto the tray.

Broome took his glass, closed his eyes and tried to obliterate the image of Heron. But, however hard he persevered, he still saw that aureole of bright hair, the delicate baby neck. Another minute and it might have snapped like a stick. It was awful, and wonderful, that he'd go to such lengths to remove obstacles from his way.

'Well?' The Frenchman demanded.

'It's not flowery like the first, nor so grapey as the second. This is sharp and fresh and will not taste so sweet.'

'You are right, of course, though I never doubted it for a moment. This is an exceptionally dry wine. Taste it.'

Broome did so.

'Do you like it?'

'Better than the others. I do not have a sweet tooth.'

'You could do well in the wine business and might be an asset, trained and sent out later to a good vineyard. How would that appeal to you?'

'I've no chance of doing any such thing. My father was so angry he'll want to rid himself of me. He'll send me to some school much further off and say it's not possible for me to come for holidays. Some spartan barracks—'

'And how could this be avoided?'

'He said I was no son of his—'

'I should not take that too literally. It was in the heat of the moment.'

'He said he knew I was not his. I should be glad. That would mean I did not belong to the gipsy.'

'You do hate her, don't you!'

'I will not belong to such—such a low person. She does not know how to speak. I hate the colours she wears. Even her smell.'

'It's obvious your father—Mr Talbot—does not share your views.'

'I do not want to go back.'

'You are too young to decide for yourself. And, however angry he may have been this morning, he'll feel differently later. Talbots have a sense of responsibility, not like we—Foredors.' Again, he laughed without amusement. 'We have few scruples.'

'Then I'll make him come for me! May I stay?'

'For a time at least. If you had murder on your mind, I'll warrant you did not break your fast?'

'I was not thinking of it until I saw her.'

'But you've had time to develop an appetite since?'

'Yes. I am quite hungry.'

'Good. Come, let us find what there is left. I've a bird or two hanging in the pantry. And the foreman brought some pies from Keswick. Do you know the town? There's an old Druid Circle on the hill overlooking the water.'

'I have never seen it.'

'Then I'll take you there if your

father agrees.'

'He says he is not that. Then to whom *do* I belong? They have places for boys like me, orphans, where I'd be shut up, put to hard labour, and something tells me I was not born to that.'

'Does it indeed?' the Frenchman enquired gently, his lace-trimmed wrist held to his mouth, as if to conceal pain or laughter. 'Does it! Now, what's it to be? Pheasant or pork pie with eggs? You decide.'

* * * *

It was Rob Dixon who came that evening saying Mr Talbot had sent him to fetch the boy home.

'I won't go,' Broome said obstinately.

'He'll be vexed, Master Broome.' Rob shuffled his feet uneasily.

'I cannot help that.'

'Let me write a note telling him I'd appreciate your company for a day or two. The time does hang in this interim stage. I'm shut out of my house proper and there's no room here for my London friends. They'd hardly appreciate a gamekeeper's cottage.'

'By rights, I ought to take the lad back, Sir?'

'Would you take him by force? A day or two could make Mr Talbot see the disagreement in a new light.'

'He'll not be pleased,' Rob reiterated, embarrassed by the whole affair.

'Nevertheless, I think a short breathing space might be to everyone's advantage. I will write to Mr Talbot and Broome will give you refreshment. Wine, Mr Dixon?'

'No thank'ee, Sir.'

'Tea?'

'I wouldn't say no to that.'

Dixon fidgeted with his cap while Broome made him tea and brought out a cake. All the time, the Frenchman's quill scratched over the paper, the only sound there was. He paused, sanded the sheet and sealed it with a flourish. 'There you are. An olive branch, I hope.'

Rob swallowed the last mouthful of plum cake and set down the fragile cup. 'I must be getting back.'

'I was down Cockermouth way recently,' the Frenchman said, handing over the folded paper, 'and I'm sure I saw you outside a cottage on the outskirts. There was a boy, around Broome's age and a collie. You were throwing sticks for it. And a dark woman came out to call you both in.'

Dixon flushed and turned pale. 'Couldn't 'a been me, Sir. Don't know nobody Cockermouth direction.'

'I could have sworn! However, it seems I was wrong. They say everyone has a double.'

'Yes, Sir,' Dixon said stolidly, then touched his cap. 'Good day, Sir.'

'Good day,' Monsieur Foredor said in apparent high humour. 'Assure Mr Talbot I'll take good care of the boy. He'll be quite safe with me.'

Once mounted, Rob urged the horse up the slope and into the copse. The palms of his hands felt clammy. Imagine that Froggie being in Cockermouth that particular day. And not only had Foredor seen him but there'd been Deborah and the lad. He'd imagined all that hidden from Janie for good but this interfering foreigner knew he'd lied about the affair. He could poke and pry, not that he'd have any proper cause to make trouble. It was the fact that someone else besides Mr Kit knowing all about an episode he'd thought buried for ever took away his sense of security and filled him with a vague foreboding.

He was half-way to Grey Ghyll when he saw the man on the skyline. There seemed only one place he could be bound for. However hard he looked, the horseman remained a stranger.

* * * *

Replete, Broome got up and wandered round the room. The portraits were overpowering in the confined space. Under one of them he read a name, half-obliterated by dust. Fanny Amberwood. She had something of Pan's bold looks but her eyes were like Foredor's. Rubbing his finger along the name-plate of another he made out Brandon Amberwood. The frame was dirtier than the others as though this portrait had been long-stored in a loft. This face was kinder than the rest though the man was undoubtedly of the same family. None of them bore Foredor's name and he thought this strange since the resemblance to the Frenchman was marked.

He wandered upstairs after the Frenchman, carrying a lantern, went out to the

329

stable to see if all was well. The candle-light showed him two poky rooms, blotched with rain, but with three more portraits standing against the wall in the larger of the attics. One in particular drew him. It was of a fair woman whose face was too like Jo's for comfort. Even the eyes were green. She had been very beautiful after a cold fashion. But what was a painting of a woman with Heron features doing in the Frenchman's cottage? The plate on this frame was missing.

By the time Monsieur returned, Broome was downstairs again, his stomach muscles tight with a curious expectancy. The Frenchman's secrecy, his habit of keeping his features half-hidden, both pointed to some mystery he longed to unravel.

'Where am I to sleep?' Broome asked as the man bolted the door, top and bottom.

'In here,' the Frenchman said and threw open another door the boy had taken to be a cupboard. There was a bed in a recess, obviously used by Foredor, and a light camp cot set along the space under the window. 'The small bed. There should be sufficient blankets for someone young and full-blooded. The fire helps. I'll make it up now and it will heat up the place in half an hour.'

The window, like all the ones downstairs, had bars across them. 'Why are they barred?'

'To keep out strangers. I have things of value I'd not want taken.'

'And those portraits.'

'As you say, the paintings. Some by famous artists. Worth a deal of money.'

'Are these all you have, these ones down here?'

'Aren't they enough! They are to be in my gallery when West Winds is completed.'

'Will that be soon?' Broome noted the evasion and was more curious than ever.

'By the summer. Then my house will be occupied at least. A phoenix rising from the ashes of the destroyed.'

'A phoenix?'

'A legendary bird, born of fire.' Foredor took off his fine coat. The crystal buttons on his waistcoat flashed.

'The house of the phoenix. I like that better than West Winds.'

'I suppose it does have a ring to it. But you are young and still romantic. And,' the Frenchman said, becoming serious, 'by your own admission, a would-be killer. Did you mean it?'

'Yes. I was already half-way to dropping that spoiled brat onto the stones. I could not have stopped myself.'

'You don't think you have made too much of an all-too-common impulse? A new arrival arouses fierce jealousies in older children. You were jealous, were you not?'

'Yes. But I was not jealous of Rose.'

'You grew up together. There lies the difference. And her disability made you treat her more gently than you might otherwise have done. I do not think you are black as you would paint yourself.'

'I am. I really meant to do it. Partly to hurt that woman, but just as much to rid myself of her.'

'I think you should not utter these sentiments to anyone else.' The Frenchman rose to poke at the fire and the flames leapt suddenly to reveal his face and body so that he looked younger and more effeminate than when he was fully clothed. Some trick of the light gave an impression of small breasts under the fitted velvet of the waistcoat, then he turned from the blaze and became himself, slender and attenuated.

'I'd say nothing. It's just that I can talk to you.'

'I could disapprove.'

'But you don't, do you.'

'What a strange boy you are. Still, it's only to be expected—'

'Oh? Why is it?'

'You ask too many questions.' Foredor went to a small cupboard set in the corner and took out a sealed paper. 'This may answer some of them. But you must promise not to open it unless something happens to me.'

'You mean—if your enemy should think of looking for you here?'

'Something like that.'

'But the bars. The bolts—'

'I cannot shut myself in for twenty-four hours a day. There must be freedom.'

'The cottage is safer than your large house.'

'Another irony. I long for the house and yet I fear the day I must move into it. I grow cowardly with age.'

'You are not old.'

The Frenchman laughed emptily. 'You have not given your word.'

'I promise only to open the letter if you die.'

There was a long silence broken by a suggestion of a sound from the darkness around them. The Frenchman snuffed out the candles and motioned Broome to follow him to the darkest corner of the room.

Something drew itself softly against the door.

Broome found himself grasping Foredor's arm tightly.

The sound was not repeated.

'A fox, I imagine,' The Frenchman said at last and released his breath on a sigh. 'I've seen them in the moonlight.'

'There's no moon tonight.'

'They must hunt, moon or no. And there will be cubs to feed.'

'I suppose so.' Broome could see the letter in the dimness, a pale oblong splotched with the bloodstain that was the seal.

He wished he had not made the promise. The document was going to burn a hole in his pocket.

* * * *

'Infernal impudence!' Kit said violently,

throwing down the Frenchman's note. 'Hasn't the boy behaved badly enough?'

'You only think he meant harm,' Jo told him. 'Jealousy's a common enough reaction. He was, at least showing some interest at last.'

'Fratricide is not so common.'

'You read too much into the—'

'Accident? He was guilty as sin. His face said everything.'

'Perhaps his Monsieur has more sense than you. Sleep on it and you'll see matters differently. Anyway, I expect Broome will have to come back tomorrow, since that cottage is not large enough for two guests.'

'Two? What are you talking about?'

'Joannie told me she'd had a stranger at the back this afternoon, looking for Monsieur Foredor. She did not care too much for his looks, a big, dark man with greying hair. Put her in mind of someone only she couldn't think who. He must have followed her instructions because Rob Dixon saw him as he came back. Passed one another the far side of the lake.'

'Did he speak to Robbie?'

'They were too far apart.'

'I'm going in the morning. Guest or no guest.'

'Perhaps you'll be more rational by then.'

'Perhaps,' Kit said grimly.

Then Pan came into the room after feeding Heron, the baby good-natured from bath and supper and no one thought any more about the difficult cuckoo in the nest.

* * * *

Broome could not think where he was. Sunlight streamed over his head and onto a white-washed wall. Boots lay on the floor, long and polished. The velvet waistcoat with the crystal buttons hung over the ladder-back chair. He raised his head, unwilling at first to emerge from the cocoon of blankets. The Frenchman was already up, the covers thrown back carelessly from the recessed bed.

It had taken Broome a long while to go to sleep. The soft slithering past the door had worked on his imagination strongly. An owl had hooted from a thicket.

The Frenchman, too, had tossed and turned for some time before his breathing

had become regular. The night had oppressed the boy, adding to the despair that
had come over him at the realisation of
his own wickedness. The awe and wonder
he'd experienced earlier had gone and the
thought of child-murder revolted him.
How could he have exulted in such an am-
bition? He no longer understood himself.
He was irredeemably degenerate and
would end up in Hell.

The cottage and the copse had begun
to seem sinister and the Frenchman a
wicked magician.

Broome slid to the flagstones and
began to dress hastily. The white oblong
on the floor attracted his attention and
again curiosity overcame disquiet. He
picked up the letter, across which the seal
spread like a padlock, then slipped it into
his inside pocket. He'd find a hiding place
for it when he got back home.

The Frenchman, breeched and white-
shirted, came to tell him breakfast was
ready. 'You must not neglect to eat. Food
will make you feel braver.' All the
time he was talking, he was putting
on the waistcoat, fastening the buttons
with slim fingers. His broad shoulders
showed off the garment, carried the black

coat admirably. Broome wished his own clothes had not suffered from lying on the floor.

'I should go after breakfast,' Broome said.

'Ah! So you've decided I was right and that second thoughts are best?'

'I don't know. But Father is sure to come seeking me himself and I'd not want him shouting and raving at you.'

'Does he? Shout and rave?'

'When he's angry.'

'He must have changed,' The Frenchman's smile was peculiar.

'You know him better than you've told me.'

'We talked in the copse where his first wife hanged herself.'

'I meant before then.' Broome had heard the facts of Judith's suicide in the kitchen.

'Perhaps I made a mistake in allowing you to stay. There's one thing you must understand. I value, above all, my privacy. Don't pry, young Broome.'

The boy went to the portrait of Brandon Amberwood. 'Who was this man?'

'A relative.'

'I thought so. And all the others?'

338

'All of them. Like a pride of lions. But that's a name I prefer to keep to myself so you'll say nothing? Have you never heard it before?'

'Not that I remember.'

'It's not a name you'd forget. Now eat, young man.'

Broome did as he was told, then got up reluctantly to go in search of his pony.

'Can you saddle him yourself?'

'Of course! I've done that for years.'

'Good.'

It was peaceful in the stable. The boy made the pony ready, then returned to the small dwelling. It must have rained in the night for the ground was soft and the slates not quite dry. There was a footprint in the mud beside the door. His heart raced. It was a much larger print than either his own or Foredor's. Remembering the sound of last night, he was troubled.

The Monsieur came out as he studied it.

'Perhaps it was not a fox,' Broome said carefully.

'One of the workmen probably. They sometimes catch their dinner in the copse. Most of them set traps. I have to turn a blind eye.'

'They'd not come so close.'

'It's time you went, Broome. I expect —another visitor. Have you the letter safe?'

'I have. You will be all right?'

'Perfectly.' The Frenchman smiled wearily. 'Now be off with you. I do not think I could face your irate father this morning.'

'Your pain troubles you?'

'It did. Now it has gone.'

'If you are sure—'

'I am sure. Goodbye, Broome.'

'Goodbye.' There seemed a terrible finality about the word. The boy stared into the Frenchman's face, seeing a trace of brightness around the eyes, then he dug his heels into the pony's flanks and was off without a backward look.

* * * *

Faro did not move until the boy had gone. An emptiness possessed her, one that could not be filled. The pain was becoming worse. Soon she would be driven to screaming, writhing on the floor, until the worst was past. It would come again relentlessly, stalking her as he did. Bender would find her and she thought now that she would welcome him. Unlike Judith, she could never kill herself, but he would do it for her.

She had chosen her heir, or rather, she had decided, at last to acknowledge him. Broome was her son and the certificate of his birth was in the possession of her lawyer, along with the rest of her official papers.

Only yesterday, the footprint in the mud would have terrified her, but the agony she'd endured while Broome was in the stable had shown her that Dr Bassett was right. Hers was to be no slow death with intermitten pain but a short and terrible one. A galloping tumour— she could not, in this present state of lassitude, remember the name he'd used —but he'd advised her to put her affairs in order as soon as possible.

It seemed a pity she'd not see the house completed, but it would be finished before it passed to Broome, together with the money she'd amassed over the years. The chandeliers from Amberwood were to be installed next week and she'd left instructions that the decorations must be white and yellow, the colours her notorious grandfather and great-grandfather favoured as much as herself.

The pockets of darkness between the trees were inimical. He was there somewhere, but she no longer feared whatever weapon he had. Chamwell had died quickly. Bender would not want her so swiftly dead. But nothing he did would be worse than the pain. After that—oblivion. Even the limbo held no real terror.

Now that she had made up her mind to accept her doom, she went inside intending to fetch her cape for the air was colder today. She would walk in the wood and he would come to her.

* * * *

Kit, distracted by the glitter of the lake and the tossing heads of the daffodils, did not see Broome until he was within earshot. Then he strove to push down the bile that rose at the sight of the boy he had come to realise was not his own. Pan had disclaimed him and Jo, on questioning, had verified the fact that the girl had not previously given birth, that Heron

342

was her first child.

Unknown to the inhabitants of Grey Ghyll, he'd taken himself over to Cockermouth, stationing himself within sight of the cottage where Deb Broome lived. He had seen both her and a boy who bore no resemblance to Broome Boswell but was obviously around the same age. He returned home thoroughly puzzled and surly as a bear.

'So you've come to your senses!' he shouted, reining in. 'I'm wasting valuable time that should be spent on the farm.'

Broome faced him defiantly. 'You told me to go.'

'Perhaps I did. But I hadn't expected you to go whining to your friend at West Winds.'

'What did you expect?'

'Now, don't take that tone with me! I thought you'd go and work off whatever it was possessed you, then come back and behave yourself.'

'I chose to go somewhere I was not resented.'

'Look, Broome. Perhaps I did mistake the situation, and if I did, I'm sorry.'

'I—don't know what's to happen to me. I can't spend all my time being

343

somewhere else because none of you want me.'

'Is that how you feel?'

'Yes.'

Kit was conscious of a twinge of pity. There was something in what the boy said. Yet he could never forgive that moment in the quadrangle with Heron bent backwards, her little body so vulnerable. 'We'll work something out.'

They rode for a short distance in silence, then he asked, 'Did Monsieur Foredor's visitor arrive?'

'Not yet.'

'But it was yesterday he asked directions.'

'Yesterday?'

'Joannie spoke to him, then Robbie saw him on his way. Somewhere past the lake.'

'Then where can he be?'

'Perhaps he was thrown from the horse. A pothole.'

'I don't think so.'

'Why not? It's wild country.'

'There's someone he's afraid of.'

'The Frenchman? Did he tell you that?'

'More than once. He said someone followed him, and last night there was a queer sound outside the door. Monsieur was always pulling the bolts—There are bars on the windows.'

'You go on to the house. I'll go back to West Winds.'

'I'd rather go with you.'

'Do as I say, Broome! Someone must tell the womenfolk I'm delayed. I'll stop at the big house first and take some of the workmen with me. I agree it might be foolish to walk into an ambush.'

'Couldn't I—?'

'No.' Kit was definite. 'He sounded a rough person from what Joannie said and it would be irresponsible of me to take you deliberately into danger. Hurry. I do not want anyone worrying at home.'

'Very well.' The boy's face was white, accentuating the blackness of his eyes.

'Go on, then.' Kit's voice sharpened.

He waited until Broome had gone some way before he set off for the Frenchman's territory.

* * * *

Two men directed Kit to the cottage when he had expressed his fears for the Frenchman's safety. The door was open and there was no reply to his urgent knocking. 'I'll take a look inside,' he said. 'Wait here and keep your eyes open.'

Daylight penetrated the deep-set window sending shivers of light across the portraits that obscured most of the walls. He stared in disbelief. Amberwoods, all of them. That sense of familiarity he'd experienced in his one meeting with the supposed Frenchman had not played him false. He knew now that it was Faro who owned the Carter property, and that revelation led him to the train of thought stemming from her seeming penchant for Broome. On his only visit to Amberwood in search of Judith, Faro had told him that Judith was Carne Amberwood's mistress and shortly to become his wife. In a violent reaction he had allowed Faro to seduce him. It was an impulse he regretted almost immediately for he had seen how she played cat and mouse with a manservant who attended them. He could not remember the man's name but he recalled perfectly the aftermath of the man's antagonism when he'd been attacked by an unseen assailant in the stable and left with a cracked skull.

That manservant could turn against

Faro should she reject him and Joannie's description of the man she saw yesterday could fit the servant's particulars.

Kit went upstairs, noting the picture of Savannah. How well the painter had caught the wintry quality of her beauty. There was no sign of anyone either in the attics or in the bedroom that led off the parlour. He saw the two unmade beds, the dishes left from breakfast, a quill and sandpot as though the Frenchman—Faro, he amended quickly—had recently penned some missive. An ink-drop on the floor still glistened wetly.

The workmen waited, one carrying a pickaxe and the other a sharp-edged shovel and a broom-handle which were the only weapons to come to hand.

'Best search the wood,' Kit told them. 'It's plain your master's not here, but whether he left by his own wish, or was taken, I cannot decide.'

'Allus said it was a chancy business being down here, alone,' the sandy-haired one said. 'Some tinker or footpad after 'is rhino, you mark my words.'

'Never came past the big 'ouse, no one did,' the other volunteered, not for the first time.

'The question is, would it be safer to stay together, or to go different ways?'

'Summat to be said for either, Mr Talbot.'

'We'd cover the ground faster if we separated. But spades and picks are no match for pistols or fowling-pieces.'

'I think Monsieur kept one in the stable.'

'Let us see, then.'

The horse was in its stall but there was no sign of the fowling-piece. 'Could 'a been the Frenchie took it,' the sandy man pointed out.

'I suppose so. Well, do we go as a unit or singly?'

The older man coughed. 'We'm used to prowling on our own, Sir. The Monsewer turns a blind eye to poaching. Not that 'es any choice for he don't see us. Doubt if a footpad would neither.'

'If you do see anything suspicious, shout. And be careful.'

'Yes, Mr Talbot. Which way does you favour?'

'I'll take that thick shrubbery, you go left and the other man right.'

Kit tested the roan's lead to ascertain if he was secure to the rotted hitching-post. The men moved silently enough. He hardly heard them as they disappeared in their appointed directions. Then he set off down an almost invisible track that led, through bracken and weeds, towards the sound of water.

The stream was narrow here, reed-choked and sluggish. Bushes grew in profusion, the soft branches springing back noiselessly after his passing. Kit, bent almost double, followed the sparse trail, thinking of Faro. There was little enough to remember. A solitary meal, an hour or two abed, the attack on him by—Bender! That was his name. Then the flight with Judith when he discovered she was, in reality, Carne Amberwood's captive, detesting the thought of the marriage arranged by her father. The tie with the Amberwoods had been broken, no news filtering through till now.

Faro remained an enigmatic figure. But she could have hated him enough to leave a foundling on his doorstep. It had not been Deborah or Pan, of that he was sure.

A rustle in the undergrowh kept him still. Another faint sound alerted him. A head rose, its back towards him, the hair black. Bender was dark.

Kit pounced forward and slid one massive arm around the unsuspecting neck.

The head twisted and Broome was staring at him with a sick terror.

'I thought I told you to go home,' Kit whispered roughly, releasing the boy so that he fell back against the bole of an alder that had survived in the waste of strangling growth.

'I couldn't. I thought of that man—'

'He is here. And your Monsieur is out of the house.'

'I've seen no one.'

'We must stay together. If there is any trouble, you must run to the big house for further help.'

'Yes, Father.'

Was he indeed Broome's father? It seemed possible. He'd put the brief episode with Faro from his mind as he had other encounters before Judith and marriage. Faro had seemed eminently capable of taking care of herself. She'd made him feel gauche and years younger than herself; a bucolic Lothario. It had been her idea to visit him in his room. She had seemed so worldly wise he'd never imagined her getting with child. But it now seemed indisputable that Broome was an Amberwood and showing unmistakable signs of following in the degenerate footsteps of his forebears. Rakes, gamblers and murderers. Blood would always out. And Amberwoods had always been fascinated by Herons, bastard or otherwise. There was some chemistry that drew them together no matter how catastrophic the results.

'Which way did you come?' Kit growled.

'From there.' Broome indicated the left. A vague furrow through the burgeoning foliage bore out his assertion.

'See anything?'

'No.'

'We'll try the other side of the water.' Kit seized the boy under the armpits and swung him across as though he had been a baby. Broome was feeling his throat as though it hurt. Kit sprang over beside him. 'That'll teach you to mind your own business.'

'It is my business.'

'It might have been this stranger. You could have been dead by now.'

Broome shivered.

'Come, lad.' They pushed forward

quietly, the tangle of briar and bramble thinning out to reveal taller tree trunks and shadowy recesses.

'There he is!' Broome hissed suddenly and Kit had a tantalising glimpse of slender darkness before the trees hid Faro from view.

* * * *

She was cold now. Secure in the rightness of her decision, Faro had simply walked out of the cottage and entered the screen of woodland without waiting to put on her cape. But the wind was keen and she was not yet dead. The knife of chill struck through her clothing and some of her resolution departed. Gritting her teeth, she went on walking with no effort at concealment. Her life seemed to have been spent to no purpose. No bond with parents or relatives, all her acquaintances and comrades dead. But there was Broome. Soon he would know his real name and the extent of his inheritance. He could go into the wine business if he wished. Perhaps he might think of her with affection and gratitude.

First she must slough off the skin of

life. She wished it were over. Her hand brushed the bole of a tree, green-filmed with damp but still beautiful. And then there was another hand with dark hairs on the back of it, a shocking hurtful thrust that brought her eyes on a level with Bender's. She smiled and he struck her heavily across the lips. A thin trickle of blood ran down towards her chin. The taste filled her mouth.

'I knew—you'd find me.'

'Then you know why I've come.'

'I did not tell the authorities that you killed Chamwell.'

'Makes no difference. I don't care what happens to me after I finish with you.'

'You're too late.'

He bent back her arm until the bone cracked. She moaned, swaying.

'I've come to send you to Chamwell. You wanted him, didn't you? Well, you can have him. You can rot together. Saw you, eating and drinking. Laughing about me! Thought you were rid of me. Well, that would never have been. I swore you'd not escape, no matter how far you ran.'

'I've stopped running, Bender, I'm going—' She was trying to tell him she was to die, but he would not listen. Repeatedly, he struck her across the mouth and her face. She saw him vaguely through a film of red. Every bone in her cheek and jaw felt splintered. Her nerve-ends screamed, or she thought they did. Someone was screaming—

The blows rained about her body and she raised her arms feebly to fend them off but he kicked out at her legs so that she crashed to the ground. She was aware, briefly, of the smell of dead leaves then the sour dampness was gone in wave after wave of agony as his booted foot crashed into her side. There was a darkness run through with lances of blood that turned thin and spiky and were gone.

* * * *

'Monsieur!' Broome said. 'Monsieur—' and he cradled the unrecognisable head in his arms. The body seemed slack and disjointed.

'We are too late, I fear,' Kit said, bending over the Frenchman's still shape. 'He could not be alive after what was done to him.'

Broome sprang to his feet. 'The stranger

must be close by!'

'Be careful. He'll have no more regard for us.'

'I think he went in that direction.' The boy looked down at the bloody face, the flaccid figure. There was a muddy scuff on one of the boots, a long raw score in the polished leather. It was brought home to him how hideously final murder was. The thought of it might be tempting but the result was always this shattered emptiness. He tried to remember what he knew about the spirit but could not see beyond the flesh.

'Someone went this way.' Kit picked up a recently broken twig. 'He must have a horse tethered in the wood. He may also have a fowling-piece. There's one missing from the stable. So do not be foolish.'

'I want him to die.'

'We do not know his motive.'

'People who kill other people, hang!'

'Have you just thought of that, Broome?'

'He'll get away if we stand talking!' The boy shifted under Kit's look.

'Very well, but we must talk sometime.'

The silent woodland was suddenly alive with the sound of crashing feet and branches thrust aside. Kit glimpsed a dark shape moving swiftly, then swallowed up as Faro had been. He and Broome began to run. Another sighting of the heavy figure, crunched like an ape, then only the tree shadows. There was a shouting, more plunging through the tangled shrubbery, the voice of the sandy-haired man bawling, 'there 'e goes!'

A shatter of sound blasted the copse. The excited voice was cut off with another appalling suddenness. 'Oh, God,' Kit whispered. 'He's done for him. But now is the time to get him, before he has time to reload.'

The second workman sprang out from the shelter of the thicket. 'Sandy's dead. Brute never gave 'im a chance.'

'Where is he now? The murderer—'

The man pointed a thick finger. 'Just seen 'im.'

They set off again. Broome's heart was bumping inside his chest. Panic fought with hate. Two people dead and one of them the Frenchman. He fought his way through a small gap to find himself separated from Kit and the workman. A narrow tunnel in the shrubbery stretched ahead. He hesitated only for a moment.

Kit would not notice that they were separated immediately. If he ran along the tunnel he might surprise the Frenchman's enemy. Now curiosity was added to his previous emotions.

The floor of the narrow passage was slimy with wet leaves. Twice he slithered and clutched out at the sides to recover his balance. Panting, he reached the end to find himself confronted by a dark, powerful man who stretched out one big, ruthless hand to grab him. The other clutched the fowling-piece. Perhaps he had not had a second charge for the weapon. If he had snatched it from the stable he most certainly would have no more shot. But the cottage door had been left open so the man could have taken it from the chest of drawers where it was kept.

'So you're the boy she had in the house.'

She! She. Broome remembered the suggestion of feminality and gaped surprise.

'Speak when you're spoken to,' the voice growled. The dark eyes were dangerous.

'I was there,' Broome forced himself to reply.

'Why should she bother with you?' The

man's expression had changed. Broome was intensely aware of the lined, cruel features, the greying hair that was once black as his own. It was as though a great pit opened in front of him. It seemed that he knew the Frenchman's killer. But how could that be? Gradually realisation came like an unwelcome guest. This was the face he saw in the mirror, only older and warped with dissipation. So would he look in thirty years. The terrible question had an equally horrifying answer.

'Who are you?' the man asked, his fingers biting into Broome's arm.

'My name is Broome Boswell.'

'And where are you from?'

He dare not mention Grey Ghyll. 'The—the house. I'm with the workmen.'

'Faro'd not take an apprentice into the cottage. Tell the truth!' Again those vicious fingers making him give a cry of pain. Faro was a game of cards, or the name of an Egyptian King, no person's name—

'You're from that gentleman's farm, aren't you. Talbot's. They're not apprentice's duds. The bitch! She never told me about you. Went off to the continent without saying a word after Mr Talbot ran off with her father's doxy and Amberwood killed the Ashton woman by mistake. Amberwood wasn't dead long of typhoid when Faro said she was going to the cemetry and not to bother coming. Never saw her again for months. But she did come back, said she'd been doing the Grand Tour. Only we know what she was really doing, don't we, lad! Spawning you in some French house—or maybe it was Italy. Mentioned Italy, Faro did. Asked her why she didn't take me and she said she'd had a lot to think about. I can see why she didn't bring you with her. You're mine. Wouldn't want *me* to get ideas above my station. But why leave you at the Talbots?' The man laughed crudely. 'I see! Wanted to pay him out for ditching her for the old man's fancy piece. Never forgot an insult, did Faro. Like all the Amberwoods. Bad enemies, they made. But I'm like that, too. Best come with me, hadn't you, seeing we're related. Think Talbot was your father, did you? But you know better now. I could see it in your eyes. You know.'

He was quiet at last. Broome felt sick. This was worse than having that sluttish gipsy for a mother.

359

'Bender!' Kit's voice coming from the trees' shelter. 'Let the boy go. He's done nothing.'

'And when I do?'

'You can't escape. The copse is ringed with men, and you've no more shot.'

'I have. Found it in the cottage. And if you don't let the boy and me go, I'll put a charge through his head. And don't think I won't. Done it before. Chamwell.'

Broome's arm had passed from pain to numbness. He wondered what would happen next. The thought of death was quite unreal. Then he started, for Kit had stepped out into the open and stood stolidly, his arms foled. 'You'll not get past me, Bender.'

'Talbot? Is it you?'

'I've changed. If it was a pretty boy you expected, you'll see you were mistaken.'

Bender's grip was relaxed, only for a moment, but it was long enough. Broome twisted, bent low and ran back into the tunnel. He heard the man's roar of rage, saw a dark, round opening to the right and dived into it just as Bender pulled aside the twigs to follow. The hole was a tight squeeze but Broome, inspired by fear of dying, thrashed through and into a soggy hollow from which small trails led in various directions. He took the one that might return him to Kit and the foliage closed around him.

* * * *

Kit saw Broome vanish. Bender make as if to follow. He began to run across the intervening space. A boulder lay in the bracken and he snatched it up, throwing as a Highlander putted the shot. It missed Bender's back by a hair's breadth crashing into the interlacing of fine twigs and branches. He swung round, the dark cruel face contorted, then raised the sporting gun.

'Don't do that!' Broome's voice came from behind Kit, making him swerve with its unexpectedness. He fell over a concealed tree stump just as the weapon was discharged, spattering the dell beyond him. As Kit rose, bruised from the tumble, he saw Bender disappear into the thicket. Limping, for his thigh hurt where the jagged stump had thrust into the flesh, he first looked to see if Broome was all right. The boy ran to him, eyes glittering, his hand bloody where a pellet had embedded itself.

'Wrap your kerchief round it,' Kit ordered, 'I'm going to fetch the roan. Bender will go for his own mount now that the fowling-piece is useless. See? He's left it on the ground. Take it back to the cottage and find something to cover—' He hesitated.

'My mother. She was my mother—He told me. The Frenchman didn't exist.'

'I only knew myself half an hour ago, when I saw the Amberwood portraits. You are Faro Amberwood's son, grandson of Sir Carne. Oh, I've not time now to tell you of your ancestry. It must wait.' And Kit made off, as fast as he was able, to his tethered horse, seeing, with relief that the hitching post had not fallen apart and the beast was where he'd left it. Just as he moved off, he saw Broome toiling up the slope, then descend towards the little house, the weapon carried carefully. 'Take care!' he called.

He felt less useless now that the horse was under him and it was not until he was nearing the spot where he had last seen Bender, that he realised he could have waited to reload the fowling gun before setting off. It would have wasted time but he'd have had Bender at a disadvantage when they came to their final encounter.

Urging the roan onwards, he saw two of the workmen from West Winds tending to another who lay with one leg doubled underneath him. 'Ran him down like a madman,' Sandy's companion said bitterly. 'First Sandy with his head blown off, now this.' The injured man moaned as he tried, feebly, to move, then lay still.

Not waiting to hear more, Kit galloped on, breaking out of the trees by the path to West Winds. He could see his quarry ahead, black coat tails flying, back crouched over the horse's head, whipping the beast's sides in senseless rage. A crowd of painters and joiners scattered at his approach, shouting curses, fists brandished. One threw a broom-handle that glanced off the horse's flanks. It reared up, neighing with pain at the unexpected blow, and Bender was thrown sideways to hang by one foot in the left-hand stirrup. He screamed at the horse to stop, but frightened, its hide lacerated by the whip, it cantered on, dragging the man over rut and stone, his head and shoulders striking any obstacle that presented itself. The screaming died to a dreadful whimpering.

The animal, blown and sweating, slowed, came to a stop, its legs trembling.

The workmen ran towards it, a thick, ugly mass, very quiet but still carrying the sharp-edged spades, the brooms, the tools of the joinery trade. Kit saw them surround the horse with a terrible intentness. They became a solid unit, not one man distinguishable from the general silhouette. The mass moved and swayed and thrust. Screams died into complete silence.

'Stand away!' Kit said, dismounting. 'Stand away—'

But no one moved. He pushed against the sturdy backs, the taut shoulders but it was not until Bender was finally dead that they broke ranks to allow him to see the body. His insides revolted.

'T'was the dragging did it,' their leader said laconically. 'Allus go that way dragged by one stirrup. But saves 'anging 'im, don't it. Won't be no need to waste money on a trial. Ain't that right, Mr Talbot?'

'That's right,' Kit whispered and turned his back on the corpse.

* * * *

364

'T'ain't right,' Pan said, beginning to take off her shift, 'for a boy to have so much at his age. Turn 'is head, it will.'

'You're dropping aitches,' Kit told her, enjoying the sight of her breasts as she bent to pull the garment over her shoulders the more easily. Her hair was the only garment his wife needed.

'It's thinking of Broome—'

'Broome is entitled to his mother's estate and it will be administered properly until he's of age. Faro made provision for that.'

'Fancy living as a man and no one the wiser!'

'She's not the first. There was the Chevalier D'Eon.'

'Who was that?'

'Favourite of the Queen of France. Dressed as a man, reputed to be a woman. Though the Queen was accused of taking the Chevalier as lover. The greatest puzzle of the age. Was she or wasn't he.'

'That's gibberish. Women's women and men's men.'

'If only everything was so simple. But I suspect the Chevalier, God rest him or her, was a person like Faro. A kind of hermaphrodite.'

Pan dropped her shift at last and stood revealed, splendid as Juno. 'A what?'

'Someone with both male and female characteristics.'

'Downright queer, that is.'

'Come here, woman. The bed's chilly.'

'You think no more of me than if I was a copper warming-pan.'

'There's a limit to the things one could do with a bed-warmer. You are different.'

'I should hope so.' She climbed up onto the bed and crouched there for a moment, looking down at him. 'Took it real bad, the boy did. Seems he liked the Frenchie—that woman, I mean.'

Kit reached out and cupped her breasts. 'I don't want to talk about Broome.'

'Oh, I know what you want! Never make any secret of it, do you. But he says he's going to buy a vineyard. Whatever for?' She pushed back the covers and wriggled slowly down the sheet, then snuffed out the candle.

'To grow grapes for wine-making. He'll probably become infernally rich.'

'Hasn't he got enough already?'

'You're just jealous because you've

never taken to him and he's the one who's come best out of all the mess. She had him registered as Brandon Amberwood. He's bar sinister, of course, but that shouldn't worry him.'

'What is he?'

'He's barred from taking the title.'

'Title, is it!'

'You mind because Heron will only be a farmer's daughter. A farmer with a grand house, too big to use fully or to furnish as it should be decked. And you are secretly annoyed because you didn't give me a son. But we can easily remedy that.'

'O' course,' Pan mused as if she'd not heard him. 'If Broome's to be living at West Winds and he's no relation to us, then he could—perhaps—well, there's Heron—'

'Broome will wed no daughter of mine!' Kit shouted. 'I told you, but you haven't listened, Amberwoods and Herons are a potent mixture. Lethal. Anyway, you don't even like him!'

'Ah, but I like his money and his fine house. I want the best for Heron.'

'She's my daughter too.'

'Are we going to quarrel about this, Kit?' She raised herself on one elbow and peered at him in the obscurity. 'He'll see a lot of Heron and she's going to be a rare beauty.'

'We will if you don't be quiet about it,' he growled. 'I'm serious.'

'Oh, well. We'll see what another fifteen years will bring,' she replied with suspicious meekness. 'Now what about that boy of yours? Don't want any Amberwood doing what you can't. Should be easy, all the practice you've had.'

'Pan.' He laughed unwillingly, then put his arms around her. One minute lying her lovely head off, the next starkly honest. It was her variety that made her so exciting. Someone else said almost the same about Cleopatra. He buried his head in her breast and pulled her close against him. Not that he'd ever quite allow himself to trust her—

* * * *

'Broome,' Rose said. 'How does it feel to know who you are? To be of some importance? Your mother was a lady—'

'And my father a murderer.'

'She sounded brave. I think I might

have liked her.'

'I don't want to talk about her.' Broome was remembering his last sight of Faro, the black moment when he wanted to dash Heron to the cobbles. He was afraid of his inherited characteristics. Revelation was a mixed blessing. But Faro had liked him, had repented of her abandonment of her only child. Between them had been a sense of kinsmanship that would surely have grown.

'Your own mother was not so praiseworthy,' Broome said cruelly.

Rose fixed her big, grey eyes on him. 'We are not to blame for our parents. One learns to overlook things. My father can be crude, bad-tempered, intolerant, but I still love him—And my mother? I'm sorry she was so unhappy.'

'You sound like a little old woman.'

'I have been made so,' she said so sadly that the same knife twisted inside him, hurting him equally.

'Poor Rose,' he replied gruffly. 'But you must not become self-pitying. I should not think so highly of you.'

'We will always be friends? I know we are no longer related—well, very distantly —but I feel the same.'

'I have not changed.'

'Then I will be welcome at West Winds when your schooling is done?'

'Yes.'

'And I can visit your vineyard?'

'If your father will allow you.'

'He will let me. He—he has Heron now. It is not quite as it was.'

'And she'll have more children, the gipsy.'

'All as beautiful as my step-sister.'

'I think she is common! The others will be the same.'

'So, Broome, we will always remain as we are.'

'Always.'

Broome, his declaration made, went to the window as though the house stifled him.

Rose, watching the strong, well-muscled back, crushed down, with a super-human effort, her momentary envy. She must not wish everyone the same as herself. She was unfortunate but there were many worse. There had been a poor man in the Keswick street, legless and strapped to a wheeled platform close to the pavement. It had taken her months to forget the look in his eyes. Shame,

370

despair and cupidity when someone tossed him a coin. Far, far worse had been the idiot boy who was strong enough in body to be sent to the mill, but had no brain with which to appreciate reading, writing, the beauty of music, the poetry of words, the cloud effects on the Lakeland hills. Without a mind one was truly nothing.

'Always,' Broome had said. But a long time ago he also said, "I love my love with an H". She did not want him to love her because she was a cripple.

Then he turned with a smile that, in spite of its attraction, made her wary.

'The sun will come out in a moment. Let us escape?'

Why not? No one would trouble to stop them now.

'We'll escape,' she agreed and held out her hand so that he might take it.